Men of the
High Calling

Men of the High Calling

Charles Neider, editor

ABINGDON PRESS
NEW YORK · NASHVILLE

MEN OF THE HIGH CALLING

Copyright MCMLIV by Pierce & Washabaugh

Library of Congress Catalog Card Number: 54-8241

"The Bishop's Beggar" is from *The Last Circle*, published by Farrar, Straus & Young, Inc.; copyright, 1942, by Curtis Publishing Company; copyright, 1942, by Estate of Stephen Vincent Benét. The selection "Dean Harcourt" is from *The Green Light* by Lloyd C. Douglas and is reprinted by permission of and arrangement with Houghton Mifflin Company, the authorized publishers, and Thomas Allen, Ltd. "The Stickit Minister" and "The Reverend John Smith Prepares His Sermon" are from *The Stickit Minister and Some Common Men* and are used by permission of the publishers, Ernest Benn, Ltd. "The Blue Cross" is reprinted by permission of Dodd, Mead & Company from *The Innocence of Father Brown*, copyright 1911 by Dodd, Mead & Company; renewal copyright 1938 by Frances Chesterton; also used by permission of Miss D. E. Collins and Messrs. Cassell & Co., Ltd. "The Altar Cloth" is copyright 1944 by The Crowell-Collier Publishing Company; reprinted by permission of the author. "A Preacher Goes to Texas" is reprinted from *Lone Star Preacher* by John W. Thomason, Jr.; copyright 1941 by John W. Thomason, Jr., copyright 1938, 1939, 1940 by Curtis Publishing Company; used by permission of the publishers, Charles Scribner's Sons. "The Three Hermits" is from *Twenty-Three Tales*, translated by Louise and Aylmer Maude, and is used by permission of Oxford University Press. "Tit for Tat" is from *The Old Country*, by Sholom Aleichem; copyright, 1946, by Crown Publishers; used by permission of Crown Publishers, Inc. "His Mother's Sermon" is from *Beside the Bonnie Brier Bush* and is used by permission of A. P. Watt & Son and the executors of the author's estate. "The Third Commandment" is from *The Ten Commandments*, copyright, 1943, by Armin L. Robinson; reprinted by permission of Simon and Schuster, publishers. "The Making of a Minister" is from *The Little Minister* and is used by permission of Cassell & Co., Ltd.

SET UP, PRINTED, AND BOUND BY THE
PARTHENON PRESS, AT NASHVILLE,
TENNESSEE, UNITED STATES OF AMERICA

for · FRITZ FAISS
and · BILL DENT

CONTENTS

The Bishop's Beggar

by STEPHEN VINCENT BENÉT

❖❖❖

It seems that in the old days there was a bishop of Remo, and he was a heedless and proud young man, though of good intentions. Now, that was possible in those days, when the fire and light of the new learning had spread through Italy, and men drank, as if intoxicated, at a new spring. There were bishops who cared less for the Word of God than for their own splendor, and cardinals who were rather men of the world—and of no good world—than sons of the Church. I do not say that our bishop was as idle and self-seeking as some of these; I do say that he was a child of his time. He would have liked to be a lord, but his eldest brother was the lord; he would have liked to be a soldier, but his second brother was the soldier. So he went into the Church, for there, too, a man who bore a great name could rise. He was clever, he was ambitious, he had great connections. Now and then, to be sure, he asked a disquieting question, but the Baldis had always been original. The path that is rugged for many was made smooth for him from the first. When he was made bishop of Remo at an early age, the fact

9

did not surprise him. Since he was to be neither lord nor soldier, he found that pleasant enough.

All went well for him, at first. They were glad to have a young and handsome bishop at Remo, for the bishop before him had been old and ill-favored. It was a pleasure to no one to kiss his ring, and he frightened the children with his peering eyes. With the coming of our bishop all this was changed. There was a great to-do and refurbishing of the bishop's palace; the smells of good cooking drifted again from the bishop's kitchens; when the bishop drove through the city, men threw their caps in the air. There were fine new frescoes in the cathedral, a new way of chanting in the choir. As for sin and suffering—well, they are always with us. The people of Remo liked to sin pleasantly and be reminded of it as little as possible.

Nevertheless, at times, a grayness would come over our bishop's spirit. He could not understand why it came. His life was both full and busy. He was a friend to art, a host to the gay and the learned, a ruler of men. He did not meddle in things which did not concern him; he felt in his heart that there was no prize in the Church which might not be within his grasp. And yet, at times, there was a grayness within him. It was singular.

He could not show that grayness before the world, he could not show it to his secretary or the witty company that gathered at his table. He could wrestle with it in prayer, and so he did. But he found it no easy task. Had the Devil appeared before him with horns and a tail, he would have known what to do. But a grayness of spirit—a cool little voice in the mind which said to him now and then, "What do you in these robes, at this place, Gianfrancesco Baldi?"—that was another matter.

He came to find by experience that motion in the open air helped him as much as anything. When the grayness oppressed him too severely, he would summon his coach and drive about the countryside. So one day, as he drove through a small country village in the hills beyond Remo, it happened. It was nobody's fault; the bishop's least of all. He saw to it that he had a skilful coachman and good horses as he saw to all such matters. But when a tall, gangling boy darts across the street right under the nose of the horses, the most skilful coachman cannot always save him. There was a cry and a scream and a soft jar. Then, where the coach had passed, the boy lay writhing in the street.

The bishop always showed at his best in emergency. When he got out of the coach, the angry shouts of the crowd died away to a respectful murmur. He lifted the boy into the coach with his strong arms and drove back with him to Remo. On the way he talked to him soothingly, though the boy was in too much pain to pay much attention to this graciousness. When they got to Remo, he had the boy carried to a servant's room in the palace and doctors summoned for him. Later on he gave instructions about cleaning the coach.

At dinner his secretary recounted the little incident, and all men praised the kindliness of the bishop. The bishop passed it off pleasantly, but, at heart, he felt a trifle irritated. He had not felt particularly drawn toward the boy; on the other hand, he could not have left him lying in the road.

By the next day, as such things go, the story had gone all over Remo, and there were unusual demonstrations of good will as the bishop passed to the cathedral. The bishop received them with dignity, but his irritation remained. He disliked ostentatious shows of virtue and distrusted the fickleness of crowds. Nevertheless, it was his duty to see the boy, and he did so.

Washed, combed, and rid of his vermin, the boy looked ordinary enough—though somewhat older than the bishop had thought him. His body was slight and emaciated, but he had a well-shaped head and large liquid eyes. These stared at the bishop with some intensity; indeed, with such intensity that the bishop wondered, at first, if the boy might not be an idiot. But a little conversation proved him sound of mind, though rustic in speech.

His name was Luigi and he was an orphan, living as best he could. In the summer he tended goats; in the winter he lived with his uncle and aunt, the tavern-keepers, who fed him and beat him. His age was about nineteen. He had made his Easter duty as a Christian. He would never walk again.

Such were the facts of the case, and the bishop thought them over clearheadedly. He wondered what to do with the boy.

"Luigi," he said, "would you like to go back to your village?"

"Oh, no," said the boy. "It is a very good village, but now that I can no longer herd goats, there is no place in it for me. Besides, one eats better in Remo—I have had white cheese twice already." And he smacked his lips. His voice was remarkably strong and cheerful, the bishop noticed with surprise.

"Very well," said the bishop patiently. "You need not go back if you do not choose. You are now, in some sense, a ward of the Church, and the wings of the Church are sheltering." He looked at the boy's legs, lying limp and motionless under the covers, and felt, though against his will, the natural

12

distaste of the hale man for the maimed. "You might learn some useful trade," he said thoughtfully. "There are many trades where the hands do all—a cobbler's, a tailor's, a basket-weaver's."

The boy shook his head joyfully. "Oh, no, your lordship," he said. "Trades take so long to learn and I am very stupid. It would not be worth the expense; your lordship would be embarrassed."

"My lordship, perhaps, is the best judge of that," said the bishop a trifle grimly. He kept thinking of the boy's remark about white cheese; it must be a spare life indeed where white cheese was such a treat. "But we are reasonable," he said. "Come, what would you be?"

"A beggar!" said the boy, and his dark eyes shone with delight.

"A beggar?" said the bishop, astonished and somewhat revolted.

"Why, yes," said the boy, as if it were the most natural thing in the world. "For ten years my father begged on the cathedral steps. That was before your lordship's time, but he was an excellent beggar and a master of his craft. True, he was subject to continual persecutions and jealousies from the honorable corporation of the beggars of Remo, coming, as he did, from outside the city. It was that which caused the ruin of our fortunes, for, in the end, when he had begun to fail, they threw him down a well, where he caught a bad cold and died of it. But in his good days he could outbeg any two of them. If your lordship would care to have me demonstrate his celebrated fainting fit, when his eyeballs rolled backward in his head—"

"I can think of nothing I should like less," said the bishop, shocked and disgusted, for it seemed to him an unworthy thing that a sturdy young man, though a cripple, should think of nothing better than beggary. "Besides," he said, "these other beggars you speak of—if they persecuted your father, no doubt they would persecute you."

"Me?" said the boy, and laughed. "Oh, once they understood, they would not dare touch me—not even Giuseppe, the Hook. I would be your lordship's beggar—the bishop's beggar!" And a light as of great peace and contentment spread over his countenance.

The bishop stared at him for a long time in silence. "That is what you wish?" he said, and his voice was dry.

"That is what I wish, your lordship," said the boy, nodding his head.

"So be it," said the bishop with a sigh, and left him. But when his coachman came to him the next morning for orders, it was all he could do to keep from reviling the man.

The bishop was not the sort of man who liked beggars. Indeed, were it not for custom and Christian charity, he would long since have cleared them from the steps of his cathedral. He could not very well do that; he knew what an impression such a move would make. Nevertheless, when he passed among them, as he must at times, he saw to it that his almoner made a suitable distribution of small coins, but he himself did his best to see and smell them as little as possible. Their whines and their supplications, their simulated sores, and their noisome rags—these were a fret and a burden to him.

Now, it seemed, he was to have a beggar of his own. He would have taken it as a suitable humiliation for pride, but he did not feel himself to be a proud man. Nor could he think

14

of the accident as anything but an accident. Had he deliberately trodden the lad beneath the hoofs of his horses—but he had not. He was well liked, able, decisive, a rising son of the Church. Nevertheless, he was to have a beggar—every day he must see his beggar on the steps of the cathedral, a living reproach, a living lesson in idleness and heedlessness. It was a small thing, to be sure, but it darkened his dinner and made him sore at heart.

Therefore, being the man he was, he put a mask upon his face. He meant to speak of the thing, so it should be known —at least *that* might ward off ridicule. He spoke of it to his secretary; the secretary agreed that it was a very seemly and Christian idea of his lordship's, while the bishop wondered if the man laughed at him in his sleeve. He spoke of it to others; there were compliments, of course. Each time he spoke of it, it turned a small knife in his breast. But that did not keep him from speaking of it, nor from seeing that every care was given Luigi.

Nevertheless, he dreaded the day when Luigi would take up his post on the steps of the cathedral. He dreaded and yearned for it, both. For then, at last, the thing would be done. After that, like many things, it would become a custom, and in time Luigi himself would fade into the mass of whining beggary that haunted the steps of the cathedral. But things were not to be quite that way.

He admired, while he detested, the thoroughness with which Luigi prepared himself for his profession. He heard the whine ring out from the servants' quarters—"Ten scudi for Luigi!"—he saw the little cart and the crutches Luigi had made for himself. Now and then he heard his own servants

15

laugh at the beggar's stories. This was hard enough to bear. But at last the day of parting came.

To his disgust, the bishop found the boy neither clean nor well-clad, as he had been since his accident, but dirty and dressed in tatters. He opened his mouth to reprove the boy, then he shut it again, for it seemed pitifully true that a beggar must dress his part. Nevertheless, the bishop did not like it. He asked Luigi, coolly, how he meant to live.

"Oh, your lordship's secretary has found me a very suitable chamber," said Luigi eagerly. "It is on the ground floor of a rookery by the river and it has room for crutches, my gear, and my cart. He will move me there tonight. Tomorrow I will be at my post on the steps of the cathedral." And he smiled gratefully at the bishop. "That will be a great day," he said.

"So," said the bishop, who could not trust himself to say anything further.

"Yet before I go," said Luigi, "I must thank your lordship for his kindness, and ask your lordship's blessing on my work. That is only suitable."

The bishop stiffened. "I may bless you, Luigi," he said, "but your work I cannot bless. I cannot give the blessing of the Church to the work of a man who lives by beggary when he might live otherwise."

"Well, then, I must go unblessed," said Luigi cheerfully. "After all, your lordship has already done so much for me! The bishop's beggar! How my uncle and aunt will stare!"

Now, of all the vainglorious, self-seeking, worthless, rascally sons of iniquity—and to think that I stand your sponsor, said the bishop, but, fortunately, he did not say it aloud. Silently he extended his ring and Luigi kissed it with such

16

innocent reverence that the bishop was sorely moved to give him his blessing after all. But he summoned up his principles and departed in silence.

The bishop slept ill that night, tormented by dreams of Luigi. He dreamed that, for his sins, he must carry Luigi on his back all the way up the steps of the cathedral. And as he mounted each step, the weight upon his back became more crushing, till at last he woke, unrefreshed.

The next day he went to the cathedral in great state, though it was an ordinary Sunday. Yet he felt the state to be, in some measure, a protection. When he passed by the steps of the cathedral, the beggars set up their usual supplications. He sent his almoner among them; it was over quicker than he thought. He did not look for Luigi and yet he felt Luigi's eyes upon him as he stood there for a moment, splendid in robe and miter. Then the thing was finished.

In the cathedral that same day, he preached passionately against the sins of idleness and heedlessness. Seldom had he been so moving—he could feel that from his congregation. When Mass was over he retired to his palace, exhausted. Yet it was pleasant for him to walk about the palace and know that Luigi was not there.

It was just after vespers when his secretary came to him and told him that a man called Giuseppe, self-styled provost of the company of the beggars of Remo, requested an audience. The bishop sighed wearily and ordered the man brought before him. He was a squat fellow of great strength and an evil cast of countenance, for one side of his face had been so burned in a fire that it was as if he had two faces, one of them inhuman. Also, his left arm terminated in an iron hook.

"This is Giuseppe, the beggar, your lordship," said the secretary with repugnance.

"Giuseppe, called Double-Face, also called the Hook, provost of the honorable company of the beggars of Remo," said Guiseppe in a rusty voice, and plumped on his knees.

The bishop raised him and asked his business.

"Well, your lordship, it's this new fellow, Luigi Lame-legs," said Giuseppe. "I've got nothing against him personal —I wouldn't hurt a fly myself in a personal way"—and he grinned horribly—"but there he is in a good place on the steps, and your lordship's servants put him there. Well, now, if he's your lordship's beggar, that's one thing—though, even so, there's fees and vails to be paid, for that's the custom. But if he isn't your lordship's beggar—and your lordship paid him no attention this morning—"

"Stop!" said the bishop with anger. "Do you mean to tell me that the very steps of the cathedral are bartered and sold among you? Why, this is simony—this is the sin of simony!"

"Your lordship can call it hard words," said Giuseppe stolidly, "but that's been the way it's been done ever since there were beggars in Remo. I paid twenty crowns for my own place, and fought old Marco too. But that's beside the point. Your lordship has a right to a beggar if your lordship wants one—we're all agreed on that. But the question is: Is this man your lordship's beggar or isn't he?"

"And supposing I said he was not my beggar?" said the bishop, trembling.

"Well, that's all we'd want to know," said Giuseppe. "And thank your lordship kindly. I had my own suspicions of the man from the first. But we've got him down by the river now —Carlo and Benito and old blind Marta; she's a tough one,

18

old blind Marta—and once we're through with him, he'll trouble your lordship no more." And sketching a clumsy salute, the man turned to go.

"Stop!" said the bishop again. "Would you have the guilt of murder upon your conscience?"

"Oh, your lordship takes it too hard," said Giuseppe, shuffling his feet. "What's one beggar more or less? We're not rich folk or learned folk to bother a mind like your lordship's. We breed and we die, and there's an end. And even at the best, it's no bed of roses on the steps of the cathedral."

The bishop wished to say many things, but he could think of only one.

"I declare to you that this man is my beggar," he said. "I stretch my hand over him."

"Well, that's very nicely spoken of your lordship," said Giuseppe in a grumbling voice, "and I dare say we can make room for him. But if the man's to keep a whole skin, your lordship had best come with me—old Marta was talking of ear-slitting when I left her."

So they found Luigi, bound but cheerful, in his first-floor chamber by the river, guarded by the persons Giuseppe had described—a hunchback, a dwarf, and a blind woman. The window which gave upon the river was open, and a large sack, weighted with stones, lay in one corner of the room. The bishop's arrival produced a certain consternation on the part of all but Luigi, who seemed to take it as a matter of course. After the boy had been unbound, the bishop addressed the beggars with some vivacity, declared that Luigi was his beggar, and gave him a piece of silver before them all, in token. This seemed to satisfy the company, who then crept away in silence.

"And yet have I done right? Have I done right?" said the bishop, striding up and down the chamber. "I greatly fear I have condoned the sin of simony! I have spent Mother Church's substance among the unworthy! And yet, even so, your blood may be upon my head," and he looked at Luigi doubtfully.

"Oh, your lordship need not take it so hard," said Luigi, rubbing his arms. "All is safe enough now. I arranged about the dues and vails with Giuseppe while your lordship was discussing her state of grace with Marta. He's an honest fellow enough, and his point is reasonable. One should not take a good place without money to keep it up. Had your lordship given me alms with your own hand this morning, our little difficulty would never have arisen. That was my fault—I assumed that your lordship knew."

"Knew?" said the bishop. "What should I know of such things? And yet, God forgive me, I am a priest and I should have knowledge of evil."

"It is merely a difference in knowledge," said Luigi gently. "Now, your lordship, doubtless, has never been in a room quite like this before."

The bishop stared at the damp walls and the mean chamber. He smelled the smell that cannot be aired from a room, the smell of poverty itself. He had never doubted his own experience before—when he had been first made a priest, he had gone on certain works of charity. Now it seemed to him that those works must have been rather carefully selected.

"No," he said, "I have never been in a room just like this one."

"And yet there are many of us who live in such rooms—and not all beggars," said Luigi. He changed his tone. "That was a fine rousing sermon your lordship gave us on idleness and heedlessness this morning," he said. "Hey, it brought the scudi forth from the good folks' pockets! An admirable sermon!"

"I am grateful for your encomiums," said the bishop bitterly. He glanced around the room again. "Is there nought else I can do?" he asked unwillingly.

"No, thank your lordship," said Luigi, and his eyes were smiling. "I have a woman to cook my dinner—it is true she is a thief, but she will not steal from a cripple—and soon, with your lordship's patronage, I shall be able to afford a charcoal brazier. Moreover, my friends seem to have left me a sack. So, after dinner I shall say my prayers and go to bed to refresh myself for tomorrow's labor."

I shall say mine, too, for I need them, said the bishop, though he did not say it to Luigi.

So that was how it began. Soon enough, the bishop's beggar was a familiar figure on the steps of the cathedral—one of the admitted curiosities of the town. He was well-liked in his trade, for he always had a merry word or a sharp one for his clients—and it passed around until "Luigi says" became a byword. The bishop became used to him as one becomes used to a touch of rheumatism. Other men had their difficulties; he had his beggar. Now and then it seemed odd to the bishop that he had ever thought of the beggars on the steps as a vague and indistinguishable heap of misery and rags. He knew them all by now—blind Marta and Carlo, the dwarf, Giuseppe Double-Face, and Benito, the hunchback. He knew their ways and their thoughts. He knew the hovels where they lived and the bread they ate. For every

21

week or so he would slip from his palace to visit Luigi's chamber.

It was necessary for him to do so, for to him Luigi represented the gravest problem of the soul that he had yet encountered. Was the man even a Christian? The bishop was not sure. He professed religion, he followed the rites of the Church. Yet sometimes when he confessed him, the bishop was appalled. Every sin that could ravage the human heart was there—if not in act, then in desire—and all told so gaily! Sometimes the bishop, angrily, would tax him with wilful exaggeration, and Luigi, with a smile, would admit the charge and ask for still another penance. This left the bishop confused.

Yet through the years there grew up between the two men a singular bond. The bishop may have been heedless, he was not stupid. Very soon he began to realize that there was another Remo than the city he had come to first—a city not of lords and scholars and tradesmen and pious ladies, but a city of the poor and the ignorant, the maimed and the oppressed. For, as Luigi said, when one lay all day on the steps of the cathedral one heard stories, and anyone will talk to a beggar. Some of the stories struck the bishop to the heart. He could hardly believe them at first, yet, when he investigated them, they were true. When he was convinced they were true, he set himself stubbornly to remedy them. He was not always successful—pleasant sinners like the Church to keep its own place. Now and then he discussed his efforts with Luigi, who listened, it seemed to the bishop, with an air of perfect cynicism. His attitude seemed to be that it was all very well for a man like the bishop to concern himself about these things and, if other folks starved and died, it was none of his concern. This irritated the bishop inordinately and made him more determined than ever.

Gradually, he noticed, the composition of his table changed. There were fewer courtiers and scholars; there were more priests from the country, smelling of poverty and chestnut bread. They came in their tattered cassocks, with their big red wrists; at first they were strange and ill at ease at his table. But the bishop was able to talk to them. After all, were they not like the old parish priests that Luigi talked of so often? When the ceremony of his table disturbed them he saw to it that there was less ceremony. Luigi mocked him for this and told him bluntly what his richer clients were saying. The bishop rebuked him for impertinence to his spiritual director and persisted.

It is strange how time flies when the heart is occupied. In no time at all, it seemed to the bishop, he was a middle-aged man with gray at his temples, and Luigi a man in his thirties. That seemed odd to the bishop; he did not know where the time had gone. He thought of it, one morning, with a sense of loss. He had meant to do many things—he was still ambitious. Now, when night came, he was often too tired to think. The troubles of many people weighed upon his heart—the troubles of the peasants in the hills, who lived from hand to mouth; the troubles of Domenico, the shoemaker, who had too pretty a daughter; the troubles of Tessa, the flower-seller, whose son was a thief. When he had first come to Remo, he had not had all these troubles. He picked up a letter on his desk— a letter that had lain there for days—and, having read it, sat staring.

The dreams of his youth came back to him, doubly hot, doubly dear. While he idled his life away in Remo, his brother and his friends had been busy. They had not forgotten him, after all. Cardinal Malaverni, the great, sage statesman whose hand was ever upon the strings of policy, meant to pass by Remo on his way to Rome. The bishop knew the cardinal—once, long ago, he had been one of the cardinal's promising young men. There was a letter also from the bishop's brother, the lord—a letter that hinted of grave and important matters. The bishop almost sobbed when he thought how long both letters had lain unanswered. He summoned his secretary and set himself about an unaccustomed bustle of preparation.

It often occured to him, sorrowfully, within the next few days, how foolish it was to leave one's letters unopened. The preparations went forward for the cardinal's visit, yet it seemed to him that they went forward ill, though he could not put his finger upon the cause. Somehow he had got out of the way of the world where such things go forward smoothly; he was more used to his country priests than to entertaining distinguished visitors. Nevertheless, he botched together a few Latin verses, saw to it that the hangings in the guest-chambers were cleaned and mended, drove his choirmaster nearly frantic, and got in the way of his servants. He noticed that these were no longer afraid of him, but treated him with tolerant patience, more like a friend than a master, and this irked him oddly. What irked him even more, perhaps, was Luigi's shameless and undisguised self-interest in the whole affair.

"Ah, your lordship, we've waited a long time for this," he said, "but it's come at last. And everyone knows that a great man like Cardinal Malaverni doesn't come to a place like Remo for nothing. So all we have to do is to play our cards

well, and then, when we move on, as we doubtless shall—
well, I, for one, won't be sorry."

"Move on?" said the bishop, astonished.

The beggar yawned.

"But how else?" he said. "I have been the bishop's beggar.
When your lordship is made a cardinal I will be the cardinal's
beggar. The post will entail new responsibilities, no doubt,
but I have confidence in my abilities. Perhaps I shall even
employ an assistant for my actual begging—after all, it is
often drafty on the steps of the cathedral."

The bishop turned and left him without a word. Yet what
Luigi had said caused trouble and disquiet in his heart, for
he knew that Luigi often had news of things to come before
even the Count of Remo had an inkling of them.

At last the great day of the cardinal's visit came.

Like all such days, it passed as a dream passes, with heat
and ceremony and worry about small things. The Latin verses
of welcome were unexpectedly well read; on the other hand,
the choristers were nervous and did not sing their best. Two
gentlemen of the cardinal's suite had to be lodged over the
stables, much to the bishop's distress, and the crayfish for
dinner had been served without sauce.

The bishop hoped that all had gone well, but he did not
know. As he sat, at last, alone with his old friend in his study
that overlooked the garden, he felt at once wrought-up and
drowsy.

This should be the real pleasure of the day, to sit with his
old friend in the cool of the evening and renew contact with
the great world. But the bishop was used to country hours
by now, and the feast had broken up late. He should be

listening to the cardinal with the greatest attention, and yet those accursed crayfish kept coming into his mind.

"Well, Gianfrancesco," said the cardinal, sipping delicately at his wine, "you have given your old tutor a most charming welcome. Your wine, your people, your guests—it reminds me somehow of one of those fine Virgilian Eclogues we used to parse together. *'Tityre, tu patulae recubans—'*"

"The choir," said the bishop—"the choir usually is—"

"Why, they sang very well!" said the cardinal. "And what good, honest, plain-spoken priests you have in your charge!" He shook his head sadly. "I fear that we do not always get their like in Rome. And yet, each man to his task."

"They have a hard charge in these hills," said the bishop wearily. "It was a great honor for them to see Your Eminence."

"Oh, honor!" said the cardinal. "To see an old man with the gout—yes, I have the gout these days, Gianfrancesco—I fear we both are not so young as we were." He leaned forward and regarded the bishop attentively. "You, too, have altered, my old friend," he said softly.

"Your Eminence means that I have rusticated," said the bishop a trifle bitterly. "Well, it is true."

"Oh, not rusticated," said the cardinal, with a charming gesture. "Not at all. But there has been a change—a perceptible one—from the Gianfrancesco I knew." He took a walnut and began to crack it. "That Gianfrancesco was a charming and able young man," he said. "Yet I doubt if he would have made the Count of his city do penance in his shirt, for his sins, before the doors of his cathedral!"

"I can explain about that," said the bishop hurriedly. "The shirt was a silk one and the weather by no means inclement.

26

Moreover, the Count's new tax would have ruined my poor. It is true we have not always seen eye to eye since then, yet I think he respects me more than he did before."

"That is just what I said to your brother, Piero," said the cardinal comfortably. "I said, 'You are wrong to be perturbed about this, Piero; it will have a good effect.' Yes, even as regards the beggar."

"My beggar?" said the bishop, and sighed.

"Oh, you know how small things get about," said the cardinal. "Some small thing is seized upon; it even travels to Rome. The bishop's beggar—the beggars' bishop—the bishop who humbles his soul to protect the poor."

"But it was not like that at all," said the bishop. "I—"

The cardinal waved him aside. "Do not hide your good works beneath a bushel, Gianfrancesco," he said. "The Church herself has need of them. These are troubled times we live in. The French king may march any day. There is heresy and dissension abroad. You have no idea what difficult days may lie ahead." He watched the bishop intently. "Our Holy Father leans much upon my unworthy shoulder," he said, "and our Holy Father is beginning to age."

"That is sore news for us all," said the bishop.

"Sore indeed," said the cardinal. "And yet, one must face realities. Should our Holy Father die, it will be necessary for those of us who truly love the Church to stand together—more especially in the college of cardinals." He paused and with a silver nutpick extracted the last meat from the walnut. "I believe that our Holy Father is disposed to reward your own labors with the see of Albano," he said.

"The see of Albano?" said the bishop as if in a dream, for, as all men knew, Albano was an old and famous diocese outside the walls of Rome, and he who was bishop of Albano wore a cardinal's hat.

"It might have a most excellent effect," said the cardinal. "I myself think it might. We have clever and able men who are sons of the Church. Indeed. And yet, just at this moment, with both the French and the German parties so active— well, there is perhaps need for another sort of man—at least as regards the people." He smiled delightfully. "You would be very close to me as cardinal-bishop of Albano—very close to us all," he said. "I should lean upon you, Gianfrancesco."

"There is nought that would please me more!" cried the bishop, like a boy. He thought for a moment of the power and the glory, of the great, crowded streets of Rome and the Church that humbles kings. "I would have to leave Remo?" he said.

"Well, yes, naturally, it would mean your having to leave Remo," said the cardinal. "Your new duties would demand it."

"That would be hard," said the bishop. "I would have to leave Luigi and all my people." He thought of them suddenly—the lame, the halt, the oppressed.

"Your people, perhaps," said the cardinal, "but certainly not Luigi. He should come with you by all means, as a living example."

"Oh, no, no, that would never do," said the bishop. "Your Eminence does not understand. Luigi is difficult enough as a bishop's beggar. As a cardinal's beggar, he would be over-weening. You have no idea how overweening he would be."

The cardinal regarded him with a puzzled stare.

"Am I dreaming, Gianfrancesco?" he said. "Or are you

28

declining the see of Albano and a cardinal's hat for no more reason than that you are attached to a beggar?"

"Oh, no, no, no!" cried the bishop, in an agony. "I am not in the least attached to him—he is my cross and my thorn. But you see, it would be so bad for him if I were to be made a cardinal. I tremble to think what would happen to his soul. And then there are all his companions—Giuseppe, the Hook, is dead, but there is still blind Marta, and Benito, the hunchback, and the new ones. No, I must stay in Remo."

The cardinal smiled—a smile of exasperation. "I think you have forgotten something, Gianfrancesco," he said. "I think you have forgotten that obedience is the first law of the Church."

"I am five times obedient," said the bishop. "Let our Holy Father do with me as he wills. Let him send me as a missionary to savages; let him strip me of my bishopric and set me to work in the hills. I shall be content. But while I have been given Remo, I have work to do in Remo. I did not expect it to be so when I first came here," he said in a low voice, "and yet, somehow, I find that it is so."

The cardinal said nothing at all for a long time.

Then at last he rose, and, pressing the bishop's hand, he retired to his own quarters. The bishop hoped that he was comfortable in them, though it occurred to him, in the uneasy sleep before dawn, that the chimney smoked.

Next morning the cardinal departed on his journey toward Rome without speaking of these matters further. The bishop felt sorry to see him go, and yet relieved. He had been very glad to see his old friend again—he told himself that. Yet from the moment of the cardinal's arrival there had been an unfamiliar grayness upon his spirit, and now that grayness was gone. Nevertheless, he knew that he must face Luigi—and that thought was hard for him.

Yet it went well enough, on the whole.

The bishop explained to him, as one explains to a child, that it did not seem as if God had intended him to be a cardinal, only bishop of Remo, and with that Luigi had to be content. Luigi grumbled about it frequently and remarked that if he had known all this in the first place, he might never have accepted the position of bishop's beggar. But he was not any more overweening than before, and with that the bishop had to be satisfied.

Then came the war with the French, and that was hard upon the bishop. He did not like wars, he did not like the thought of his people being killed. Yet, when the Count of Remo fled with most of his soldiery, and the mayor locked himself in his house and stayed there, shaking, there was no one to take over the rule of the town but the bishop. The very beggars in the streets cried out for him; he could not escape the task.

He took it with a heavy heart, under the mocking eyes of Luigi. With Luigi in his cart, he inspected the walls and defenses.

"Well, your lordship has a very pretty problem," said Luigi. "Half a dozen good cannon shot and the city will be taken by storm."

"I thought so, I feared so," said the bishop, sighing. "And yet my people are my people."

"Your lordship might easily compromise with the enemy," said Luigi. "They are angry with the Count, it is true—they thought they had him bought over. Yet it would mean but two score hangings or so, and a tribute, properly assessed."

30

"I cannot permit my flock to be harried and persecuted," said the bishop.

"Well, if your lordship must die, I will die with your lordship," said Luigi. "Meanwhile, we might set the townsfolk to work on the walls—at least it will give them something to do. And yet, there may be another way."

So it was done, and the bishop worked day and night, enheartening and encouraging his people. For once, all Remo was one, and the spirit and will that burned within it were the bishop's. Yet it seemed no time at all before the French sat down before Remo.

They sent a trumpet and a flag to demand the surrender of the city. The bishop received the young officer who came with the trumpet—a dark-faced man he was, with a humorous twist to his mouth. The bishop even took him on a tour of the walls, which seemed to surprise him a little.

"You are well defended," said the Frenchman politely.

"Oh, no, we are very ill defended," said the bishop. "My good children have been trying to strengthen the wall with sandbags, but, as you perceive, it is rotten and needs rebuilding. Moreover, the Count was badly cheated on his powder. I must speak to him of it sometime, for hardly a gun we have is fit to fire."

The Frenchman's astonishment grew. "I do not wish to doubt your lordship's word," he said, "but if those things are so, how does your lordship propose to defend Remo?"

"By the will of God," said the bishop very simply. "I do not wish my poor people killed; neither do I wish them oppressed. If needs must, I shall die in their stead, but they shall go scatheless. Ere you hang one man of Remo, I shall

31

take the noose from around his neck and put it around my own."

"Your lordship makes things very difficult," said the Frenchman, thoughtfully. "My King has no desire to attack the Church—and, indeed, the walls of Remo seem stronger than your lordship reckons."

Then he was conscious of a plucking at his sleeve. It was Luigi, the beggar, in his little cart, who, by signs and grimaces, seemed to wish the Frenchman to follow him.

"What is it, Luigi?" said the bishop wearily. "Ah, yes, you wish to show our friend the room where we store the powder. Very well. Then he may see how little we have."

When the Frenchman rejoined the bishop, he was wiping sweat from his forehead, and his face was white. The bishop pressed him to stay for a glass of wine, but he said he must return to his camp, and departed, muttering something incoherent about it being indeed the will of God that defended Remo.

When he had gone, the bishop looked severely upon Luigi. "Luigi," he said sternly, "I fear you have been up to some of your tricks."

"How your lordship mistakes me," said the beggar. "It is true I showed him three of my fellow-beggars—and they did not seem to him in the best of health. But I did not say they had plague; I let him draw his own conclusions. It took me four days to school them in their parts, but that I did not tell him either."

"That was hardly honest, Luigi," said the bishop. "We know there is no plague in the town."

"We know also that our walls are rotten," said Luigi, "but the French will not believe that, either. Men of war are extremely suspicious—it is their weakness. We shall wait and see."

They waited and saw, for that night a council of war was held in the French camp and the officer who had come with the trumpet reported (a) that Remo was held in great force and strongly defended; (b) that its bishop was resolved to die in the breach; and (c) that there was a plague in the city. Taking all these factors into account, the French wisely decided, after some forty-eight hours' delay, to strike camp and fall back on their main army—which they did just in time to take part in the historic defeat of the whole French invasion a week later. This defeat sealed for all time the heroic defense of Remo; for, had the part of the French army occupied before Remo rejoined their main body before, the historic defeat might have been as historic a victory for the French. As it was, all Italy rang with the name of the bishop of Remo.

But of all this the bishop knew nothing, for his beggar, Luigi, was dying.

As the French moved away they had loosed off a few cannon shot, more in irritation than for any real military purpose. However, one of the cannon shot, heedlessly aimed, struck the steps of the cathedral, and you may still see the scars. It also struck the cart wherein Luigi lay directing his beggars at one task of defense or another. When the bishop first heard that his beggar was hurt, he went to him at once. But there was little that a man could do but wait, and the waiting was long. It was not until seven weeks later that Luigi passed from this earth. He endured, indeed, till the messengers came from Rome.

After they had talked with the bishop, the bishop went alone to his cathedral and prayed. Then he went to see Luigi.

33

"Well?" said the dying man eagerly, staring at him with limpid eyes.

"His Holiness has been graciously pleased to make of me the first archbishop of Remo, placing under my staff, as well, the dioceses of Ugri and Soneto," said the bishop slowly. "But I have the news from Cardinal Malaverni, and I may remain here till I die." He stared at Luigi. "I do not understand," he said.

"It is well done. You have stood by the poor in their poverty and the wretched in their hour of trial," said Luigi, and for once there was no trace of mockery in his voice.

"I do not understand. I do not understand at all," said the bishop again. "And yet I think you deserve recompense rather than I, Luigi."

"No," said Luigi, "that I do not."

The bishop passed his hand across his brow. "I am not a fool," he said. "It was well done, to humble my spirit. And yet, why did you do so, Luigi?"

"Why, that was my great sin," said Luigi. "I have confessed many vain and imaginary sins, but never the real one till now." He paused, as if the words hurt him. "When your lordship's coach rolled over my legs, I was very bitter," he said. "A poor man has little. To lose that little—to lose the air on the hills and the springing step, to lie like a log forever because a bishop's coachman was careless—that made me very bitter. I had rather your lordship had driven over me again than taken me back to your palace and treated me with kindness. I hated your lordship for your indifferent kindness—I hated you for everything."

"Did you so, Luigi?" said the bishop.

"Yes," said Luigi. "And I could see that your lordship

hated me—or, if not hated, loathed, like a crippled dog that one must be kind to without liking. So I set myself out to tease and torment your lordship—at first by being your beggar, then in other ways. I could not believe in goodness; I could not believe there would not come a moment when your lordship would turn upon me and drive me forth."

He paused a moment and wiped his mouth with a cloth.

"Yes, I could not believe that at all," he said. "But you were not to be broken, Gianfrancesco, my brother. The evil I showed you daily was like a knife in your heart and a burden on your back, but you bore the knife and the burden. I took delight in showing you how ill things went in your city—how, below the fair surface, there was misery and pain. And had you once turned aside from that misery and pain, I would have been satisfied, for then, bishop or no bishop, you would have lost your soul. Was that evil of me, Gianfrancesco?"

"Very evil in intent," said the bishop steadily, "for, while it is permitted to be tempted, it is evil to tempt. And yet proceed."

"Well," said Luigi, with a sudden and childlike stare, "it did not work. The more I tried to make you a bad man, the better man you became. You would not do what was ill; you would not depart from your poor, once you had known them —not even for a red hat or a count's favor. You would not do ill at all. So now we have defended Remo, the two of us, and I am dying." He stirred uneasily in his bed. "It is just as well," he said, with a trace of his old mockery. "I told my uncle I would live to be a cardinal's beggar, but I am not sure that I would have liked it. I have been the bishop's beggar so long. And yet, from the first I have loved you also, Gianfrancesco.

35

Will you give me your blessing now, on me and my work—the blessing you denied me once?"

The bishop's face was wrung. Yet he lifted his hand and absolved and blessed Luigi. He blessed Luigi and his work in the name of the Father and of the Son and of the Holy Ghost. When that had been done, a smile appeared on Luigi's face.

"A very fine blessing," he said. "I must tell that to the Hook when I see him; he will be envious. I wonder is it drafty on the steps of heaven? A very fine blessing, your lordship . . . ten . . . scudi . . . for . . . Luigi." And with that his jaw dropped, and it was over. But the bishop knelt beside the bed with streaming eyes.

And all that, to be sure, was a long time ago. But they still tell the story in Remo when they show the bishop's tomb. He lies upon it, fairly carven in marble. But carved all around the tomb are a multitude of beggars, lame, halt, and misshapen, yet all praising God. And there are words in Latin which say, "It is not enough to have knowledge—these also are my sheep." Of the tomb of Luigi, the beggar—that no man knows. They say it is beside the bishop's but, in one war or another, it was destroyed and there is no trace of it now. Yet Luigi was an arrogant spirit; perhaps he would have liked that best.

The Two Churches of 'Quawket

by HENRY CUYLER BUNNER

❖❖❖

THE REVEREND COLTON M. PURSLY, OF AQUAWKET (COM-
monly pronounced 'Quawket), looked out of his study window over a remarkably pretty New England prospect, stroked
his thin, grayish side-whiskers, and sighed deeply. He was a
pale, sober, ill-dressed Congregationalist minister of forty-
two or three. He had eyes of willow-pattern blue, a large
nose, and a large mouth, with a smile of forced amiability in
the corners. He *was* amiable, perfectly amiable and in-
nocuous—but that smile sometimes made people with a strong
sense of humor want to kill him. The smile lingered even
while he sighed.

Mr. Pursly's house was set upon a hill, although it was a
modest abode. From his window he looked down one of those
splendid streets that are the pride and glory of old towns in
New England—a street fifty yards wide, arched with grand
Gothic elms, bordered with houses of pale yellow and white,
some in the homelike, simple yet dignified colonial style, some
with great Doric porticos at the street end. And above the
billowy green of the tree-tops rose two shapely spires, one to

37

the right, of granite, one to the left, of sand-stone. It was the sight of these two spires that made the Reverend Mr. Pursly sigh.

With a population of four thousand five hundred, 'Quawket had an Episcopal Church, a Roman Catholic Church, a Presbyterian Church, a Methodist Church, a Universalist Church (very small), a Baptist Church, a Hall for the "Seventh-Day Baptists" (used for secular purposes every day but Saturday), a Bethel, and—"The Two Churches"—as every one called the First and Second Congregational Churches. Fifteen years before, there had been but one Congregational Church, where a prosperous and contented congregation worshiped in a plain little old-fashioned red brick church on a side-street. Then, out of this very prosperity, came the idea of building a fine new freestone church on Main Street. And, when the new church was half-built, the congregation split on the question of putting a "rain-box" in the new organ. It is quite unnecessary to detail how this quarrel over a handful of peas grew into a church war, with ramifications and interlacements and entanglements and side issues and undercurrents and embroilments of all sorts and conditions. In three years there was a First Congregational Church, in freestone, solid, substantial, plain, and a Second Congregational Church in granite, something gingerbready, but showy and modish—for there are fashions in architecture as there are in millinery, and we cut our houses this way this year and that way the next. And these two churches had half a congregation apiece, and a full-sized debt, and they lived together in a spirit of Christian unity, on Capulet and Montague terms. The people of the First Church called the people of the Second Church the "Sadduceeceders," because there was no future for them, and the people of the Second Church called the people of the First Church the "Phariseemes." And this went on year after year, through the winters when the foxes hugged their holes in the ground within the woods about 'Quawket, through the summers when the birds of the air twittered in their nests in the great elms of Main Street.

If the First Church had a revival, the Second Church had a fair. If the pastor of the First Church exchanged with a distinguished preacher from Philadelphia, the organist of the Second Church got a celebrated tenor from Boston and had a service of song. This system after a time created a class in both churches known as "the floats," in contradistinction to the "pillars." The floats went from one church to the other according to the attractions offered. There were, in the end, more floats than pillars.

The Reverend Mr. Pursly inherited this contest from his predecessor. He had carried it on for three years. Finally, being a man of logical and precise mental processes, he called the head men of his congregation together, and told them what in worldly language might be set down thus:

There was room for one Congregational Church in 'Quawket, and for one only. The flock must be reunited in the parent fold. To do this a master stroke was necessary. They must build a Parish House. All of which was true beyond question—and yet—the church had a debt of $20,000 and a Parish House would cost $15,000.

And now the Reverend Mr. Pursly was sitting at his study window, wondering why all the rich men *would* join the Episcopal Church. He cast down his eyes, and saw a rich man coming up his path who could readily have given $15,000 for a Parish House, and who might safely be expected to give

$1.50, if he were rightly approached. A shade of bitterness crept over Mr. Pursly's professional smile. Then a look of puzzled wonder took possession of his face. Brother Joash Hitt was regular in his attendance at church and at prayer meeting; but he kept office hours in his religion, as in everything else, and never before had he called upon his pastor.

Two minutes later, the minister was nervously shaking hands with Brother Joash Hitt.

"I'm very glad to see you, Mr. Hitt," he stammered, "very glad—I'm—I'm—"

"S'prised?" suggested Mr. Hitt, grimly.

"Won't you sit down?" asked Mr. Pursly.

Mr. Hitt sat down in the darkest corner of the room, and glared at his embarrassed host. He was a huge old man, bent, heavily-built, with grizzled dark hair, black eyes, skin tanned to a mahogany brown, a heavy square underjaw, and big leathery dewlaps on each side of it that looked as hard as the jaw itself. Brother Joash had been all things in his long life— sea captain, commission merchant, speculator, slave dealer even, people said—and all things to his profit. Of late years he had turned over his capital in moneylending, and people said that his great claw-like fingers had grown crooked with holding the tails of his mortgages.

A silence ensued. The pastor looked up and saw that Brother Joash had no intention of breaking it.

"Can I do anything for you, Mr. Hitt?" inquired Mr. Pursly.

"Ya-as," said the old man. "Ye kin. I b'leeve you gin'lly git sump'n' over 'n' above your sellery when you preach a fun'l sermon?"

"Well, Mr. Hitt, it—yes—it is customary."

40

"How much?"

"The usual honorarium is—h'm—ten dollars."

"The—*whut?*"

"The—the fee."

"Will you write me one for ten dollars?"

"Why—why—" said the minister, nervously; "I didn't know that any one had—had died—"

"There hain't no one died, ez I know. It's *my* fun'l sermon I want."

"But, my dear Mr. Hitt, I trust you are not—that you won't —that—"

"Life's a rope of sand, parson—you'd ought to know that— nor we don't none of us know when it's goin' to fetch loost. I'm most ninety now, an' I don't cal'late to git no younger."

"Well," said Mr. Pursly, faintly smiling; "when the time *does* come—"

"No, *sir!*" interrupted Mr. Hitt, with emphasis; "when the time *doos* come, I won't have no use for it. Th' ain't no sense in the way most folks is berrid. Whut's th' use of puttin' a man into a mahog'ny coffin, with a silver plate big's a dishpan, an' preachin' a fun'l sermon over him, an' costin' his estate good money, when he's only a poor deef, dumb, blind fool corpse, an' don't get no good of it? *Naow,* I've be'n to the undertaker's, an' hed my coffin made under my own sooperveesion—good wood, straight grain, no knots—nuthin' fancy, but doorable. I've hed my tombstun cut, an' chose my text to put onto it— 'we brung nuthin' into the world, an' it is certain we can take nuthin' out'—an' now I want my fun'l sermon, jes' as the other folks is goin' to hear it who don't pay nuthin' for it. Kin you hev it ready for me this day week?"

"I suppose so," said Mr. Pursly, weakly.

"I'll call fer it," said the old man. "Heern some talk about a Perrish House, didn't I?"

"Yes," began Mr. Pursly, his face lighting up.

" 'Tain't no sech a bad *i*dee," remarked Brother Joash. "Wal, good day." And he walked off before the minister could say anything more.

One week later, Mr. Pursly again sat in his study, looking at Brother Joash, who had a second time settled himself in the dark corner.

It had been a terrible week for Mr. Pursly. He and his conscience, and his dream of the Parish House, had been shut up together working over that sermon, and waging a war of compromises. The casualties in this war were all on the side of the conscience.

"Read it!" commanded Brother Joash. The minister grew pale. This was more than he had expected. He grew pale and then red and then pale again.

"Go ahead!" said Brother Joash.

"Brethren," began Mr. Pursly, and then he stopped short. His pulpit voice sounded strange in his little study.

"Go ahead!" said Brother Joash.

"We are gathered together here to-day to pay a last tribute of respect and affection—"

"Clk!" There was a sound like the report of a small pistol. Mr. Pursly looked up. Brother Joash regarded him with stern intentness.

"—to one of the oldest and most prominent citizens of our town, a pillar of our church, and a monument of the civic virtues of probity, industry and wisdom, a man in whom we all took pride, and—"

42

"Clk!" Mr. Pursly looked up more quickly this time, and a faint suggestion of an expression just vanishing from Mr. Hitt's lips awakened in his unsuspicious breast a horrible suspicion that Brother Joash had chuckled.

"—whose like we shall not soon again see in our midst. The children on the streets will miss his familiar face—"

"Say!" broke in Brother Joash, "how'd it be for a delegation of child'n to foller the remains, with flowers or sump'n? They'd volunteer if you give 'em the hint, wouldn't they?"

"It would be—unusual," said the minister.

"All right," assented Mr. Hitt, "only an *i*dee of mine. Thought they might like it. Go ahead!"

Mr. Pursly went ahead, haunted by an agonizing fear of that awful chuckle, if chuckle it was. But he got along without interruption until he reached a casual and guarded allusion to the widows and orphans without whom no funeral oration is complete. Here the metallic voice of Brother Joash rang out again.

"Say! Ef the widders and orphans send a wreath—or a Gates-Ajar—*ef* they do, mind ye!—you'll hev it put a-top of the coffin, where folks'll see it, wun't ye?"

"Certainly," said the Reverend Mr. Pursly, hastily; "his charities were unostentatious, as was the whole tenor of his life. In these days of spendthrift extravagance, our young men may well—"

"Say!" Brother Joash broke in once more. "Ef any one wuz to git up right there, an' say that I wuz the derndest meanest, miserly, penurious, parsimonious old hunks in 'Quawket, you wouldn't let him talk like that, would ye?"

"Unquestionably not, Mr. Hitt!" said the minister, in horror.

"Thought not. On'y thet's whut I heern one o' your deacons

43

say about me the other day. Didn't know I heern him, but I did. I thought you wouldn't allow no such talk as that. Go ahead!"

"I must ask you, Mr. Hitt," Mr. Pursly said, perspiring at every pore, "to refrain from interruptions—or I—I really— can not continue."

"All right," returned Mr. Hitt, with perfect calmness. "Continner."

Mr. Pursly continued to the bitter end, with no further interruption that called for remonstrance. There were soft inarticulate sounds that seemed to him to come from Brother Joash's dark corner. But it might have been the birds in the *Ampelopsis Veitchii* that covered the house.

Brother Joash expressed no opinion, good or ill, of the address. He paid his ten dollars, in one-dollar bills, and took his receipt. But as the anxious minister followed him to the door, he turned suddenly and said:

"You was talkin' 'bout a Perrish House?"

"Yes—"

"Kin ye keep a secret?"

"I hope so—yes, certainly, Mr. Hitt."

"The' 'll be one."

"I feel," said the Reverend Mr. Pursly to his wife, "as if I had carried every stone of that Parish House on my shoulders and put it in its place. Can you make me a cup of tea, my dear?"

The summer days had begun to grow chill, and the great elms of 'Quawket were flecked with patches and spots of yellow, when, early one morning, the meagre little charity-boy whose duty it was to black Mr. Hitt's boots every day—it was a luxury he allowed himself in his old age—rushed, pale and frightened, into a neighboring grocery, and cried:

"Mist' Hitt's dead!"

"Guess not," said the grocer, doubtfully. "Brother Hitt's gut th' Old Nick's agency for 'Quawket, 'n' I ain't heerd th't he's been discharged for inattention to dooty."

"He's layin' there smilin'," said the boy.

"Smilin'?" repeated the grocer. "Guess I'd better go 'n' see."

In very truth, Brother Joash lay there in his bed, dead and cold, with a smile on his hard old lips, the first he had ever worn. And a most sardonic and discomforting smile it was.

The Reverend Mr. Pursly read Mr. Hitt's funeral address for the second time, in the First Congregational Church of 'Quawket. Every seat was filled; every ear was attentive. He stood on the platform, and below him, supported on decorously covered trestles, stood the coffin that enclosed all that was mortal of Brother Joash Hitt. Mr. Pursly read with his face immovably set on the line of the clock in the middle of the choir gallery railing. He did not dare to look down at the sardonic smile in the coffin below him; he did not dare to let his eye wander to the dark left-hand corner of the church, remembering the dark left-hand corner of his own study. And as he repeated each complimentary, obsequious, flattering platitude, a hideous, hysterical fear grew stronger and stronger within him that suddenly he would be struck dumb by the "clk!" of that mirthless chuckle that had sounded so much like a pistol-shot. His voice was hardly audible in the benediction.

The streets of 'Quawket were at their gayest and brightest when the mourners drove home from the cemetery at the close of the noontide hour. The mourners were principally the deacons and elders of the First Church. The Reverend Mr. Pursly lay back in his seat with a pleasing yet fatigued consciousness of duty performed and martyrdom achieved. He was exhausted, but humbly happy. As they drove along, he looked with a speculative eye on one or two eligible sites for the Parish House. His companion in the carriage was Mr. Uriel Hankinson, Brother Joash's lawyer, whose entire character had been aptly summed up by one of his fellow-citizens in conferring on him the designation of "a little Joash for one cent."

"Parson," said Mr. Hankinson, breaking a long silence, "that was a fust-rate oration you made."

"I'm glad to hear you say so," replied Mr. Pursly, his chronic smile broadening.

"You treated the deceased right handsome, considerin'," went on the lawyer Hankinson.

"Considering what?" inquired Mr. Pursly, in surprise.

"Considerin'—well, *considerin'*—" replied Mr. Hankinson, with a wave of his hand. "You must feel to be reel disapp'inted 'bout the Parish House, I sh'd s'pose."

"The Parish House?" repeated the Reverend Mr. Pursly, with a cold chill at his heart, but with dignity in his voice. "You may not be aware, Mr. Hankinson, that I have Mr. Hitt's promise that we should have a Parish House. And Mr. Hitt was—was—a man of his word." This conclusion sounded to his own ears a trifle lame and impotent.

"Guess you had his promise that there *should* be a Parish

46

House," corrected the lawyer, with a chuckle that might have been a faint echo of Brother Joash's.

"Well?"

"Well—the Second Church gits it. I draw'd his will. Good day, parson, I'll 'light here. Air's kind o' cold, ain't it?"

Dean Harcourt

by LLOYD C. DOUGLAS

᛫᛫

IT IS PRESUMABLE THAT AMONG THE MORE THOUGHTFUL OF those who sought the counsel of Dean Harcourt, some were impressed by the fact that, although he was a unique personality, not too easily evaluable, his mind and mood were essentially the product of the Cathedral.

For more than three quarters of a century, Trinity Cathedral had been one of the most highly respected institutions of the entire Middle West.

This distinction may have been due partly to her imposing architecture, a stately Gothic strongly reminiscent of York Minster. It may have been accounted for also by her commanding location, for the Cathedral close was bounded by four spacious streets, one of them Lake Boulevard, the most prominent avenue in the city. Moreover, the great edifice faced beautiful Madison Park, to the considerable advantage of her massive towers and old-worldish buttresses.

But Trinity's influential position rested upon something more consequential than these fortunate external phenomena. There had grown up a general public sentiment to the effect that you always knew where to find her. She was not subject to the sudden chills and fevers which wobbled the erratic pulse of many another institution displaying similar symbols in the windows. Trinity had been singularly immune to widespread emotional epidemics. Sometimes neighboring churches of clamorous importance were exasperated over her reluctance or downright refusal to participate in their tempestuous crusades of reform, and many an ardent front-paged apostle of despair had eloquently berated her for her cold-blooded indifference to society's imminent collapse. A devastating crisis was on, shouted the gloomsters, and Trinity had merely sat there and mumbled, "In all time of our tribulation; in all time of our prosperity, Good Lord, deliver us."

She had even kept her poise throughout the war, remaining discreetly neutral until the Government had officially declared itself otherwise, a difficult position which had drawn the fire of several downtown prophets who were eager to be early on the field of battle and hotly impatient of these lackadaisical delays.

Then she had loyally advocated patriotic sacrifice, but without the prevalent hysteria, which had been interpreted by many as another proof of her habitual unconcern. One zealous pulpiteer preached a widely quoted sermon on the Laodiceans, who were neither hot nor cold, and pointed in the direction of the well-known Yorkish towers as a deplorable case of such apathy.

But Trinity did not allow herself to be disconcerted. When most of the other churches were hanging the Kaiser, Sunday after Sunday, she continued to intone, with a dispassionateness that infuriated the swashbucklers, "Save and deliver

us, we humbly beseech thee, from the hands of our enemies."
That was all you could expect, rasped the militants, of prayers
that had to be read from a book! They had no capacity to
arouse moral indignation!

When peace arrived and it was again prudent for Christian
pacifism to put forth foliage and blossoms, Trinity's neighbors
had given themselves to an orgy of increasingly bold resolu-
tions that they would never, under any circumstance whatso-
ever, take up arms in an aggressive movement. Heartened by
response to this endeavor, they took the next step fearlessly,
declaring that they would never fight even in the defense of
their country. Trinity did not go on record with convictions
on this subject, and when heavily pressed for a declaration,
announced that so far as she was concerned all such matters
would have to be dealt with on their own merits when and
if they called for a decision. The younger fry among the clergy
pointed a disapproving finger toward her, asserting that Trinity
was dead on her feet and didn't realize that she was stricken
of a disease that would presently carry her off. But she continued to carry on as if unaware of the lethal nature of her
infirmity.

In the northeast tower a carillon of great value and wide
repute played on weekdays, from four to five, the historic
hymns of the Anglican faith, and it was traditional that
this daily program always began and ended with "O God,
Our Help in Ages Past," which seemed to be Trinity's theme
song. On certain occasions of national grief or gratification,
when the emotional tide ran high, these serenely confident
measures may have stirred many people who, ordinarily, did
not think much about their own spiritual reliances, and it is
not inconceivable that some of the more discriminating, who

50

had been bullied and badgered from one extreme opinion to another by institutions given to noisy tantrums of ecstasy or woe, were at least momentarily stabilized.

A high wrought-iron fence enveloped on three sides the Cathedral close. This gave the whole establishment an air of sequestration from the raucous hurly-burly of secular affairs, a redundant precaution, perhaps, for it was hardly necessary that Trinity should thus emphasize her insular aloofness from the contemporary fret.

At the rear of the main edifice, and facing on Marlborough, were the Bishop's Mansion, the Parish House, and the residence of the Dean.

It was rumored that there were telephones, typewriters, an adding device, a few clerks, and the inevitable paraphernalia of business covertly tucked away in a remote corner of the Parish House, but the casual visitor who had occasion to call there was not assaulted at the front door by the metallic racket of modern machinery.

Latterly there had been a fad, originated by city churches and amusingly imitated by the less busy elsewhere, to give the impression that the operation of "The Kingdom" should be pursued by up-to-date techniques consonant with the methods of great factories engaged in the fabrication and distribution of commercial commodities. In such enterprising strongholds the prophet's desk was cluttered with telephones dangling from adjustable brackets. A row of buttons served his urgency in buzzing the various members of his staff into his presence to report on the success of last night's "banquet" of the Carpenter's Apprentices, to present printer's proofs of the weekly bulletin and the newspaper advertising for Sunday, the program for the Advance Club, and what had been ascertained about the leak in the roof. His stenographer sat with her pad on her knee, licking the point of her pencil, poised for action. The Millennium was about to be delivered, F.O.B., as per yours of the thirteenth which, if you have further occasion to advert to it in future negotiations, should be keyed MBX13579.

Trinity had never railed at this nonsense, considering it none of her business, but she had not gone in for it herself. The people who entered her quiet precincts were asked the nature of their errands by unflustered employees trained to understand that the less professional they were, the more ably they would discharge their duties.

George Harcourt was a product of Trinity Cathedral. Her mind and his were in complete accord. Perhaps they may have influenced one another somewhat during the twenty years of his deanship. His serenity had become so potent that persons of every conceivable type came to him for advice, consolation, and encouragement. It was a heavy load to carry, but he never complained of it.

Every weekday but Saturday a procession of men tarried in the reception parlor of his residence taking turns in conference with him, keeping him at his desk from ten to one. In the afternoon, from three to six, women of all ages and ranks appeared there for the same purpose. He never referred to it or thought of it as a "clinic." He compiled no statistics, posted no records, permitted no clerical fussiness in the handling of this strange business. An unassuming volunteer for the day welcomed the callers and seated them. In due time they would have their turn.

Every morning at eight, two young curates placed strong hands under the Dean's elbows and led him—for he was a cripple—into the dimly lighted chancel of the Cathedral, where, whatever storms might be blowing outside, whatever tumultuous issues might be agitating the city or the nation or the world, his resonant voice intoned a petition "for all sorts and conditions of men; that thou wouldst be pleased to make thy ways known unto them."

When the early morning service was ended, the curates would assist the Dean to a chair placed for him in the center of the chancel, facing the high altar, and leave him alone for a half-hour.

And thus it was that when broken people came to Dean Harcourt for reconditioning, most of them, it was said, went out of his presence with the feeling that they had been very close to Headquarters.

She entered the Dean's office-library and crossed it with the agile, elastic, assured stride of complete physical fitness under superb control, seated herself gracefully in the chair he indicated, directly facing him, laid an expensive hand-bag on the spacious mahogany desk which separated them, and loosened the collar of an exquisite Persian-lamb coat.

"Sonia Duquesne," she said, in response to his low-voiced query.

The interview did not proceed any farther than that for a long moment.

Bearing most of his weight on the broad arms of his tall-backed churchly chair, the Dean leaned forward, pursed his lips thoughtfully, and took friendly stock of her. The rather hard, sophisticated smile she had brought along was gradually replaced by an almost entreating expression of self-defense, of meekness, of tenderness too, for it was now apparent to her

53

that his deep-lined face bore unmistakable evidence of suffering.

They studied each other silently, with candid concern, Sonia so impressed and stilled by the spiritual majesty of the man that she accepted his scrutiny of her without the slightest sensation of self-consciousness.

It was a singularly interesting face. The upper lip was extraordinarily long, giving the firm but generous mouth an appearance of being securely locked. Perhaps, reflected Sonia, it was his mouth that encouraged strangers to confide in him. A friend had told her that people found it easy to tell him all about themselves without embarrassment or restraint. Doubtless it was the mouth that made them confident. It seemed to have been built especially for the safekeeping of secrets. And there was something uncannily prescient in his eyes. They were dark, almost cavernous. A veritable sunburst of crow's-feet at the outer corners gave the effect of a residual smile of compassion which softened the penetrating search and interpreted it as a comradely quest. His thick white hair shone silver in the single light suspended above his head, a light that intensified, by strong shadows, the ruggedness of his face.

"That is your real name?" asked the Dean.

"Yes. I know it is a bit fantastic. But it is mine. My father's people were of French descent and my mother thought Sonia a pretty name. She saw it in a story."

"It is a pretty name, and I had not thought it incongruous, but you do not look foreign. When was it and where—that your mother read the story?"

"In 1901—Cedar Rapids."

"You are unmarried?"

"Yes," replied Sonia, her eyes occupied with the gloves which she had unbuttoned and was tugging off, finger by finger. Glancing up, she met his gaze, and added, "No—I was never married."

"Am I right in surmising that you are engaged in something theatrical?"

"Again I must answer—yes and no——"

The Dean acknowledged her honest candor with a slight inclination of the head. Sonia saw that she had said the right thing.

"I am the proprietor of a little shop, dealing in exclusive gowns. My clients—my customers prefer to think I am Parisian. I make no effort to counteract that belief. The place does have a foreign atmosphere. Perhaps I am theatrical—to the extent of playing a part in the course of my daily business."

"Do you attend the services of the Cathedral?" asked the Dean, still smiling a little over her frank confession.

"No, sir; I have no religion."

"Very well, then. Let us begin. Tell me all about it. What brought you here? . . . And remember that the more directly you come at it, the more time we will have to talk—profitably. . . . What has he done to you?"

She sat for a while with a perplexed expression, her lips parted, slightly baring pretty teeth, tensely locked.

"No—I am not a mind reader," explained the Dean gently, "but I have had much experience in listening."

"I believe that," said Sonia. "Well—he has decided to go back to his wife. She is not very well, and thinks she wants him. She has treated him very shabbily. It was her fault that he lost interest in their home. Now she begs him to return. I urged him to go. And I intend never to see him again. . . . That was yesterday." Sonia finished pulling off her gloves and laid them on the desk beside the handbag with a little gesture of finality. Her hands were white and well cared for.

"So—I really did not come to you for advice," she continued. "For there is nothing to decide. They told me you were able to help people who had trouble. That's why I came. I'm glad I did. . . . This is a very restful place. . . . You will not scold me. I've had all the punishment I can take."

"You love him—I think."

"Devotedly! And he loves me. He needs me, too, for he has been very unfortunate recently—since the crash."

"Did he contribute to your support?"

"Never! It wasn't on that basis, at all. In fact, for the past few weeks——"

Dean Harcourt's lips tightened, and he slowly raised a hand.

"Don't you want me to tell you?" asked Sonia, wide-eyed, shaking her head girlishly.

"Not that . . . I think you will feel better afterward if you do not confide that part of it."

Sonia looked puzzled; then nodded approval.

"I take it that you bear his wife no ill will?"

"Oh, no, not at all," she replied quickly. "In fact, lately, since he has been so hard-pressed, and I knew she was ill, I have ——"

"Don't!" commanded the Dean, so sternly that she winced under his unexpected rebuke. "You mustn't tell that to anybody—not even to me!" His voice grew gentle. "And may I add that I consider you a very fortunate woman to be possessed of such a soul . . . If you were my daughter I would be proud of you."

Her lips trembled as she replied, "Soul? I hardly knew I had one."

56

"Yes," sighed the Dean, running his long fingers through the shaggy hair at his temples. "Yes—that's the trouble. People collide with circumstances that push them off the commonly accepted moral reservation—and then they assume that they have lost their souls. . . . See here! Do you know anything about football?"

"A little. I often go. I did—last Saturday."

"Very good. You will have noticed then that a player sometimes runs out of bounds. Often it's his own fault, though frequently he is *forced* over the chalk-line. But, however it may have happened, he isn't sent home in disgrace. The game officials mark the spot where he went out, and carry the ball back into the field from that point."

"And then," said Sonia, "he loses his right to carry it."

"Only temporarily," corrected the Dean, pleased with this feature of his allegory. "He may quickly regain his right to carry the ball. There is no telling but the next time he lays hands on it, he will go through for a touchdown."

"You don't think I've lost my soul, then?"

"I should be more disposed to think," declared the Dean warmly, "that you have just now come to the place in your life where the essential fineness of you is about to have its great chance."

"What would you have me do?" asked Sonia sincerely.

"You must find somebody or something to absorb your love—a child, perhaps, or a worthy charity in which you may invest yourself personally. Your case is not so difficult as you think. You came to grief through love. It is the people who get into trouble through hate—they're the ones I worry over. Sometimes it is very hard to help them. Love is a gift—abused,

57

demoted, misdirected, quite frequently—but a gift, neverthe-less. Hate is a disease. And you, obviously, are not a hater.

"This encourages me to believe that you may be able to understand to what an extent the happiness of the world depends upon the clear vision of people who have a natural talent for love—to neutralize the bad influence of the people who are diseased by hate. Let me show you what I mean . . ."

The Dean edged himself far forward in his chair, rested his elbows on the desk, and looked Sonia steadily in the eyes, urging her earnest concentration.

"You see—not many people take time to consider how they are related to the Long Parade. They snatch their little pleas-ures; they bemoan their little disappointments; they smile and smirk and sigh and sulk, reacting variously to events affecting them as individuals. But they do not think of them-selves as component parts of *an era*. They fail to understand that we are all trudging along, elbow to elbow, in an endless, tightly integrated procession, in which our most important interests are held in common.

"Sometimes they sense it a little when some large catastrophe has frightened them into a huddle. It is often reported of groups that they have felt it keenly in time of shipwreck, battle, or some mass tragedy. Then they live, for an hour, in a previously unexperienced state of nobility, discovering them-selves to be brave, and suddenly impressed by the fact that human beings are all related.

"People with an extraordinary talent for love should be able to understand this in the ordinary process of living, and get the same thrill out of uneventful daily life that the ship-wrecked experience when tugged together by sudden mis-fortune.

58

"Now—this brings us up to your case. . . . Your love has been so urgent that it has led you to defy the social canons. You would like to atone for it, or at least try to justify your possession of a love so reckless. . . . Very well—I say! . . . You can do it! You *must* do it! . . . Try to begin your thinking about this by believing that the successful onward push of the human procession is the important thing, after all; far more important than any of the trifling ups and downs of the individuals. . . . Sometimes I like to think of Civilization as a ship. That ship, my friend, is more important than any member of the crew! . . . If you want to pay for the privilege of your love—and the mistakes of your love—believe that!"

They sat for a little while in silence. The Dean had made a platitude sound vital, dynamic. Sonia distinctly felt the strong tug of it. Her eyes were contemplative.

"That's all," said the Dean, rousing from the reverie into which he had momentarily drifted. "I shall be thinking of you. We will try to find something specific for you to do. Are you agreed?"

She arose to go, apparently reluctant to leave.

"I hope I can hold this feeling when I am outside again—in the street," she said meditatively. "There is something about this place—and you—that has made my worries seem very small. . . . Forgive my asking—if this isn't the thing to say—but shouldn't I pay somebody for this interview—pay it to the Cathedral, maybe?"

"Yes," replied the Dean, "I was just coming to that. . . . You are to go through that door at the right. You will find a small dressing room. Take off your hat and coat, and return to me."

She stood for a moment, mystified; then smiled, and obeyed. Presently she was back, waiting orders, her face full of inquiry.

"Now I want you to go out to the reception parlor where you waited when you came here, and inquire who is next. You will take that woman, whoever she is, into the small adjacent room: you know the one I mean."

"Where your secretary took me," said Sonia. "Really—she was the sweetest person I ever met, Dean Harcourt. She was so tender—and understanding."

"I am glad you found her so. . . . Well—you take your lady into that little room and let her tell you all she wants to about her reasons for coming here, asking her the same general questions you were asked. And then you come back and tell me. After that, you may bring her to my door. Then you will be free to recover your belongings and go your way. There is another exit from the dressing room, leading into the hall."

Sonia hesitated.

"But, Dean Harcourt"—she protested—"it seems such a pity to ask *me* to do this when I have had no experience—and there is your secretary, outside, who knows exactly what to say to people. I never met anyone so—so thoroughly fitted to deal with a person in trouble."

The Dean smiled enigmatically.

"That woman is not my secretary," he said quietly. "She was my last caller—just before you came."

Sonia's amazement parted her lips and narrowed her eyes.

"Do you always make them do that?" she asked.

"No—just the ones I think I can trust to do it well."

"I'll try," she said.

She was gone for about five minutes and returned with a distressed face. It was quite evident that she had been crying.

"Well?"

"Oh—Dean Harcourt—it's about her little girl. The doctors told her this morning that the little thing isn't ever going to be right, mentally; a brain tumor, or something. She's simply heartbroken. . . . And there wasn't a thing I could say that would have been of any comfort to her. . . . I just held her— and couldn't talk. I'm afraid you made a mistake in sending me out there."

"It was very well done, I think," said the Dean. "Now go and bring her in. And then you go around to the dressing-room and powder your nose—and run along. It has been a good day's work."

Sonia impulsively clasped his hand.

"I think you're wonderful!" she exclaimed, smiling pensively through her tears.

"No, Sonia," he replied, measuring his words slowly, "I'm not wonderful. . . . But you have made connection with something, this afternoon, that *is wonderful—wonderful!*" Drawing himself out of the introspective mood in which he seemed to have been speaking more to himself than to her, he added: "When you leave the dressing room, if you turn to the right the hallway will lead you directly into the nave of the Cathedral. . . . Go out that way. And when you are there, tarry a moment, sit down, face the altar, and say a little prayer for me. . . . I am not very strong, you know. I need the co-operation of people like you."

The clock in the great bell-tower was striking four. Trinity's theme song vibrated in the air.

61

Sonia sank to her knees beside the Dean's chair and murmured, brokenly, "People like *me!* . . . *Oh, my God!*"

He laid a firm hand on her quivering shoulder.

"Come," he said gently, "your friend is waiting."

She rose to her feet and walked unsteadily to the door, stood for a moment with her hand on the knob, wiping her eyes and striving valiantly to regain her self-control. Then she glanced back at the Dean, who sat with his elbows on the desk, his seamed face cupped in his hands, and a rapt expression in his eyes, listening to the bells.

Sonia smiled bravely, and turned the knob.

"I think I'll be all right now," she said.

"Yes—child," replied the Dean, as one answering from a dream, "you'll be—all right—now."

The Stickit Minister

by S. R. CROCKETT

THE CROWS WERE WHEELING BEHIND THE PLOUGH IN scattering clusters, and plumping singly upon the soft, thick grubs which the ploughshare was turning out upon an unkindly world. It was a bask blowy day in the end of March, and there was a hint of storm in the air—a hint emphasised for those skilled in weather lore by the presence of half a dozen sea gulls, white vagrants among the black coats, blown by the south wind up from the Solway—a snell, Scotch, but not unfriendly day altogether. Robert Fraser bent to the plough handles, and cast a keen and wary eye towards his guide posts on the ridge. His face was colourless, even when a dash of rain came swirling across from the crest of Ben Gairn, whose steep bulk heaved itself a blue haystack above the level horizon of the moorland. He was dressed like any other ploughman of the south uplands—rough homespun much the worse for wear, and leggings the colour of the red soil which he was reversing with the share of his plough. Yet there was that about Robert Fraser which marked him no common man. When he paused at the top of the ascent, and stood with his back against the horns of the plough, the country man's legacy from Adam of the Mattock, he pushed back his weather-beaten straw hat with a characteristic gesture, and showed a white forehead with blue veins channelling it—a damp, heavy lock of black hair clinging to it as in Severn's picture of John Keats on his deathbed. Robert Fraser saw a couple of black specks which moved smoothly and evenly along the top of the distant dyke of the highway. He stood still for a moment or two watching them. As they came nearer, they resolved themselves into a smart young man sitting in a well-equipped gig drawn by a showily actioned horse, and driven by a man in livery. As they passed rapidly along the road the hand of the young man appeared in a careless wave of recognition over the stone dyke, and Robert Fraser lifted his slack reins in staid acknowledgment. It was more than a year since the brothers had looked each other so nearly in the eyes. They were Dr. Henry Fraser, the rising physician of Cairn Edward, and his elder brother Robert, once Student of Divinity at Edinburgh College, whom three parishes knew as "The Stickit Minister."

When Robert Fraser stabled his horses that night and went in to his supper, he was not surprised to find his friend, Saunders M'Quhirr of Drumquhat, sitting by the peat fire in the "room." Almost the only thing which distinguished the Stickit Minister from the other small farmers of the parish of Dullarg was the fact that he always sat in the evening by himself *ben the hoose,* and did not use the kitchen in common with his housekeeper and herd boy save only at meal-times. Robert had taken to Saunders ever since—the back of his ambition broken—he had settled down to the farm, and he welcomed him with shy cordiality.

"You'll take a cup of tea, Saunders?" he asked.

64

"Thank ye, Robert, I wadna be waur o't," returned his friend.

"I saw your brither the day," said Saunders M'Quhirr, after the tea cups had been cleared away, and the silent housekeeper had replaced the books upon the table. Saunders picked a couple of them up, and, having adjusted his glasses, he read the titles—"Milton's Works," and a volume of a translation of "Dorner's Person of Christ."

"I saw yer brither the day; he maun be gettin' a big practice!"

"Ay!" said Robert Fraser, very thoughtfully.

Saunders M'Quhirr glanced up quickly. It was, of course, natural that the unsuccessful elder brother should envy the prosperous younger, but he had thought that Robert Fraser was living on a different plane. It was one of the few things that the friends had never spoken of, though every one knew why Dr. Fraser did not visit his brother's little farm. "He's gettin' in wi' the big fowk noo, an' thinks maybe that his brither wad do him nae credit." That was the way the clash of the countryside explained the matter.

"I never told you how I came to leave the college, Saunders," said the younger man, resting his brow on a hand that even the horn of the plough could not make other than diaphanous.

"No," said Saunders quietly, with a tender gleam coming into the humorsome kindly eyes that lurked under their bushy tussocks of grey eyebrow. Saunders' humour lay near the Fountain of Tears.

"No," continued Robert Fraser, "I have not spoken of it to so many; but you've been a good frien' to me, Saunders, and I think you should hear it. I have not tried to set myself right with folks in the general, but I would like to let *you* see clearly before I go my ways to Him who seeth from the beginning."

"Hear till him," said Saunders; "man, yer hoast [cough] is no' near as sair as it was i' the back-end. Ye'll be here lang efter me; but lang or short, weel do ye ken, Robert Fraser, that ye need not to pit yersel' richt wi' me. Hev I no' kenned ye sins ye war the size o' twa scrubbers?"

"I thank you, Saunders," said Robert, "but I am well aware that I'm to die this year. No, no, not a word. It is the Lord's will! It's more than seven year now since I first kenned that my days were to be few. It was the year my faither died, and left Harry and me by our lane.

"He left no sillar to speak of, just plenty to lay him decently in the kirkyard among his forebears. I had been a year at the Divinity Hall then, and was going up to put in my discourses for the next session. I had been troubled with my breast for some time, and so called one day at the infirmary to get a word with Sir James. He was very busy when I went in, and never noticed me till the hoast took me. Then on a sudden he looked up from his papers, came quickly over to me, put his own white handkerchief to my mouth, and quietly said, 'Come into my room, laddie!' Ay, he was a good man and a faithful, Sir James, if ever there was one. He told me that with care I might live five or six years, but it would need great care. Then a strange prickly coldness came over me, and I seemed to walk light-headed in an atmosphere suddenly rarified. I think I know now how the mouse feels under the air-pump."

"What's that?" queried Saunders.

"A cruel ploy not worth speaking of," continued the Stickit Minister. "Well, I found something in my throat when I tried to thank him. But I came my ways home to the Dullarg, and night and day I considered what was to be done, with so much to do and so little time to do it. It was clear that both Harry

66

and me could not go through the college on the little my faither had left. So late one night I saw my way clear to what I should do. Harry must go, I must stay. I must come home to the farm, and be my own 'man'; then I could send Harry to the college to be a doctor, for he had no call to the ministry as once I thought I had. More than that, it was laid on me to tell Jessie Loudon that Robert Fraser was no better than a machine set to go five year.

"Now all these things I did, Saunders, but there's no use telling you what they cost in the doing. They were right to do, and they were done. I do not repent any of them. I would do them all over again were they to do, but it's keen bitterer than I thought."

The Stickit Minister took his head off his hand and leaned wearily back in his chair.

"The story went over the country that I had failed in my examinations, and I never said that I had not. But there were some that knew better who might have contradicted the report if they had liked. I settled down to the farm, and I put Harry through the college, sending all but a bare living to him in Edinburgh. I worked the work of the farm, rain and shine, ever since, and have been for these six years the 'stickit minister' that all the world kens the day. Whiles Harry did not think that he got enough. He was always writing for more, and not so very pleased when he did not get it. He was aye different to me, ye ken, Saunders, and he canna be judged by the same standard as you and me."

"I ken," said Saunders M'Quhirr, a spark of light lying in the quiet of his eyes.

"Well," continued Robert Fraser, lightened by Saunders' apparent agreement, "the time came when he was clear from the college, and wanted a practice. He had been ill-advised that he had not got his share of the farm, and he wanted it selled to share and share alike. Now I kenned, and you ken, Saunders, that it's no' worth much in one share let alone two. So I got the place quietly bonded, and bought him old Dr. Aitkin's practice in Cairn Edward with the money.

"I have tried to do my best for the lad, for it was laid on me to be my brother's keeper. He doesna come here much," continued Robert, "but I think he's not so ill against me as he was. Saunders, he waved his hand to me when he was gaun by the day!"

"That was kind of him," said Saunders M'Quhirr.

"Ay, was it no'," said the Stickit Minister, eagerly, with a soft look in his eyes as he glanced up at his brother's portrait in cap and gown, which hung over the china dogs on the mantelpiece.

"I got my notice this morning that the bond is to be called up in November," said Robert. "So I'll be obliged to flit."

Saunders M'Quhirr started to his feet in a moment. "Never," he said, with the spark of fire alive now in his eyes, "never as lang as there's a beast on Drumquhat, or a poun' in Cairn Edward Bank," bringing down his clenched fist upon the Milton on the table.

"No, Saunders, no," said the Stickit Minister, very gently; "I thank you kindly, but *I'll be flitted before that!*"

The Blue Cross

by G. K. Chesterton

❖❖

Between the silver ribbon of morning and the green glittering ribbon of sea, the boat touched Harwich and let loose a swarm of folk like flies, among whom the man we must follow was by no means conspicuous—nor wished to be. There was nothing notable about him, except a slight contrast between the holiday gaiety of his clothes and the official gravity of his face. His clothes included a slight, pale grey jacket, a white waistcoat, and a silver straw hat with a grey-blue ribbon. His lean face was dark by contrast, and ended in a curt black beard that looked Spanish and suggested an Elizabethan ruff. He was smoking a cigarette with the seriousness of an idler. There was nothing about him to indicate the fact that the grey jacket covered a loaded revolver, that the white waistcoat covered a police card, or that the straw hat covered one of the most powerful intellects in Europe. For this was Valentin himself, the head of the Paris police and the most famous investigator of the world; and he was coming from Brussels to London to make the greatest arrest of the century.

Flambeau was in England. The police of three countries had tracked the great criminal at last from Ghent to Brussels, from Brussels to the Hook of Holland; and it was conjectured that he would take some advantage of the unfamiliarity and confusion of the Eucharistic Congress, then taking place in London. Probably he would travel as some minor clerk or secretary connected with it; but, of course, Valentin could not be certain; nobody could be certain about Flambeau.

It is many years now since this colossus of crime suddenly ceased keeping the world in a turmoil; and when he ceased, as they said after the death of Roland, there was a great quiet upon the earth. But in his best days (I mean, of course, his worst) Flambeau was a figure as statuesque and international as the Kaiser. Almost every morning the daily paper announced that he had escaped the consequences of one extraordinary crime by committing another. He was a Gascon of gigantic stature and bodily daring; and the wildest tales were told of his outbursts of athletic humour; how he turned the *juge d'instruction* upside down and stood him on his head, "to clear his mind"; how he ran down the Rue de Rivoli with a policeman under each arm. It is due to him to say that his fantastic physical strength was generally employed in such bloodless though undignified scenes; his real crimes were chiefly those of ingenious and wholesale robbery. But each of his thefts was almost a new sin, and would make a story by itself. It was he who ran the great Tyrolean Dairy Company in London, with no dairies, no cows, no carts, no milk, but with some thousand subscribers. These he served by the simple operation of moving the little milk cans outside people's doors to the doors of his own customers. It was he who had kept up an unaccountable and close correspondence with a young lady whose whole letter-bag was intercepted, by the extraordinary trick of photographing his messages infinitesimally small upon the slides of a microscope. A sweeping simplicity, however, marked many of his experiments. It is said that he once re-painted all the numbers in a street in the dead of night merely to divert one traveller into a trap. It is quite certain that he invented a portable pillar-box, which he put up at corners in quiet suburbs on the chance of strangers dropping postal orders into it. Lastly, he was known to be a startling acrobat; despite his huge figure, he could leap like a grasshopper and melt into the tree-tops like a monkey. Hence the great Valentin, when he set out to find Flambeau, was perfectly aware that his ad-ventures would not end when he had found him.

But how was he to find him? On this the great Valentin's ideas were still in process of settlement.

There was one thing which Flambeau, with all his dexterity of disguise, could not cover, and that was his singular height. If Valentin's quick eye had caught a tall apple-woman, a tall grenadier, or even a tolerably tall duchess, he might have ar-rested them on the spot. But all along his train there was nobody that could be a disguised Flambeau, any more than a cat could be a disguised giraffe. About the people on the boat he had already satisfied himself; and the people picked up at Harwich or on the journey limited themselves with certainty to six. There was a short railway official travelling up to the terminus, three fairly short market gardeners picked up two stations afterwards, one very short widow lady going up from a small Essex town, and a very short Roman Catholic priest going up from a small Essex village. When it came to the last case, Valentin gave it up and almost laughed. The little priest was so much the essence of those Eastern flats; he had a face as round and dull as a Norfolk dumpling; he had eyes as empty as the North Sea; he had several brown paper parcels, which he was

71

quite incapable of collecting. The Eucharistic Congress had doubtless sucked out of their local stagnation many such creatures, blind and helpless, like moles disinterred. Valentin was a sceptic in the severe style of France, and could have no love for priests. But he could have pity for them, and this one might have provoked pity in anybody. He had a large, shabby umbrella, which constantly fell on the floor. He did not seem to know which was the right end of his return ticket. He explained with a moon-calf simplicity to everybody in the carriage that he had to be careful, because he had something made of real silver "with blue stones" in one of his brown-paper parcels. His quaint blending of Essex flatness with saintly simplicity continuously amused the Frenchman till the priest arrived (somehow) at Tottenham with all his parcels, and came back for his umbrella. When he did the last, Valentin even had the good nature to warn him not to take care of the silver by telling everybody about it. But to whomever he talked, Valentin kept his eye open for someone else; he looked out steadily for anyone, rich or poor, male or female, who was well up to six feet; for Flambeau was four inches above it.

He alighted at Liverpool Street, however, quite conscientiously secure that he had not missed the criminal so far. He then went to Scotland Yard to regularise his position and arrange for help in case of need; he then lit another cigarette and went for a long stroll in the streets of London. As he was walking in the streets and squares beyond Victoria, he paused suddenly and stood. It was a quaint, quiet square, very typical of London, full of an accidental stillness. The tall, flat houses round looked at once prosperous and uninhabited; the square of shrubbery in the centre looked as deserted as a green Pacific islet. One of the four sides was much higher than the rest, like a daïs; and the line of this side was broken by one of London's admirable accidents—a restaurant that looked as if it had strayed from Soho. It was an unreasonably attractive object, with dwarf plants in pots and long, striped blinds of lemon yellow and white. It stood specially high above the street, and in the usual patchwork way of London, a flight of steps from the street ran up to meet the front door almost as a fire-escape might run up to a first-floor window. Valentin stood and smoked in front of the yellow-white blinds and considered them long.

The most incredible thing about miracles is that they happen. A few clouds in heaven do come together into the staring shape of one human eye. A tree does stand up in the landscape of a doubtful journey in the exact and elaborate shape of a note of interrogation. I have seen both these things myself within the last few days. Nelson does die in the instant of victory; and a man named Williams does quite accidentally murder a man named Williamson; it sounds like a sort of infanticide. In short, there is in life an element of elfin coincidence which people reckoning on the prosaic may perpetually miss. As it has been well expressed in the paradox of Poe, wisdom should reckon on the unforeseen.

Aristide Valentin was unfathomably French; and the French intelligence is intelligence specially and solely. He was not "a thinking machine"; for that is a brainless phrase of modern fatalism and materialism. A machine only *is* a machine because it cannot think. But he was a thinking man, and a plain man at the same time. All his wonderful successes, that looked like conjuring, had been gained by plodding logic, by clear and commonplace French thought. The French electrify the world not by starting any paradox, they electrify it by carrying out a truism. They carry a truism so far—as in the French Revolution. But exactly because Valentin understood reason, he understood the limits of reason. Only a man who knows nothing of motors talks of motoring without petrol; only a man who knows nothing of reason talks of reasoning without strong, undisputed first principles. Here he had no strong first principles. Flambeau had been missed at Harwich; and if he was in London at all, he might be anything from a tall tramp on Wimbledon Common to a tall toastmaster at the Hôtel Métropole. In such a naked state of nescience, Valentin had a view and a method of his own.

In such cases he reckoned on the unforeseen. In such cases, when he could not follow the train of the reasonable, he coldly and carefully followed the train of the unreasonable. Instead of going to the right places—banks, police stations, rendezvous —he systematically went to the wrong places; knocked at every empty house, turned down every *cul de sac,* went up every lane blocked with rubbish, went round every crescent that led him uselessly out of the way. He defended this crazy course quite logically. He said that if one had a clue this was the worst way; but if one had no clue at all it was the best, because there was just the chance that any oddity that caught the eye of the pursuer might be the same that had caught the eye of the pursued. Somewhere a man must begin, and it had better be just where another man might stop. Something about that flight of steps up to the shop, something about the quietude and quaintness of the restaurant, roused all the detective's rare romantic fancy and made him resolve to strike at random. He went up the steps, and sitting down at a table by the window, asked for a cup of black coffee.

74

It was half-way through the morning, and he had not break-fasted; the slight litter of other breakfasts stood about on the table to remind him of his hunger; and adding a poached egg to his order, he proceeded musingly to shake some white sugar into his coffee, thinking all the time about Flambeau. He re-membered how Flambeau had escaped, once by a pair of nail scissors, and once by a house on fire; once by having to pay for an unstamped letter, and once by getting people to look through a telescope at a comet that might destroy the world. He thought his detective brain as good as the criminal's, which was true. But he fully realised the disadvantage. "The criminal is the creative artist; the detective only the critic," he said with a sour smile, and lifted his coffee cup to his lips slowly, and put it down very quickly. He had put salt in it.

He looked at the vessel from which the silvery powder had come; it was certainly a sugar-basin; as unmistakably meant for sugar as a champagne-bottle for champagne. He wondered why they should keep salt in it. He looked to see if there were any more orthodox vessels. Yes; there were two salt-cellars quite full. Perhaps there was some speciality in the condiment in the salt-cellars. He tasted it; it was sugar. Then he looked round at the restaurant with a refreshed air of interest, to see if there were any other traces of that singular artistic taste which puts the sugar in the salt-cellars and the salt in the sugar-basin. Except for an odd splash of some dark fluid on one of the white-papered walls, the whole place appeared neat, cheerful and ordinary. He rang the bell for the waiter.

When that official hurried up, fuzzy-haired and somewhat blear-eyed at that early hour, the detective (who was not without an appreciation of the simpler forms of humour) asked him to taste the sugar and see if it was up to the high reputation of the hotel. The result was that the waiter yawned suddenly and woke up.

"Do you play this delicate joke on your customers every morning?" inquired Valentin. "Does changing the salt and sugar never pall on you as a jest?"

The waiter, when this irony grew clearer, stammeringly assured him that the establishment had certainly no such intention; it must be a most curious mistake. He picked up the sugar-basin and looked at it; he picked up the salt-cellar and looked at that, his face growing more and more bewildered. At last he abruptly excused himself, and hurrying away, returned in a few seconds with the proprietor. The proprietor also examined the sugar-basin and then the salt-cellar; the proprietor also looked bewildered.

Suddenly the waiter seemed to grow inarticulate with a rush of words.

"I zink," he stuttered eagerly, "I zink it is those two clergymen."

"What two clergymen?"

"The two clergymen," said the waiter, "that threw soup at the wall."

"Threw soup at the wall?" repeated Valentin, feeling sure this must be some singular Italian metaphor.

"Yes, yes," said the attendant excitedly, and pointing at the dark splash on the white paper, "threw it over there on the wall."

Valentin looked his query at the proprietor, who came to his rescue with fuller reports.

"Yes, sir," he said, "it's quite true, though I don't suppose it has anything to do with the sugar and salt. Two clergymen came in and drank soup here very early, as soon as the shutters

were taken down. They were both very quiet, respectable people; one of them paid the bill and went out; the other, who
seemed a slower coach altogether, was some minutes longer
getting his things together. But he went at last. Only, the
instant before he stepped into the street he deliberately picked
up his cup, which he had only half emptied, and threw the
soup slap on the wall. I was in the back room myself, and so
was the waiter; so I could only rush out in time to find the
wall splashed and the shop empty. It don't do any particular
damage, but it was confounded cheek; and I tried to catch the
men in the street. They were too far off though; I only noticed
they went round the next corner into Carstairs Street."

The detective was on his feet, hat settled and stick in hand.
He had already decided that in the universal darkness of his
mind he could only follow the first odd finger that pointed; and
this finger was odd enough. Paying his bill and clashing the
glass doors behind him, he was soon swinging round into the
other street.

It was fortunate that even in such fevered moments his eye
was cool and quick. Something in a shop-front went by him
like a mere flash; yet he went back to look at it. The shop was
a popular greengrocer and fruiterer's, an array of goods set
out in the open air and plainly ticketed with their names and
prices. In the two most prominent compartments were two
heaps, of oranges and of nuts respectively. On the heap of
nuts lay a scrap of cardboard, on which was written in bold,
blue chalk, "Best tangerine oranges, two a penny." On the
oranges was the equally clear and exact description, "Finest
Brazil nuts, 4d. a lb." M. Valentin looked at these two placards
and fancied he had met this highly subtle form of humour
before, and that somewhat recently. He drew the attention of

the redfaced fruiterer, who was looking rather sullenly up and down the street, to this inaccuracy in his advertisements. The fruiterer said nothing, but sharply put each card into its proper place. The detective, leaning elegantly on his walking-cane, continued to scrutinise the shop. At last he said, "Pray excuse my apparent irrelevance, my good sir, but I should like to ask you a question in experimental psychology and the association of ideas."

The red-faced shopman regarded him with an eye of menace; but he continued gaily, swinging his cane, "Why," he pursued, "why are two tickets wrongly placed in a greengrocer's shop like a shovel hat that has come to London for a holiday? Or, in case I do not make myself clear, what is the mystical association which connects the idea of nuts marked as oranges with the idea of two clergymen, one tall and the other short?"

The eyes of the tradesman stood out of his head like a snail's; he really seemed for an instant likely to fling himself upon the stranger. At last he stammered angrily: "I don't know what you 'ave to do with it, but if you're one of their friends, you can tell 'em from me that I'll knock their silly 'eads off, parsons or no parsons, if they upset my apples again."

"Indeed?" asked the detective, with great sympathy. "Did they upset your apples?"

"One of 'em did," said the heated shopman; "rolled 'em all over the street. I'd 'ave caught the fool but for havin' to pick 'em up."

"Which way did these parsons go?" asked Valentin.

"Up that second road on the left-hand side, and then across the square," said the other promptly.

"Thanks," replied Valentin, and vanished like a fairy. On the other side of the second square he found a policeman, and said: "This is urgent, constable; have you seen two clergymen in shovel hats?"

The policeman began to chuckle heavily. "I 'ave, sir; and if you arst me, one of 'em was drunk. He stood in the middle of the road that bewildered that——"

"Which way did they go?" snapped Valentin.

"They took one of them yellow buses over there," answered the man; "them that go to Hampstead."

Valentin produced his official card and said very rapidly: "Call up two of your men to come with me in pursuit," and crossed the road with such contagious energy that the ponderous policeman was moved to almost agile obedience. In a minute and a half the French detective was joined on the opposite pavement by an inspector and a man in plain clothes.

"Well, sir," began the former, with smiling importance, "and what may——?"

Valentin pointed suddenly with his cane. "I'll tell you on the top of that omnibus," he said, and was darting and dodging across the tangle of the traffic. When all three sank panting on the top seats of the yellow vehicle, the inspector said: "We could go four times as quick in a taxi."

"Quite true," replied their leader placidly, "if we only had an idea of where we were going."

"Well, where *are* you going?" asked the other, staring.

Valentin smoked frowningly for a few seconds; then, removing his cigarette, he said: "If you *know* what a man's doing, get in front of him; but if you want to guess what he's doing, keep behind him. Stray when he strays; stop when he stops; travel as slowly as he. Then you may see what he saw and may act as he acted. All we can do is to keep our eyes skinned for a queer thing."

"What sort of queer thing do you mean?" asked the inspector.

"Any sort of queer thing," answered Valentin, and relapsed into obstinate silence.

The yellow omnibus crawled up the northern roads for what seemed like hours on end; the great detective would not explain further, and perhaps his assistants felt a silent and growing doubt of his errand. Perhaps, also, they felt a silent and growing desire for lunch, for the hours crept long past the normal luncheon hour, and the long roads of the North London suburbs seemed to shoot out into length after length like an infernal telescope. It was one of those journeys on which a man perpetually feels that now at last he must have come to the end of the universe, and then finds he has only come to the beginning of Tufnell Park. London died away in draggled taverns and dreary scrubs, and then was unaccountably born again in blazing high streets and blatant hotels. It was like passing through thirteen separate vulgar cities all just touching each other. But though the winter twilight was already threatening the road ahead of them, the Parisian detective still sat silent and watchful, eyeing the frontage of the streets that slid by on either side. By the time they had left Camden Town behind, the policemen were nearly asleep; at least, they gave something like a jump as Valentin leapt erect, struck a hand on each man's shoulder, and shouted to the driver to stop.

They tumbled down the steps into the road without realising why they had been dislodged; when they looked round for enlightenment they found Valentin triumphantly pointing his finger towards a window on the left side of the road. It was a large window, forming part of the long façade of a gilt and palatial public-house; it was the part reserved for respectable dining, and labelled "Restaurant." This window, like all the rest along the frontage of the hotel, was of frosted and figured glass; but in the middle of it was a big, black smash, like a star in the ice.

"Our cue at last," cried Valentin, waving his stick; "the place with the broken window."

"What window? What cue?" asked his principal assistant. "Why, what proof is there that this has anything to do with them?"

Valentin almost broke his bamboo stick with rage.

"Proof!" he cried. "Good God! the man is looking for proof! Why, of course, the chances are twenty to one that it has *nothing* to do with them. But what else can we do? Don't you see we must either follow one wild possibility or else go home to bed?" He banged his way into the restaurant, followed by his companions, and they were soon seated at a late luncheon at a little table, and looking at the star of smashed glass from the inside. Not that it was very informative to them even then.

"Got your window broken, I see," said Valentin to the waiter as he paid the bill.

"Yes, sir," answered the attendant, bending busily over the change, to which Valentin silently added an enormous tip. The waiter straightened himself with mild but unmistakable animation.

"Ah, yes, sir," he said. "Very odd thing, that sir."

"Indeed? Tell us about it," said the detective with careless curiosity.

"Well, two gents in black came in," said the waiter; "two of those foreign parsons that are running about. They had a cheap and quiet little lunch, and one of them paid for it and went out. The other was just going out to join him when I

81

looked at my change again and found he'd paid me more than three times too much. 'Here,' I says to the chap who was nearly out of the door, 'you've paid too much.' 'Oh,' he says, very cool, 'have we?' 'Yes,' I says, and picks up the bill to show him. Well, that was a knock-out."

"What do you mean?" asked his interlocutor.

"Well, I'd have sworn on seven Bibles that I'd put 4s. on that bill. But now I saw I'd put 14s., as plain as paint."

"Well?" cried Valentin, moving slowly, but with burning eyes, "and then?"

"The parson at the door he says all serene, 'Sorry to confuse your accounts, but it'll pay for the window.' 'What window?' I says. 'The one I'm going to break,' he says, and smashed that blessed pane with his umbrella."

All three inquirers made an exclamation; and the inspector said under his breath, "Are we after escaped lunatics?" The waiter went on with some relish for the ridiculous story:

"I was so knocked silly for a second, I couldn't do anything. The man marched out of the place and joined his friend just round the corner. Then they went so quick up Bullock Street that I couldn't catch them, though I ran round the bars to do it."

"Bullock Street," said the detective, and shot up that thoroughfare as quickly as the strange couple he pursued.

Their journey now took them through bare brick ways like tunnels; streets with few lights and even with few windows; streets that seemed built out of the blank backs of everything and everywhere. Dusk was deepening, and it was not easy even for the London policemen to guess in what exact direction they were treading. The inspector, however, was pretty certain that they would eventually strike some part of Hampstead Heath.

Abruptly one bulging gas-lit window broke the blue twilight like a bull's-eye lantern; and Valentin stopped an instant before a little garish sweetstuff shop. After an instant's hesitation he went in; he stood amid the gaudy colours of the confectionery with entire gravity and bought thirteen chocolate cigars with a certain care. He was clearly preparing an opening; but he did not need one.

An angular, elderly young woman in the shop had regarded his elegant appearance with a merely automatic inquiry; but when she saw the door behind him blocked with the blue uniform of the inspector, her eyes seemed to wake up.

"Oh," she said, "if you've come about that parcel, I've sent it off already."

"Parcel!" repeated Valentin; and it was his turn to look inquiring.

"I mean the parcel the gentleman left—the clergyman gentleman."

"For goodness' sake," said Valentin, leaning forward with his first real confession of eagerness, "for Heaven's sake tell us what happened exactly."

"Well," said the woman a little doubtfully, "the clergymen came in about half an hour ago and bought some peppermints and talked a bit, and then went off towards the Heath. But a second after, one of them runs back into the shop and says, 'Have I left a parcel?' Well, I looked everywhere and couldn't see one; so he says, 'Never mind; but if it should turn up, please post it to this address,' and he left me the address and a shilling for my trouble. And sure enough, though I thought I'd looked everywhere, I found he'd left a brown paper parcel, so I posted it to the place he said. I can't remember the address now; it was somewhere in Westminster. But as the thing seemed so important, I thought perhaps the police had come about it."

"So they have," said Valentin shortly. "Is Hampstead Heath near here?"

"Straight on for fifteen minutes," said the woman, "and you'll come right out on the open." Valentin sprang out of the shop and began to run. The other detectives followed him at a reluctant trot.

The street they threaded was so narrow and shut in by shadows that when they came out unexpectedly into the void common and vast sky they were startled to find the evening still so light and clear. A perfect dome of peacock-green sank into gold amid the blackening trees and the dark violet distances. The glowing green tint was just deep enough to pick out in points of crystal one or two stars. All that was left of the day-light lay in a golden glitter across the edge of Hampstead and that popular hollow which is called the Vale of Health. The holiday makers who roam this region had not wholly dispersed; a few couples sat shapelessly on benches; and here and there a distant girl still shrieked in one of the swings. The glory of heaven deepened and darkened around the sublime vulgarity of man; and standing on the slope and looking across the valley, Valentin beheld the thing which he sought.

Among the black and breaking groups in that distance was one especially black which did not break—a group of two figures clerically clad. Though they seemed as small as insects, Valentin could see that one of them was much smaller than the other. Though the other had a student's stoop and an inconspicuous manner, he could see that the man was well over six feet high. He shut his teeth and went forward, whirling his stick impatiently. By the time he had substantially diminished the distance and magnified the two black figures as in a vast microscope, he had perceived something else; something which startled him, and yet which he had somehow expected. Whoever was the tall priest, there could be no doubt about the identity of the short one. It was his friend of the Harwich train, the stumpy little *curé* of Essex whom he had warned about his brown paper parcels.

Now, so far as this went, everything fitted in finally and rationally enough. Valentin had learned by his inquiries that morning that a Father Brown from Essex was bringing up a silver cross with sapphires, a relic of considerable value, to show some of the foreign priests at the congress. This undoubtedly was the "silver with blue stones"; and Father Brown undoubtedly was the little greenhorn in the train. Now there was nothing wonderful about the fact that what Valentin had found out Flambeau had also found out; Flambeau found out everything. Also there was nothing wonderful in the fact that when Flambeau heard of a sapphire cross he should try to steal it; that was the most natural thing in all natural history. And most certainly there was nothing wonderful about the fact that Flambeau should have it all his own way with such a silly sheep as the man with the umbrella and the parcels. He was the sort of man whom anybody could lead on a string to the North Pole; it was not surprising that an actor like Flambeau, dressed as another priest, could lead him to Hampstead Heath. So far the crime seemed clear enough; and while the detective pitied the priest for his helplessness, he almost despised Flambeau for condescending to so gullible a victim. But when Valentin thought of all that had happened in between, of all that had led him to his triumph, he racked his brains for the smallest rhyme or reason in it. What had the stealing of a

blue-and-silver cross from a priest from Essex to do with chuck-
ing soup at wall paper? What had it to do with calling nuts
oranges, or with paying for windows first and breaking them
afterwards? He had come to the end of his chase; yet somehow
he had missed the middle of it. When he failed (which was
seldom), he had usually grasped the clue, but nevertheless
missed the criminal. Here he had grasped the criminal, but
still he could not grasp the clue.

The two figures that they followed were crawling like black
flies across the huge green contour of a hill. They were evidently sunk in conversation, and perhaps did not notice where
they were going; but they were certainly going to the wilder
and more silent heights of the Heath. As their pursuers gained
on them, the latter had to use the undignified attitudes of the
deer-stalker, to crouch behind clumps of trees and even to
crawl prostrate in deep grass. By these ungainly ingenuities the
hunters even came close enough to the quarry to hear the murmur of the discussion, but no word could be distinguished
except the word "reason" recurring frequently in a high and
almost childish voice. Once over an abrupt dip of land and a
dense tangle of thickets, the detectives actually lost the two
figures they were following. They did not find the trail again
for an agonising ten minutes, and then it led round the brow
of a great dome of hill overlooking an amphitheatre of rich
and desolate sunset scenery. Under a tree in this commanding
yet neglected spot was an old ramshackle wooden seat. On
this seat sat the two priests still in serious speech together.
The gorgeous green and gold still clung to the darkening
horizon; but the dome above was turning slowly from peacock-
green to peacock-blue, and the stars detached themselves more
and more like solid jewels. Mutely motioning to his followers,

Valentin contrived to creep up behind the big branching tree, and, standing there in deathly silence, heard the words of the strange priests for the first time.

After he had listened for a minute and a half, he was gripped by a devilish doubt. Perhaps he had dragged the two English policemen to the wastes of a nocturnal heath on an errand no saner than seeking figs on its thistles. For the two priests were talking exactly like priests, piously, with learning and leisure, about the most aerial enigmas of theology. The little Essex priest spoke the more simply, with his round face turned to the strengthening stars; the other talked with his head bowed, as if he were not even worthy to look at them. But no more innocently clerical conversation could have been heard in any white Italian cloister or black Spanish cathedral.

The first he heard was the tail of one of Father Brown's sentences, which ended: ". . . what they really meant in the Middle Ages by the heavens being incorruptible."

The taller priest nodded his bowed head and said:

"Ah, yes, these modern infidels appeal to their reason; but who can look at those millions of worlds and not feel that there may well be wonderful universes above us where reason is utterly unreasonable?"

"No," said the other priest, "reason is always reasonable, even in the last limbo, in the lost borderland of things. I know that people charge the Church with lowering reason, but it is just the other way. Alone on earth, the Church makes reason really supreme. Alone on earth, the Church affirms that God himself is bound by reason."

The other priest raised his austere face to the spangled sky and said:

"Yet who knows if in that infinite universe——?"

"Only infinite physically," said the little priest, turning sharply in his seat, "not infinite in the sense of escaping from the laws of truth."

Valentin behind his tree was tearing his fingernails with silent fury. He seemed almost to hear the sniggers of the English detectives whom he had brought so far on a fantastic guess only to listen to the metaphysical gossip of two mild old parsons. In his impatience he lost the equally elaborate answer of the tall cleric, and when he listened again it was again Father Brown who was speaking:

"Reason and justice grip the remotest and the loneliest star. Look at those stars. Don't they look as if they were single diamonds and sapphires? Well, you can imagine any mad botany or geology you please. Think of forests of adamant with leaves of brilliants. Think the moon is a blue moon, a single elephantine sapphire. But don't fancy that all that frantic astronomy would make the smallest difference to the reason and justice of conduct. On plains of opal, under cliffs cut out of pearl, you would still find a notice-board, 'Thou shalt not steal.'"

Valentin was just in the act of rising from his rigid and crouching attitude and creeping away as softly as might be, felled by the one great folly of his life. But something in the very silence of the tall priest made him stop until the latter spoke. When at last he did speak, he said simply, his head bowed and his hands on his knees:

"Well, I still think that other worlds may perhaps rise higher than our reason. The mystery of heaven is unfathomable, and I for one can only bow my head."

Then, with brow yet bent and without changing by the faintest shade his attitude or voice, he added:

"Just hand over that sapphire cross of yours, will you? We're all alone here, and I could pull you to pieces like a straw doll."

The utterly unaltered voice and attitude added a strange violence to that shocking change of speech. But the guarder of the relic only seemed to turn his head by the smallest section of the compass. He seemed still to have a somewhat foolish face turned to the stars. Perhaps he had not understood. Or, perhaps, he had understood and sat rigid with terror.

"Yes," said the tall priest, in the same low voice and in the same still posture, "yes, I am Flambeau."

Then, after a pause, he said:

"Come, will you give me that cross?"

"No," said the other, and the monosyllable had an odd sound.

Flambeau suddenly flung off all his pontifical pretensions. The great robber leaned back in his seat and laughed low but long.

"No," he cried, "you won't give it me, you proud prelate. You won't give it me, you little celibate simpleton. Shall I tell you why you won't give it me? Because I've got it already in my own breast-pocket."

The small man from Essex turned what seemed to be a dazed face in the dusk, and said, with the timid eagerness of "The Private Secretary":

"Are—are you sure?"

Flambeau yelled with delight.

"Really, you're as good as a three-act farce," he cried. "Yes, you turnip, I am quite sure. I had the sense to make a duplicate of the right parcel, and now, my friend, you've got the duplicate and I've got the jewels. An old dodge, Father Brown—a very old dodge."

"Yes," said Father Brown, and passed his hand through his hair with the same strange vagueness of manner. "Yes, I've heard of it before."

The colossus of crime leaned over to the little rustic priest with a sort of sudden interest.

"*You* have heard of it?" he asked. "Where have *you* heard of it?"

"Well, I mustn't tell you his name, of course," said the little man simply. "He was a penitent, you know. He had lived prosperously for about twenty years entirely on duplicate brown paper parcels. And so, you see, when I began to suspect you, I thought of this poor chap's way of doing it at once."

"Began to suspect me?" repeated the outlaw with increased intensity. "Did you really have the gumption to suspect me just because I brought you up to this bare part of the heath?"

"No, no," said Brown with an air of apology. "You see, I suspected you when we first met. It's that little bulge up the sleeve where you people have the spiked bracelet."

"How in Tartarus," cried Flambeau, "did you ever hear of the spiked bracelet?"

"Oh, one's little flock, you know!" said Father Brown, arching his eyebrows rather blankly. "When I was a curate in Hartlepool, there were three of them with spiked bracelets. So, as I suspected you from the first, don't you see, I made sure that the cross should go safe, anyhow. I'm afraid I watched you, you know. So at last I saw you change the parcels. Then, don't you see, I changed them back again. And then I left the right one behind."

"Left it behind?" repeated Flambeau, and for the first time there was another note in his voice beside his triumph.

"Well, it was like this," said the little priest, speaking in the same unaffected way. "I went back to that sweet-shop and asked if I'd left a parcel, and gave them a particular address if it turned up. Well, I knew I hadn't; but when I went away again I did. So, instead of running after me with that valuable parcel, they have sent it flying to a friend of mine in Westminster." Then he added rather sadly: "I learnt that, too, from a poor fellow in Hartlepool. He used to do it with handbags he stole at railway stations, but he's in a monastery now. Oh, one gets to know, you know," he added, rubbing his head again with the same sort of desperate apology. "We can't help being priests. People come and tell us these things."

Flambeau tore a brown-paper parcel out of his inner pocket and rent it in pieces. There was nothing but paper and sticks of lead inside it. He sprang to his feet with a gigantic gesture, and cried:

"I don't believe you. I don't believe a bumpkin like you could manage all that. I believe you've still got the stuff on you, and if you don't give it up—why, we're all alone, and I'll take it by force!"

"No," said Father Brown simply, and stood up also, "you won't take it by force. First, because I really haven't still got it. And, second, because we are not alone.

Flambeau stopped in his stride forward.

"Behind that tree," said Father Brown, pointing, "are two strong policemen and the greatest detective alive. How did they come here, do you ask? Why, I brought them, of course! How did I do it? Why, I'll tell you if you like! Lord bless you, we have to know twenty such things when we work among the criminal classes! Well, I wasn't sure you were a thief, and it would never do to make a scandal against one of our own clergy. So I just tested you to see if anything would make you show yourself. A man generally makes a small scene if he finds salt in his coffee; if he doesn't, he has some reason for keeping quiet. I changed the salt and sugar, and *you* kept quiet. A man generally objects if his bill is three times too big. If he pays it, he has some motive for passing unnoticed. I altered your bill, and *you* paid it."

The world seemed waiting for Flambeau to leap like a tiger. But he was held back as by a spell; he was stunned with the utmost curiosity.

"Well," went on Father Brown, with lumbering lucidity, "as you wouldn't leave any tracks for the police, of course somebody had to. At every place we went to, I took care to do something that would get us talked about for the rest of the day. I didn't do much harm—a splashed wall, spilt apples, a broken window; but I saved the cross, as the cross will always be saved. It is at Westminster by now. I rather wonder you didn't stop it with the Donkey's Whistle."

"With the what?" asked Flambeau.

"I'm glad you've never heard of it," said the priest, making a face. "It's a foul thing. I'm sure you're too good a man for a Whistler. I couldn't have countered it even with the Spots myself; I'm not strong enough in the legs."

"What on earth are you talking about?" asked the other.

"Well, I did think you'd know the Spots," said Father Brown, agreeably surprised. "Oh, you can't have gone so very wrong yet!"

"How in blazes do you know all these horrors?" cried Flambeau.

The shadow of a smile crossed the round, simple face of his clerical opponent.

"Oh, by being a celibate simpleton, I suppose," he said. "Has it ever struck you that a man who does next to nothing but hear men's real sins is not likely to be wholly unaware of human evil? But, as a matter of fact, another part of my trade, too, made me sure you weren't a priest."

"What?" asked the thief, almost gaping.

"You attacked reason," said Father Brown. "It's bad theology."

And even as he turned away to collect his property, the three policemen came out from under the twilight trees. Flambeau was an artist and a sportsman. He stepped back and swept Valentin a great bow.

"Do not bow to me, *mon ami,*" said Valentin with silver clearness. "Let us both bow to our master."

And they both stood an instant uncovered while the little Essex priest blinked about for his umbrella.

The Altar Cloth

by Katherine Lyon

PASTOR BORKMAN CAREFULLY REMOVED THE CLOTH FROM the altar, and the wide sleeves of his black gown fell like dark wings about him as he stretched his arms to shake the cloth straight. His hands held the heavy white silk gently. He never allowed Jens Clausen, the sexton, to handle this finest altar cloth. Nearly five years ago old Marja had presented it to the church, and he had kept it as cleanly white as the day she gave it. True, it was not used every Sunday, only on special days. Today had been St. Olav's Day, and this was St. Olav's Church, standing plain and white at the top of the village street above the blue-green fiord.

The pastor folded the cloth into its accustomed creases, smiling a little as he remembered the feeling of dismay with which he had first heard that old Marja had made an altar cloth for the church.

Old Marja lived in a tiny house surrounded by gooseberry bushes, on the cliff at the other end of the village, overlooking the harbor. She was weathered and wrinkled, and her hands were knotted with rheumatism and blackened with toil, but though she had been called "old Marja" for a long time, she never seemed to get any older. She lived alone in her little house, taking care of her pig and cow, hoeing in her garden, and rowing her boat down the fiord to catch fish. She was a good fisherman, if the rotting pile of heads and entrails on the edge of the cliff was any sign.

When she came to church on Sundays, a shapeless bundle of petticoats with a black handkerchief tied over her wispy gray hair, and took her accustomed seat well to the front, the pastor was often guilty of wishing that she had chosen to sit farther back. He was ashamed of this unworthy thought, and in atonement he always spoke to her after the service with special friendliness, holding her work-roughened hand in both of his.

But when his wife, Birthe, told him that old Marja had made an altar cloth of white satin for the church, he could not withhold a groan of despair.

"If it were linen or cotton," he said, "it could at least be washed. But satin! I don't see how we can use it." He frowned and shook his head. *I must think of her good intentions,* he told himself. *I can be careful what I say, now I am prepared.*

But he was not prepared, after all, when old Marja brought the big parcel into his study and untied the string which held it. Inside the crumpled newspaper was heavy brown paper, and, inside that, a package done up in a clean white cloth. The pastor waited while old Marja, breathing heavily, turned back the edges and disclosed her handiwork.

The pastor gazed at it awestruck. He felt as though he were observing a miracle—the shining whiteness of the silk, the bright, untarnished gold of the cross and crown, the delicate perfection of the fine, careful stitches. It seemed incredible that old Marja, with her roughened, swollen fingers and fading sight, could have made it.

"It is beautiful," he said at last.

Old Marja's small blue eyes nearly disappeared into the wrinkles of her cheeks, so wide was her smile. "There is no altar cloth so fine anywhere in the diocese," she said complacently. "I have made it myself, that the glory of God might shine brightly at St. Olav's—I, and the good Lord, Who has helped me."

The pastor had the fleeting thought that the Lord had seldom undertaken a more difficult task, but he said aloud, "The Lord has blessed your effort. St. Olav's will be grateful."

"Since a year ago Whitsuntide have I worked on it. I am glad it is finished. It has been a great care to me." Marja gathered up the papers and began to wind the string about her fingers. "In a way, I shall be lonely without it."

The pastor repeated, "It is very beautiful," and smoothed the satin appreciatively with his finger tips.

Marja caught her breath. "Be careful," she said. "Excuse me, but it is so easy to soil."

The pastor felt the blood mount to his forehead. "I know," he said, "I will take care of it."

So the cloth had been presented to St. Olav's, blessed and sanctified by the bishop when he paid his quarterly visit, and all the parish was proud of Marja's gift. The pastor was both humble and happy when it adorned the altar; humble for his own frailties and errors, and happy for this evidence of a human's devotion and God's guidance.

Now, at the close of this St. Olav's Day, he carried the cloth into the vestry and laid it in the big chest under the windows, automatically smoothing out the wrinkles. He was no longer thinking of Marja's offering; today the burden in his heart was too great to be eased by the softness of silk or an old woman's careful stitches.

He stood looking down on the village of Lilleby, so green and white beneath the bright midsummer sun, and remembered all that had happened there since Marja had given the cloth to St. Olav's. He thought of the day when the German soldiers had marched down the cobbled street to their barracks in the schoolhouse, and the German officers had sat stiffly in the parlor of the little hotel above the quay and told the citizens of Lilleby how it must be with them.

Since that dreadful day nothing had been as before in the village. Life had gone on in a maze of restriction and uncertainty. Fear and hunger and death had towered above the fiord like ancient giants let loose from the mountains. One by one the young men had disappeared from the farms and wharves, some escaping to England to fight the battle for Norway's freedom, others caught in the Nazi mesh of work drafts and forced labor. The school had been suspended and Herr Lange, the teacher, deported to the north because he would not ally himself with the Quislings. Nowhere in Lilleby was there any peace, least of all in the heart of the pastor, but he alone realized the mockery of the phrase which came so often to his lips: "I am a man of peace."

He had tried to put the church first. By no unconsidered act must he endanger St. Olav's and the solace it offered to the troubled parishioners.

"The church is for all and above all," he had said to Birthe. "As a minister of the Lord, my first duty is to Him and my second to the people I serve here."

"But the church is the state church," Birthe had said, "under the control of the new government. You will have to do what they tell you."

"I know," the pastor had admitted. "But if I take no part in these political quarrels I can keep the church free for our people. I must yield where I have to. If I am careful it can be managed."

Birthe knitted to the end of a row. The rings on her once plump fingers had grown loose and slipped back and forth with her movements. "Appeasement is an ugly word," she said.

"Godlessness is worse," said the pastor calmly. "I must do as my conscience bids me."

But he was not as certain as he sounded, and often his duty as a servant of the Lord and his inclination as a man warred within him. At such times he envied old Marja, who, of all the village, seemed undisturbed by the Nazi domination.

She went her way much as usual, working in her garden and rowing her little boat along the fiord to catch what fish she could. Perhaps she did not come quite so often to the church, but if the day was fine and the fog did not hang over the headlands, she would be sitting in her accustomed seat in the second row from the front. If it were a saint's day, and her cloth hung at the altar, she would lean forward and scrutinize it carefully, her face relaxing into a smile when she saw that all was well.

Sometimes the pastor thought bitterly, "That is the one gift which she has made to the Lord, the single proof of her devotion. It does not matter to her what goes on in the village. She is only concerned about the altar cloth." And then he would chide himself for being unjust, for he knew that Marja's soul was as simple as it was good.

So the pastor had served his flock, marrying, baptizing,

burying, as in the days of peace. He treated the German commandant with politeness, yielding deferentially to his authority when the need arose.

Pastor Borkman had proved he could take the expedient way in the matter of the church bells, which had been requisitioned to make Nazi bullets. He resigned the bells from St. Olav's without protest, and when Jens, the sexton, and one of the younger deacons had come to him with a proposal to steal the bells and hide them from the Germans, he had counseled against it.

"You would only get us all into trouble," he said. "Our visitors would be needlessly incensed and doubly hard on us. Truly, it is best to give up the bells with what grace we can. As a matter of fact, they are hopelessly out of tune, anyhow. When these hard days are over we shall have a fine new set of chimes for St. Olav's." And he had smiled so confidently that they had agreed to do as he wished.

But as time passed and the conflict between the church and the Nazi authorities spread openly over Norway, he found it increasingly hard to hold his self-appointed middle way. When the Department of Church and Education put out the new catechism, he was faced with an issue that he could not avoid.

"Never," he declared to Birthe, "never will I permit our children to be taught that Adolf Hitler is a colleague of the Lord Almighty. It is unthinkable. Not even to keep St. Olav's would the Lord want such company."

Birthe had nodded approvingly. "But what will you do?"

"I shall postpone the adoption of the catechism on one pretext and another." And so he had done as long as possible, but at last he had been forced to make a plain statement of ac-

99

ceptance or refusal. He had couched his refusal in the most diplomatic terms, but he knew its meaning was clear.

It was on the same morning when he sent his letter to the State Department of Church and Education that the American fighter plane crashed on the mountain behind the village. A few hours later the pilot died in the little room back of Dr. Lassen's office. But not before he told them his name, which was as Norwegian as their own, and that of his home, a Norwegian-American community.

Pastor Borkman was with him as he died, reading from the prayer book which he had slipped into his pocket when the doctor called him.

Over the lifeless form, the doctor and the pastor exchanged glances. "Where can he be buried?" asked the doctor.

"At the top of the churchyard," said the pastor, after a moment, "facing the sea."

The doctor was folding his stethoscope into its case. "I'm afraid it will mean trouble." He knew the pastor's usual caution. "We could do it quietly tonight."

The pastor shook his head. Perhaps the knowledge that the letter to the State Department was already in the mail made him reckless. "He is one of us. He must have a proper and Christian burial. We will hold the funeral tomorrow noon."

So the American boy, whose father was born in Norway, was committed to the hard, cold earth of Lilleby cemetery, under the sighing pines which pointed to the sky from which he had fallen. Pastor Borkman read the ritual beside the mound, which the children had heaped with flowers. Nearly all the village stood around the grave or lined the path leading to the top of the churchyard. The pastor was surprised to see old Marja on the outskirts of the crowd.

When the pastor and the sexton, the last to leave the grave, came down from the churchyard, they were met by a lieutenant and a squad of six men.

"Herr Pastor," said the lieutenant, "you did not obtain a permit from the commandant to bury the American soldier in the churchyard. It is not permitted that he can rest there. He was an enemy of Norway."

The pastor's voice was gentle: "The dead are no man's enemies. They belong to God, and they shall rest with Him."

"I have given my men orders to disinter the body," said the lieutenant. "It must be placed elsewhere."

The pastor saw that the villagers were coming slowly back into the churchyard and he heard the threatening murmur of their voices. "Look, my friend," he said; "you would be making a great mistake. You know me for a man of peace and opposed to violence. Everywhere in Lilleby the authority of your state is recognized, but here in the churchyard among the dead, what does it matter? Now there is quiet in the village. Do not stir up trouble."

"I have my orders," said the lieutenant.

"Then wait; let me see the commandant first," said the pastor. He raised his voice a little: "It is very unlucky to move the dead."

The lieutenant had hesitated, then grumbled that it was most irregular, but he would do nothing for the present.

The pastor's interview with the commandant had not been pleasant, but in the end he had got his way. Temporarily, at least, until the feeling in the village had died down, the American pilot should be undisturbed. But the pastor knew he had offended the commandant, and this knowledge marred his satisfaction. If this victory had been won at the cost of his parish, he had been wrong to claim it.

Weeks went by, and the Department of Church and Education seemed to have forgotten the pastor. Gradually he began to feel more secure. Perhaps such a big and powerful department was willing to overlook the idiosyncrasy of one pastor in a small parish.

But today, as he stood beside the chest where Marja's altar cloth lay folded so neatly, he knew how wrong he had been. The Nazis overlooked nothing. The letter from the Department of Church and Education crackled under his robe as his arm brushed across it. Its phrases were indelibly impressed upon his memory:

"Because of the non-co-operative spirit of the minister of this diocese . . . the fomenting of unrest by a spiritual leader of the people . . . the unwillingness to accept the regulations of the Department . . . Andreas Borkman, Pastor of St. Olav's Church at Lilleby, is hereby relieved of his charge, and Per Pedersen is appointed to the vacant pastorate."

Per Pedersen. The pastor knew him well as a thorough-going scoundrel and hypocrite. Per Pedersen of Bergen, formerly a member of the Bergen Mission, deposed years ago for misuse of funds. Per Pedersen, to be shepherd of St. Olav's fold. So the State Department had decreed and, had the letter ended there, the pastor must have recognized there was no recourse from its finality. He had done what he could and the responsibility was no longer his. It was the next sentence which offered him yet another chance for compromise:

"Because of the frequent refusal of local congregations to accept a change in leadership, it is hoped that Herr Pastor

Borkman will find it possible to remain with this parish as assistant to the new pastor and, by his example, to bring about a spirit of obedience and allegiance to the legally appointed representative of God."

There it was. If he bowed his neck to the Nazi yoke, if he took orders from Per Pedersen, some part of St. Olav's might still be preserved for Lilleby parish.

He looked through the small-paned vestry window at the village lying so deceptively quiet at the edge of the fiord under the great, dark mountain. He knew there was hardly a house in all the village where sorrow and despair did not keep watch by the fireside. His people who had need of him.

With his knee he shoved the drawer shut and began to take off his vestments. He knew what his decision must be....

The Sunday after St. Olav's Day, Pastor Borkman walked with Per Pedersen into St. Olav's Church. Tall and calm, the pastor led the way through the church into the vestry.

"Here we keep the vessels for the sacrament," he said. "Here is the cupboard for your robes." With his key he unlocked the wide chest. "Here are the cloths for the altar." And then, although it was not a special day, he took out Marja's altar cloth.

"What a handsome cloth!" said Per Pedersen effusively. "So lovely, really exquisite. Let me help you put it on."

Pastor Borkman brushed past him. "I can manage alone."

No sound of bells summoned the parishioners up the hill to St. Olav's, yet they all came together, as though, in some hidden recess of their memory, they still heard the bells. From the vestry window the pastor watched them. He had told no one save Birthe of the State Department's decree, but he was

103

certain that these people coming toward him were aware of a crisis.

In spite of the swelling music from the organ, Pastor Borkman could almost hear the ripple which ran across the congregation as he and Per Pedersen came slowly up to the altar, bowed their heads, and went to their places. Per Pedersen climbed up to the high pulpit, tripping over his gown in his nervousness, while the pastor seated himself behind the lower reading desk.

He shaded his eyes with his hand and looked out over the church as he had done for so many Sundays. He noticed that old Marja was not in her accustomed seat, and then he saw her coming down the aisle. She sat down in the second row, peering intently at the altar before she bent her head in prayer.

At the back of the church there was a little disturbance. The pastor saw four State Police enter and take their stand beside the door. So the Department of Church and Education was making doubly sure. Per Pedersen would have his congregation, even if Pastor Borkman's words failed to keep them.

The music ceased with a little sigh, and the pastor rose to begin the service.

"The Lord be with you."

"And with thy spirit," came the full response from the congregation.

Through the opening hymn, the collect, and the epistle, the pastor's voice did not falter. Then he stepped from the desk to the middle of the chancel. In his hand he held a sheet of paper. Behind him Marja's altar cloth glowed whitely, outlining his graying head and broad shoulders. He began to read.

He finished the official announcement of Per Pedersen's appointment, then went on quickly: "And I, your former pastor, will remain as assistant in the parish. I ask your continued support and allegiance to St. Olav's. You who have been my friends so many years will help me to carry on the work of the church under a new leadership. I appeal to you to remember that God is above all, and in the end must prevail. Only by doing His work on earth, can we make His kingdom come."

When he stopped speaking, there was not a sound in the church, but as he turned back to his desk a low-voiced murmur rose from all sides. No one stirred from his place, however, and the pastor let out his breath in a sigh of relief. Nothing had happened. Perhaps it was going to be all right.

The new pastor switched on his reading light and cleared his throat impressively, but, before he could speak, old Marja got up from her seat and walked across the space to the chancel. She looked neither to the right nor to the left, but began to climb the steps to the altar.

Pastor Borkman started to rise, then sank back into his chair, his hands gripping its arms. He knew why she had come, and he could not stop her.

Marja unfastened the gold-and-white cloth from the altar and began to fold it carefully. Then Per Pederson found his voice. He came tumbling down from his pulpit to face her.

"Woman!" he shouted. "You are profaning the sacred altar. Put down that cloth."

Marja folded the cloth in front of her. Even now she held it away from her body so that she should not soil it against her shawl. Her eyes burned blue in her puckered old face, and she did not draw back an inch before Per Pedersen's uplifted hand.

"I made this cloth," she said, and, though her voice was low and hoarse, it carried to every part of the church, so great was the quiet. "I made it for the glory of Our Lord and the Church of St. Olav's. I did not make it for the Nazi-appointed traitors who take the name of the Lord in vain. I gave it to this church, and now I take it back, for this church no longer belongs to God."

She moved down the steps until she stood opposite Pastor Borkman. "You must forgive me, but you are wrong. Look in your heart and you will know."

Then she walked awkwardly down the aisle toward the door, holding the altar cloth in her arms.

Pastor Borkman felt as though he were in a dream from which he could not wake. He was standing naked in a bright light before his congregation for them to see his shame. He wanted to speak, but he had no voice. Then he heard the sound of heavy boots on the floor, and as Marja neared the door, he saw the State Police seize her, one on either side. The power of life flowed back to the pastor.

"Stop!" he called. "You cannot arrest this woman. She has done no crime. She has only taken back her own. Let her go."

The two troopers who were hurrying Marja out the door did not turn, but one of the others stepped back into the church. "No, no," he said, "we do not arrest her for what she has done here. 'Tis merely an old woman's spite. We arrest her for treason. The silly old fool has been using her boat to run escaping Norwegians up the fiord." Then, he, too, was gone.

106

The pastor moved so quickly that his gown billowed out behind him. Per Pedersen caught at it, but the pastor jerked himself free. He strode down the aisle, the congregation standing aside to let him through. He caught glimpses of their faces as he passed—faces sad, shocked, sympathetic, stern, but still the faces of his friends. As he reached the door he heard the sound of a starting motor and knew he was too late.

He came out onto the porch to see a small brown truck pull away from the gates and tear madly down the hill. Marja was gone. He understood that she was gone forever. He looked after the truck with eyes as empty as the eyes of the newly dead.

Then he saw the altar cloth. It lay like a shining pool on the dark, bare earth outside the gates. He walked toward it and picked it up, trying to brush away the dirt. On the steps of the church behind him, his congregation stood in silent uncertainty. Per Pedersen was stamping up and down, ordering them to come back to the house of the Lord, but they were not listening. Their faces were turned toward Pastor Borkman.

The pastor knew what he must do, what Marja would have wanted. Holding the altar cloth in his hands, he walked slowly up the slope along the fence leading to the top of the churchyard. He could hear the others coming after him, the murmur of their voices, and a child's high question, "Where's he going, Mother? What's he going to do?"

At the top of the churchyard, where the pines sang above the grave of the American flier, he stopped and laid Marja's altar cloth on the dark rock wall, holding it in place with two clean stones. Then he turned to face his people.

"From old Marja," he said, "have I learned the truth. Norway's right is the Lord's right. The church lies not in brick and wood and stone, but in men's hearts." His face was white as the altar cloth behind him, but his voice was strong and exultant. "The Lord is in His holy temple. Here let us worship Him."

A Preacher Goes to Texas

by JOHN W. THOMASON, JR.

❖❖

IT IS ONE OF THOSE STORIES UNCLE JIMMY FARROW USED TO tell, at Mr. Lee Rodgers' place on Patterson Lake in Houston County, when we sat, after supper, on the porch through summer evenings: How the Rev. Praxiteles Swan appeared in Texas and preached his first sermon at Washington on the Brazos, to the notable confusion of the devil in those parts. In his years of achievement, they called Praxiteles Swan "the Hurricane of God." He was superannuated before my time, but all my old folks had trembled under his thunders, and he loomed vast and legendary, even in the country where Sam Houston and Davy Crockett were remembered.

Uncle Jimmy, a dried-up little fox squirrel of a man who claimed to have served with Quantrell, and who, for sixty years after the war, never sat in line with a window, day or night, was a shirttail boy in Washington County in the 1850's, and saw the preacher arrive. But the actual beginnings of that career I found myself, years after Uncle Jimmy told the tale, in an old thick book dealing with the saints of early Texas Methodism. In it is preserved, besides other edifying material, Praxiteles Swan's own journal of his life and acts.

Uncle Jimmy's narrative style was of the leisurely contemplative type, best enjoyed by persons having no other engagements. It owed much of its effectiveness, I think, to the setting —the deep and timeless peace of the Trinity River bottom, the noises of the night and the woods, and the dark shimmer of the lake under the stars. And the journal, although it recorded immense and laborious travels in a wilderness, and fiery contests for immortal souls, is also the chronicle of an elder and unhurried time—it is, in fact, long-winded. Therefore, I abridge the one and paraphrase the other.

Of Praxiteles' beginnings, it is enough to know that he came of a regretted *mésalliance* between a Yankee schoolteacher named Swan, and Miss Cassandra Pelham, a lady of imperious Virginia blood. He was orphaned early. His uncle, Colonel Marius Pelham, raised him, as they say, on his place in the pleasant Piedmont country outside of Charlottesville, where the Colonel lived, withdrawn and feudal, among his Negroes, his fighting cocks and his blood horses; drinking brandy juleps before dinner, port after, and Madeira between meals, and reading the more outrageous of the Augustan poets in the original Latin. An Army officer until it bored him, a member of the Congress until, he said, the tone of the lower house became too degraded for a refined person's stomach, and a duelist always, he instructed his nephew in the accomplishments and prejudices of the Virginia gentry; and through Praxiteles' adult life, the violent old autocrat stood sneering over the shoulder of the man of God—although I am sure Praxiteles would never have admitted this.

His uncle sent him to Princeton College for his education, because he regarded Mr. Jefferson as a nauseous demagogue, and could not abide his works; and after that he designed the

110

young man for the law. But, unaccountably, the nephew came under other influences. In his twenty-second year, the summer after his graduation—he being then six feet and upward of lank red-headed youth—he faced his uncle in his own garden, and told him plainly he was called to the Methodist ministry.

Praxiteles records the interview at length, and it must have been of a nature to make the house servants turn gray under their dark skins and seek places of safety. He quotes his own remarks, which are elevated and improving, but his uncle's statements he barely suggests, with the explanation that they were horrid blasphemies, and he feared his aged relative to be already in Satan's waistcoat pocket. He comments sadly that Colonel Pelham was a man of honor, infatuated in the delusion that a man of honor could live a decent life according to his personal standards, without dependence on higher guidance. "In such there is no hope; they are worse than the most dissolute and hardened sinners, for whom there is at least repentance and salvation. 'Drunk with wine, as Ephraim in his fat valleys——' "

The upshot of it was, his uncle threw him out, and they never saw each other again; they came of the same violent blood. But you identify Colonel Pelham as the unrepentant sinner; a figure at once moving and repellent and somehow glamorous, which Praxiteles thereafter used effectively through fifty years of sermons. The same afternoon he departed from his home, taking some gold pieces left out of his quarterly allowance, his riding cloak, and a change of linen in his saddlebags, astride the big, hammer-headed, three-quarter-bred mare given him when a colt. He went to Baltimore.

Baltimore was the outpost of Southern Methodism, lately split away from the Northern brethren on the vexatious question of Negro slavery. I abridge his account of what he did there, and how he was ordained; and how old Bishop Andrew, a shrewd prince of the church, had him in for an interview and detailed him to the Texas mission. Because, nowhere else, the bishop said, indicating the letters and memorials on the episcopal desk, were the shepherds so sorely tried as in the Texas missions; nowhere else were the sheep so black and the wolves so bold. You conceive him appraising Praxiteles' lean length of bone and sinew, his shock of red hair, his purposeful green eyes, aggressive nose, and the thin firm mouth over the long jaw and the pointed chin, and considering that such a young soldier belonged in the forefront of the battle. Perhaps he thought of King David, who was also white and ruddy. No bishop would have wanted to be responsible for King David's discipline, and Texas was a long way off. He cautioned Praxiteles about Texas. The people were sensitive in unexpected spots, he warned, and it would be better not to refer to his calling as missionary work, or to his colleagues as missionaries. Up here, of course; but down there "be ye therefore wise as serpents, and harmless as doves." Praxiteles, he ordered, would proceed forthwith to the settlement called Washington-on-the-Brazos, in the Rutersville District, pending the yearly assembly of the Texas Conference and a permanent assignment. The pastor of that flock, he explained, had succumbed to a lung fever induced by his toils. In Texas, the bishop warned him, a minister's body needed to be as robust as his soul. His honorarium, he thought, would be a hundred and sixty dollars a year, the years his congregation made a crop. When they didn't, the Lord would provide. At the end, he blessed Praxiteles and sent him forth, quoting the appropriate scriptures.

112

Praxiteles neglected his journal for two months; he states, merely, that he rode down to Texas after Christmas. And he resumed his entries in early March, 1852, the day he crossed into the state by Gaines' Ferry on the Sabine. A cold rain drove on a northeast wind, he mentions, and the roads were trying to his mare, who was not now up into her bridle as when they left Virginia. He refers to great discomfort from his breeches, which were worn through inside the knees— "Mem. . . . get some good woman to patch them for me."

Texas was excessively well-watered that year. He listed the creeks between the Sabine and the Neches rivers, all of them high and some of them overflowing from the rains, and never a bridge in the country, and no bottom to the roads. He discovered that his mare could swim, which was probably a surprise to both of them when the ford went out from under in an innocent-looking brown creek east of the Trinity, and they all but drowned. He pressed on, as only circuit riders and fugitives did in those parts, resting where darkness overtook him; one night in a verminous tavern, another in a loft above a barn full of horned cattle, and once in the attic of a poor man's house—man who received him hospitably enough, fed him bacon and greens and corn bread, showed a readiness to discuss spiritual affairs, and then, when Praxiteles disclosed his denomination, tried to eject him into the wet and stormy wilderness. The journal briefly states that Praxiteles declined to be ejected, but it contains this entry: "I had rather associate with howling savages than with Campbellites."

By Swartout he came to the Trinity, booming along at flood stage, and found a ferry, and had directions to Washington. "Just keep goin' west," they told him helpfully. "Don't

113

turn neither north nor south. There ain't but one road goin' west."

He passed Cold Spring and Montgomery, climbed the watershed between the Trinity and the San Jacinto, with its solemn pine forests, and plunged again into bottom land, smothered under pin oak, walnut, pecan, hickory and sweet gum, every tree trailing Spanish moss, mournful in the rain as dripping beards on hanged men. Miles of road were under water, and the occasional higher stretches marched, rutted, between rain-dappled lagoons that carried a current, more often than not. Houses were a day's ride apart, and there were no settlements, and nobody on the road beyond occasional glum mud-plastered mail riders. He spent a night in the bottom, huddled under a tree, his mare trembling and the water making noises all around. There was a panther—the first he had encountered—hunting in the neighborhood, and its squalls were dreadful in his ears. He took comfort, he recorded, from singing hymns, and felt that the Lord's hand was over him. He forded the East Fork, which was not bad, and swam Winter's Creek and Peach Creek, and late on a gray March evening he approached the Middle Fork of the San Jacinto; two days' ride, he calculated, from the Brazos. It was still raining.

The Middle Fork ran banks full, foul with floating brush. Where it lapped into the road, one stood with a sodden quilt on his shoulders and a shotgun under his arm, gazing downstream into the last of the light. That man was, in fact, our Uncle Jimmy Farrow; then a sort of roustabout for the cook on Old Man Locke's wagon train, that did hauling between Cincinnati on the Trinity and Brenham. The cook had given him a ten-gauge double gun, and told him to go get a mess of

114

ducks, because the teamsters were promising to fry him over his own fire if he fed them any more side meat and corn pone; the high water had detained the wagon train for days and they were in the worst possible humor.

Uncle Jimmy, telling us the story, says he was watching so sharp down the river for the evening flight that he let the fellow get right up on him before he noticed. Long-legged fellow on a big gaunted mare; all he could see was a white face between a hat brim and a turned-up cloak collar, stopping to speak to him. As he turned his head, Uncle Jimmy saw ducks from the corner of his eye, and he told the man, blast his bowels, if he moved he'd kill him.

The fellow sat there, frozen—it's not what a duck sees that scares him, Uncle Jimmy claims; it's what moves—and five hundred mallards came along the river about as high as the treetops. Right at the ford they flared out over the bank, making for a stubble field back in the woods, and Uncle Jimmy picked his correct second of time and let them have both barrels, knocking down a dozen or so. Those old ten-gauges, with thirty-inch, cylinder-bored barrels, scattered fine. The ducks fell on the land, but some were crippled, and he had to be mighty spry to beat them to the water and twist their necks; and this man dismounted and helped; had legs like a sandhill crane, Uncle Jimmy says, and a reach like a hayrake. When they collected the ducks—nice mallards in prime condition from the winter on the Gulf Coast—Uncle Jimmy saw the stranger was just a youngster—little older than he was—and he took him to the wagon camp on some higher ground a quarter of a mile upstream.

The boys—half a dozen teamsters—were playing brag under the lean-to shelter they knocked up and covered with a wagon sheet, and they were sullen and ugly, and down to ten gallons of whisky, which Old Man Locke was sitting on with his pistol in his waistband, and dealing out just a tin cupful at a time, before meals. Old Man Locke told the stranger he reckoned he was welcome to what grub there was, and he could sleep under a wagon; if he was stayin', he could turn to and help the cook. Old Man Locke was rough-talkin', they said, in those days.

Well, there was nothing finicky about the stranger; first he unsaddled and scraped the mud off his mare, then he helped with the ducks. The cook had boiling water ready to scald them, and Uncle Jimmy and this man snatched the feathers right off of them, all in no time.

Here Uncle Jimmy digressed to describe at length the way they broiled the ducks; something we all knew and did in those parts, and liked to talk about, but need not here repeat. Uncle Jimmy recalls, the teamsters were in a better humor after supper. Nobody really paid any attention to the stranger until he declined the slug of bitters that Old Man Locke courteously offered him. Then they wanted to know who he was and where he came from.

He stood up, as tall as a tree, Uncle Jimmy remembers, and told them he was a preacher of the gospel, a-bound for Washington on the Brazos.

"Well," says Old Man Locke, who was strong on religion himself, "you must be a Methodist. Either they're Methodists over thar, or they ain't anything."

"I am," says the preacher, "an unworthy servant of the Methodist Episcopal Church, South. The name is Swan."

"Well," Old Man Locke answered, "I'm a man that takes my religion serious. I'm a blue-light Presbyterian, I am, and so is all my folks. Young man—Reverend, I should say, though you look mighty young and mighty redheaded to be a shepherd —even a Methody shepherd—it mought turn out your luck, one of these days, to sit under ouah preacher, down in Victoria— the Elder Calvin Knox Singletree. When he talks, you can smell hell, brother—that's what you can! And the way Elder Singletree puts it, I like a religion that's a religion, not spoon vittles, or sugar-tits fer babes, but strong meat fer men! A religion, as Elder Singletree says, a man kain get his tushes into. No, young man, you're a foreigner here, and far from home, and you're welcome to yo' share of my grub an' camp-fire, but you're unfortunate. So are a lot of folks. Elder Single-tree's religion is the only religion fer grown folks. No other kind will be preached in my wagon train. But if you want to read us a Psa'm before we turn in, I'm agreeable and the boys will listen."

Uncle Jimmy says they sat quiet while the Reverend Swan read them a scripture and prayed them a prayer; and I found the story briefed in Praxiteles' journal.

Next morning, the rain blew off and the Middle Fork went down, and they got across in good shape; and Old Man Locke sent Uncle Jimmy ahead on a mule to make some arrangements for him in Washington. He rode with Praxiteles, who, Uncle Jimmy remembers, asked all sorts of questions about every-thing, and they made good time, for before dark they came out on the river, and the ferryman set them across, of a Saturday afternoon.

There was not a great deal to Washington, although the orators referred to it freely as the cradle of Texas independence, the town on the great river the Spaniards call *Brazos de Dios* —Arms of God.

There were some log cabins and barns, and a few clapboarded houses, the wide whipsawed boards cleated on over the original logs and whitewashed. Some stores were ranked out of alignment; the most elaborate building in sight, a rambling unpainted structure behind a false front, was Gadsen's Saloon and Billiard Parlors. Patient horses stood on three legs in front of it; elsewhere, dejected mules and phlegmatic oxen labored through the mud, drawing high-slung wagons. There was a cotton shed and a platform handy to the river, but the steelyards over the weighing stand hung rusty on a rusty wire, and the dull yellow sky lowered over all. Razorback hogs moved importantly across the road, or stood to scratch their ticks against the corner posts of the buildings. Everywhere there was mud; all the men wore their trousers inside their boots.

Praxiteles came up from the ferry with Uncle Jimmy and rode toward the saloon, from which proceeded loud shouts of laughter and considerable swearing in bad-tempered, drawling voices. Elsewhere, sallow men lounged in front of stores, whittled and chewed tobacco; only around the saloon was there life and movement. As Praxiteles drew in his horse and sat, undecided, looking about him, a man came with great dignity from the saloon, caromed off the hitch rail, and walked into Praxiteles' mare. He leaned against her shoulder, his hand going uncertainly to the rider's knee.

"Well, I declar'," he said, amiably—"I declar'. Gettin' to be so many people in town, a man can't make his way thoo 'em, noways." He got his chin up, beamed at the preacher, and said, with interest, "I never seed you befo'. You strangeh hyar? My name's Medary; ev'ybody knows me."

Praxiteles confirmed him. Yes. A pilgrim and a stranger.

118

The Reverend Swan. Would he be so good as to point out the tavern?

The other brought his eyes into coincidence and studied him gravely. Tallest preacher, he remarked, he ever did see. But there wasn't no tavern. Could get a shakedown, now, in Goat Gadsen's place, but nothing fitten for a preacher. He, the man continued, always slept the preachers—that is, the Methodist preachers. He wasn't a Methodist, himself—reckoned he was a kind of backslidden sinner—but his wife was the all-fired out-prayingest Methodist between the Sabine and the Colorado rivers; had a preacher in the house right now. "Come on, preacher," he added hospitably. "Come on. Come on out to my place. I'll show you."

He cast his weight against the mare and paid no attention to Praxiteles' courteous protest. He would walk, he stated. Little walk do him good. He feared he was sort of overtaken. If he'd knowed the preacher was comin', he wouldn't—this he swore roundly—have smoked so many seegyars. He then recognized Uncle Jimmy, and told him to come along, too, and lead his horse for him.

He was a very persuasive man, and Praxiteles was tired, and they went willingly, Mr. Medary hanging to a stirrup leather, and recovering an admirable equilibrium as the heavy walking brought the sweat out on him. They plodded a mile down the road, plunged into the woods, then proceeded between new-cleared land where raw furrows ran under trees, girdled and dead, to a sprawling house in a grove of moss-draped oaks. It was as good a house as Praxiteles had seen in Texas. Its original logs had been sheathed in weatherboarding; it was roofed with cypress shingles and had a huge stone chimney at each end. All around it ran a deep porch, and the kitchen and outbuildings and barn, as well as the house itself, were smartly whitewashed. Chickens and turkeys scratched in the yard, and a whole congregation of potlikker hounds boiled out noisily to greet the master. Hard behind the dogs came two little Negroes; then a couple of towheaded children, very bashful, and a brisk, neat lady with a humorous dark eye and a firm mouth, evidently mistress of herself and others. An older girl appeared at the door, looked out, and withdrew hastily.

" 'Light down, rev'rend, 'light down!" cried Mr. Medary, now perfectly steady on his legs. "Gimme those saddlebags. Walk right in, seh; you' in yo' own house! . . . Nigger, take the rev'rend's mar'. Rub her down with a snatch of hay befo' you water her, and give her a feed of cawn in the corner stall. . . . She stand quiet in the stable, rev'rend? . . . Nigger, I'll be out to look at her, an' if she ain't bedded right, I'll cut yo' years off and make you eat 'em!" He led the way to the house and did the honors: "Mrs. Medary, hyar's the Rev'rend Swan— him that the presidin' elder was tellin' us was coming. . . . Rev'rend, this is Nick, an' this is Bubber, and this is Lucindy. Chillun air the po' man's blessin', rev'rend! . . . Mrs. Medary, whar's Jinny?"

They hustled him into the house. A fine fire snapped and crackled in a deep fireplace, taking the chill out of the wet March air.

By the fire in a rocking chair, with a shawl over his shoulders, sat a lean man in a rusty black store suit which was weather-stained and mottled with age. He got painfully to his feet, extending a limp hand; he had a sad sallow face, thinly bearded, and hot-tempered dyspeptic eyes.

"Hyar's Brother Grebs—Rev'rend Brother Grebs," continued

120

Mr. Medary cordially. "He's passin' thoo, goin' up to Marshall. He was took sick."

"I'm mighty po'ly," agreed the Rev. Elkanah Grebs. "I'm mighty po'ly. The Lord's hand has been heavy on me, brother. Boils, even as Job, and a touch of the bloody flux."

The good man was vastly depressed; the ills of the spirit, he asserted, graveled him worse than the weaknesses of the flesh. He had proposed to conduct services for the little flock in Washington; they having been without spiritual food since the late Brother Haggers passed to his reward last November. He had sent the word ahead that he would preach tomorrow, and the good folks were making ready to come in, by buggy, oxcart and wagon, from Dan even to Beersheba—that is, from as far west as Brenham, and from Anderson and Big Sandy, the other way. There would surely be young olive branches, born during the winter, for baptism, and probably couples to be church-married—maybe things you wouldn't want to keep waiting. But the Methodist Church, called Gilgal Chapel, was struck by lightning last fall and burned. The cotton warehouse was full up to the rafters. About the only place a gathering might be held was Mr. Gadsen's Saloon and Billiard Parlors; and Reverend Grebs had approached Mr. Gadsen in the matter with confidence, for the faithful those days congregated in eccentric places when the weather was too bad to sit under the trees.

Mr. Gadsen, Praxiteles was informed, hardened his heart like Pharaoh and said he wasn't going to lose his Sunday-afternoon trade for a parcel of howling Methodists; he was a Campbellite himself, and his customers would be put out with him. No, seh. He wasn't even polite about it. And while they talked within, young sinners placed cockleburs under the saddle of the preacher's mule; so that when he came out and mounted, he was flung off into a mud puddle and further humiliated. Here Mr. Medary felt constrained to interrupt. It wasn't, he told Praxiteles, as though the community was down on preachers. They treated them right well—everybody did. That was just a bunch of young hellions who'd been heating their coppers with Goat Gadsen's forty-rod, and sort of hellin' around. They didn't mean anything by it—just boys, reely.

The sad feature, Brother Grebs concluded, was that the good folks would be coming along, and no way to stop them. They'd have that haul over heavy roads—His voice trailed off sadly. Praxiteles, listening with concern, recalled something of his furious uncle's conversation—philosophic reminiscences to the effect that, coming on a new scene, the superior man always does something impressive; something to command public attention—like the time, in Natchez, Colonel Pelham, on arrival, called Col. Marmaduke Astley out and shot him within an hour. Like the time, again, in his first term with the Federal Congress, he caned the congressman from Rhode Island.

Praxiteles announced, a cold fire behind his green eyes: "There'll be services, as God willeth, in this publican's place of business. I'll conduct them myself."

About that time, Uncle Jimmy says, Miss Jinny entered the room, having primped herself up for company; she was the oldest girl in the family, peart as a red heifer, and fat as a butterball—fine a gyu'l as you ever did see, Uncle Jimmy asserted, slapping his leg. It was time she was married off, everybody was saying in those parts; and it was her own fault she wasn't. The young bucks were around her thick as flies in fly time, but she just couldn't seem to make up her mind. The Lord only knew, Uncle Jimmy recollected, how many gougings and kneeings and general ruckuses there had been over her in the settlement. The field was narrowed down to Bud Pike and Jim Pike, two cousins that farmed up the river a ways. They'd had their eye on her, and between them they whipped off the others—being, Uncle Jimmy says, as mean a pair of wildcats as ever came out of the Brazos Bottom—and now they were running each other for her, nip and tuck.

First one would be ahead, and then the other, said Uncle Jimmy; the whole community was watching it, and there were bets made every day in Goat Gadsen's Saloon and Billiard Parlors.

As for the Reverend Praxiteles, he wrote that night in his diary, how he was made acquainted, at Mr. Medary's house, with a most comely young lady, Miss Jael Medary; and he notes that, before retiring, he read from the Book of Judges the story of Jael, and the decisive steps Jael took in the case of the soldier Sisera, as celebrated by the great triumphant song Deborah the prophetess made about her on that occasion. It edified him considerably. And he added to his diary: "Genesis ii, 23 & 24. Mayhap the Lord sends me an helpmeet."

Meantime, they all went in to supper.

Never, anywhere, Praxiteles reflected, looking through half-shut lids as Brother Grebs delivered a comprehensive grace, had he seen so much, or such a variety, of food on a table. Whatever else Mr. Medary did with his talents, it was evident that he was a good provider; and when the grace was finished, Mr. Medary exhorted his guests to eat hearty. A man shouldn't let himself die in debt to his stomach, he stated, and he, for one, did not intend to.

"That's right. Plenty more in the kitchen!" cried Mrs. Medary.

Uncle Jimmy remembers that Miss Jinny—only her mother called her Jael—kept looking sideways at the preacher, and he looking back at her, in a way to make you sick. He never could see, Uncle Jimmy remarked, why the women in them days took on so over a preacher. And they still did, he was told.

The family possessed an organ capable of music. It was not in tune, and the dampness had done unfortunate things to its keys, but Miss Jinny was able to coax recognizable melody out of it, and after supper, her father, who, by frequent trips out to the smokehouse—from which he returned wiping his mouth and chewing a clove—maintained himself in a state of geniality, insisted that they sing. His wife reminded him that it was Saturday night, and too near Sunday for ballads and breakdowns, especially with preachers in the house.

Mr. Medary replied that, like nothing on earth, he honed and hankered for a hymn tune.

They placed the lamps and Miss Jinny sat herself to the organ. Praxiteles admired the bronze lights in her hair and the lines of her flat back. He came gallantly near to turn the music, and made bold to recommend a noble hymn of praise, Mount Zion—No. 36. She struck the chords with confident strong hands, and he led boldly:

> *"O Love divine, how sweet thou art,*
> *When shall I find my willing heart*
> *All taken up by thee?"* . . .

Mrs. Medary lifted a thin soprano, some beats behind the rest; Mr. Medary amiably contributed a growling bass, far from the key; and Miss Jinny, whose voice was untrained, but sweet and fresh, came along effectively with Praxiteles' baritone. The Reverend Elkanah, wrapped in a quilt by the fire, beat time with a slippered foot and hummed approvingly.

Somebody hollered outside, "Hello, the house!" and there entered Mr. Bud Pike and Mr. Jim Pike, two of the ugliest young men Praxiteles had ever seen; when their eyes fell on him, they bristled visibly. One was tall—not so tall as Praxiteles, but tall enough—and very solidly built; he had a broad dark face and hard black eyes, and a shock of hair, well-greased, and huge hairy hands. The other was shorter and more compact, with a bullethead, little piggish eyes, and a flat face, all of him as square and stocky as a blockhouse.

No need for Mr. Medary to whisper, after introducing them, that they were cousins—for the family favor was strong—and no need to add that they were sparking Miss Jinny—for both looked at her like she was something good to eat—and their enmity to Praxiteles, simply because he was in the room with her, was evident and immediate. He saw, also, the bright blush that rose from Jael's neck to the roots of her hair.

But when Mr. Medary added, behind his hand, that she would be making up her mind which one to choose, right soon, and that the reverend might have a wedding on his hands any day now, Praxiteles was conscious of a wave of revulsion. He realized at once that he didn't want this to happen; he was later to search his soul in prayer over the violence that suddenly filled his heart, without receiving light on the matter.

The singing was resumed, Praxiteles standing manfully in his place by the organ, while Miss Jinny appeared to be nervous. She did not incline her body modestly away from him as he leaned to turn a leaf, and once or twice her hand went up and touched his on the music. When this happened, a pleasant excitement surged in him. The two boys were glooming like thunderclouds.

The atmosphere in the room was no longer friendly; you could, Uncle Jimmy says, fair smell the blood and guts on the floor.

The Reverend Grebs announced that it was his bedtime, and he reckoned his young brother had come a long way and was ready for the shucks—"only, it's not shucks, under this godly rooftree, brother; it's the finest goose feathers under elegant eiderdown quilts," he explained, so that Mrs. Medary colored with pleasure.

Let them, suggested Brother Grebs, have a lesson, and a sweet season of prayer before they sought their rest; ask a blessing on their labors in the morning.

Here the biggest Pike spoke his first word: "What labors, pahson?"

"Friend," Praxiteles answered him, "it is my intention to hold services at the settlement in the morning."

"Whar'bouts?" asked Mr. Pike.

"It is my intention to request your Mr.—Gadsen?—Gadsen to allow us the use of his place of business for two hours in the morning."

"Does Goat Gadsen know about it? Well, we was just ridin' on. We'll tell him what you want," said Mr. Pike ominously.

Praxiteles thanked him with the blandest air imaginable. "Do so, I beg, Mr. Pike. It is the Lord's work."

They departed without ceremony. Mr. Medary looked at Praxiteles thoughtfully, and the Reverend Grebs said he hoped his afflictions would let him out of bed tomorrow, but he was afraid they wouldn't. Nonetheless, he prayed at length and powerfully, and they all retired.

126

In the morning, they rode into town; the women and children in a wagon, Reverend Grebs, still feeble, riding with them, and the others on horseback.

Praxiteles hitched his mare to the rack and approached the front of the saloon steadily, his saddlebags, which contained his Bible and his hymn books, in his hand. A dozen unkempt individuals, not all of them sober, observed his approach. Within, the cheerful murmur of godless entertainment ceased. At once the door was crowded.

Two detached themselves from the knot of observers and stood out to meet the preacher—Bud Pike and Jim Pike, the gallants of the night before. Praxiteles was aware of a stiffening of the hair at the back of his neck, and a quiver along his bones, a sort of bugle call to action in his blood, for the aspect of the two was not peaceful. They were squarely in front of him, their arms hanging, but out a little from their bodies, and their faces dark and sneering—what a family resemblance they had, Praxiteles noted. He said, the skin around his mouth feeling stiff, "A good morrow to you, friends!"

"No friend of yours, pahson," snarled Jim Pike.

"That's right," agreed the other.

Praxiteles stopped because another step would have brought him into collision. "Young men—" he began.

"Listen, preacher. What would you do if we was to give you a damn good whippin'?"

"My friends," Praxiteles told them, keeping his voice under control, "if the Lord give me grace, I will bear it. But if He don't, woe to your hides!"

With that, Bud Pike slapped him—a slap at the end of a full-arm swing. Praxiteles might have taken a blow, but a slap, now—A second later, Jim Pike put his head down and charged, butting like a bull. Praxiteles side-stepped. Bud came in, his arms flailing, exactly in time to receive his cousin's bullethead in his stomach. The air went out of Bud with a great "whuff!" and the two fell, entangled, in a mud puddle. Before they could sit up, Praxiteles, his temper flaming like his hair, was upon them; he squatted on Jim Pike's shoulders, whipped a long thigh over his neck and ground his face into the mud. Bud Pike, dizzy from the impact, he seized by the stock as he came to his knees, hauled him close to, and began to buffet him with mighty short-arm punches that rocked his head loose on his shoulders. Jim, underneath him, threshed about like a chicken with a wrung neck, but never really got his head high enough to breathe.

The engagement was like San Jacinto fight in its brevity and violence and its astonishing and improbable outcome. The eagerness and fury of his enemies, together with the soft footing, delivered them into Praxiteles' hand. In time the action would assume legendary proportions, and take its place in the folklore of the region, but Uncle Jimmy Farrow, there present, swears it occurred exactly as he tells it.

It did not last long. The one was smothered and the other's face beat into a bloody pulp. But Praxiteles was conscious of a wild joy, and quite heedless of his cut knuckles. He heard, at first dimly, then with reluctant attention, the genial voice of Mr. Medary, and felt that gentleman's hand on his shoulder.

"Rev'rend! Rev'rend! They got enough, seh, sholy! Don't kill 'em, rev'rend; they's just boys!"

Giving the completely groggy Bud one last terrific backhander in the mouth, Praxiteles flung him away and rose from Jim's back, turning that one over, not gently, with his foot. Jim's face was completely masked with mud, and he made distressed blowing noises through it as he tried to sit up. Bud Pike came to his elbow, spat out a tooth and opened one eye. When Praxiteles looked at him, he lay down again, hastily. And from the saloon fifty men whooped in Homeric laughter.

"Boys, did you see his arms going? Like Old Man Weyser's windmill with the governor off in a blue norther!"

"Ol' Jim, with the reverend sittin' on his head!"

"Make way for the reverend, boys! He's a bobcat with bristles on his belly. He's a cross between a catamount and a alligator!"—this from an enthusiast well-drunken, who was immediately suppressed; for the ladies were getting down from the wagons. The men stood silent as Praxiteles Swan came toward them, having retrieved his saddlebags. They made way for him respectfully; some of them touched their hats.

One called, "Oh, Dutch, get the reverend a towel an' a basin, in case he wants to spruce up!"

Behind him walked Mr. Medary, his chest out a foot, saying to this acquaintance and that: "Reverend Swan, boys, from old Virginyeh. Particular friend of mine—stayin' at my house. They say he's a powerful preacher too."

The ladies followed. Miss Jael Medary, her skirts lifted daintily from the mud, disclosing the neatest ankles in the world, passed her fallen suitors with the effect of shying away from leprosy, but she was not thinking of them; she never thought of them again. Her cheeks flamed deliciously, and her eyes were at once speculative and tender, following the tall figure of Praxiteles Swan.

In Mr. Gadsen's Saloon and Billiard Parlors, saints and willing sinners hustled together with chairs and benches. The Negro bottle washer snatched the goboons out of sight behind the bar.

In his little room at one side, Mr. Goat Gadsen himself brought water and helped in the removal of the worst of the blood and mud with which the Church Militant was spattered; his expert judgment was, the eye where one of Bud's wild swings had landed wouldn't close altogether; he recommended a chunk of raw liver as soon as services was over. And the ladies would be glad to mend his coat, where it was split up the back. Uncle Jimmy passed out the hymnbooks.

The Rev. Elkanah Grebs, assisting, said he was miraculously restored in health, and he'd be pleased to deliver the opening prayer.

"You sho'ly smote the Amalekites hip and thigh, brother," he exulted. "'The sword of the Lord and of Gideon'! And what, if I might make so bold, will be yore text this morning?"

"I'll give 'em a lesson from First Samuel, the ninth chapter —how Saul went looking for his father's asses," Praxiteles told him.

Brother Grebs knew his Bible; Uncle Jimmy says he rubbed his hands and allowed that he couldn't do better. It was the passage describing young Saul as being "from his shoulders and upward . . . higher than any of the people."

"And I don't know what you're looking for, exactly, but I do know what you've found, brother," he added, as Praxiteles pulled his coat on and went into the bar, where the congregation was settled down.

Uncle Jimmy laughed. "Reverend Grebs, he was right about it. He married the new preacher to Miss Jinny the next Sunday morning, and Brother Swan was the first man in Washington County that got married and was not shivareed by the neighbors."

The Three Hermits

AN OLD LEGEND CURRENT IN THE VOLGA DISTRICT

by LEO NIKOLAEVICH TOLSTOY

❖❖❖

And in praying use not vain repetitions, as the Gentiles do: for they think that they shall be heard for their much speaking. Be not therefore like them: for your Father knoweth what things ye have need of, before ye ask Him.

—Matt. 6:7-8

A BISHOP WAS SAILING FROM ARCHANGEL TO THE SOLOVÉTSK Monastery, and on the same vessel were a number of pilgrims on their way to visit the shrines at that place. The voyage was a smooth one. The wind favorable and the weather fair. The pilgrims lay on deck, eating, or sat in groups talking to one another. The Bishop, too, came on deck, and as he was pacing up and down he noticed a group of men standing near the prow and listening to a fisherman, who was pointing to the sea and telling them something. The Bishop stopped, and looked in the direction in which the man was pointing. He could see nothing, however, but the sea glistening in the sunshine. He drew nearer to listen, but when the man saw him,

131

he took off his cap and was silent. The rest of the people also took off their caps and bowed.

"Do not let me disturb you, friends," said the Bishop. "I came to hear what this good man was saying."

"The fisherman was telling us about the hermits," replied one, a tradesman, rather bolder than the rest.

"What hermits?" asked the Bishop, going to the side of the vessel and seating himself on a box. "Tell me about them. I should like to hear. What were you pointing at?"

"Why, that little island you can just see over there," answered the man, pointing to a spot ahead and a little to the right. "That is the island where the hermits live for the salvation of their souls."

"Where is the island?" asked the Bishop. "I see nothing."

"There, in the distance, if you will please look along my hand. Do you see that little cloud? Below it, and a bit to the left, there is just a faint streak. That is the island."

The Bishop looked carefully, but his unaccustomed eyes could make out nothing but the water shimmering in the sun.

"I cannot see it," he said. "But who are the hermits that live there?"

"They are holy men," answered the fisherman. "I had long heard tell of them, but never chanced to see them myself till the year before last."

And the fisherman related how once, when he was out fishing, he had been stranded at night upon that island, not knowing where he was. In the morning, as he wandered about the island, he came across an earth hut, and met an old man standing near it. Presently two others came out, and after having fed him and dried his things, they helped him mend his boat.

"And what are they like?" asked the Bishop.

132

"One is a small man and his back is bent. He wears a priest's cassock and is very old; he must be more than a hundred, I should say. He is so old that the white of his beard is taking a greenish tinge, but he is always smiling, and his face is as bright as an angel's from heaven. The second is taller, but he also is very old. He wears a tattered peasant coat. His beard is broad, and of a yellowish grey color. He is a strong man. Before I had time to help him, he turned my boat over as if it were only a pail. He too is kindly and cheerful. The third is tall, and has a beard as white as snow and reaching to his knees. He is stern, with overhanging eyebrows; and he wears nothing but a piece of matting tied round his waist."

"And did they speak to you?" asked the Bishop.

"For the most part they did everything in silence, and spoke but little even to one another. One of them would just give a glance, and the others would understand him. I asked the tallest whether they had lived there long. He frowned, and muttered something as if he were angry; but the oldest one took his hand and smiled, and then the tall one was quiet. The oldest one only said: 'Have mercy upon us,' and smiled."

While the fisherman was talking, the ship had drawn nearer to the island.

"There, now you can see it plainly, if your Lordship will please to look," said the tradesman, pointing with his hand.

The Bishop looked, and now he really saw a dark streak—which was the island. Having looked at it a while, he left the prow of the vessel, and going to the stern, asked the helmsman:

"What island is that?"

"That one," replied the man, "has no name. There are many such in this sea."

"Is it true that there are hermits who live there for the salvation of their souls?"

"So it is said, your Lordship, but I don't know if it's true. Fishermen say they have seen them; but of course they may only be spinning yarns."

"I should like to land on the island and see these men," said the Bishop. "How could I manage it?"

"The ship cannot get close to the island," replied the helmsman, "but you might be rowed there in a boat. You had better speak to the captain."

The captain was sent for and came.

"I should like to see these hermits," said the Bishop. "Could I not be rowed ashore?"

The captain tried to dissuade him.

"Of course it could be done," said he, "but we should lose much time. And if I might venture to say so to your Lordship, the old men are not worth your pains. I have heard say that they are foolish old fellows, who understand nothing, and never speak a word, any more than the fish in the sea."

"I wish to see them," said the Bishop, "and I will pay you for your trouble and loss of time. Please let me have a boat."

There was no help for it; so the order was given. The sailors trimmed the sails, the steersman put up the helm, and the ship's course was set for the island. A chair was placed at the prow for the Bishop, and he sat there, looking ahead. The passengers all collected at the prow, and gazed at the island. Those who had the sharpest eyes could presently make out the rocks on it, and then a mud hut was seen. At last one man saw the hermits themselves. The captain brought a telescope and, after looking through it, handed it to the Bishop.

"It's right enough. There are three men standing on the shore. There, a little to the right of that big rock."

The Bishop took the telescope, got it into position, and he saw the three men: a tall one, a shorter one, and one very small and bent, standing on the shore and holding each other by the hand.

The captain turned to the Bishop.

"The vessel can get no nearer in than this, your Lordship. If you wish to go ashore, we must ask you to go in the boat, while we anchor here."

The cable was quickly let out; the anchor cast, and the sails furled. There was a jerk, and the vessel shook. Then, a boat having been lowered, the oarsmen jumped in, and the Bishop descended the ladder and took his seat. The men pulled at their oars and the boat moved rapidly towards the island. When they came within a stone's throw, they saw three old men: a tall one with only a piece of matting tied round his waist: a shorter one in a tattered peasant coat, and a very old one bent with age and wearing an old cassock—all three standing hand in hand.

The oarsmen pulled in to the shore, and held on with the boathook while the Bishop got out.

The old men bowed to him, and he gave them his blessing, at which they bowed still lower. Then the Bishop began to speak to them.

"I have heard," he said, "that you, godly men, live here saving your own souls and praying to our Lord Christ for your fellow men. I, an unworthy servant of Christ, am called, by God's mercy, to keep and teach His flock. I wished to see you, servants of God, and to do what I can to teach you, also."

The old men looked at each other smiling, but remained silent.

"Tell me," said the Bishop, "what you are doing to save your souls, and how you serve God on this island."

The second hermit sighed, and looked at the oldest, the very ancient one. The latter smiled, and said:

"We do not know how to serve God. We only serve and support ourselves, servant of God."

"But how do you pray to God?" asked the Bishop.

"We pray in this way," replied the hermit. "Three are ye, three are we, have mercy upon us."

And when the old man said this, all three raised their eyes to heaven, and repeated:

"Three are ye, three are we, have mercy upon us!"

The Bishop smiled.

"You have evidently heard something about the Holy Trinity," said he. "But you do not pray aright. You have won my affection, godly men. I see you wish to please the Lord, but you do not know how to serve Him. That is not the way to pray; but listen to me, and I will teach you. I will teach you, not a way of my own, but the way in which God in the Holy Scriptures has commanded all men to pray to Him."

And the Bishop began explaining to the hermits how God had revealed Himself to men; telling them of God the Father, and God the Son, and God the Holy Ghost.

"God the Son came down on earth," said he, "to save men, and this is how He taught us all to pray. Listen, and repeat after me: 'Our Father.'"

And the first old man repeated after him, "Our Father," and the second said, "Our Father," and the third said, "Our Father."

"Which art in heaven," continued the Bishop.

The first hermit repeated, "Which art in heaven," but the second blundered over the words, and the tall hermit could not say them properly. His hair had grown over his mouth so that he could not speak plainly. The very old hermit, having no teeth, also mumbled indistinctly.

The Bishop repeated the words again, and the old men repeated them after him. The Bishop sat down on a stone, and the old men stood before him, watching his mouth, and repeating the words as he uttered them. And all day long the Bishop labored, saying a word twenty, thirty, a hundred times over, and the old men repeated it after him. They blundered, and he corrected them, and made them begin again.

The Bishop did not leave off till he had taught them the whole of the Lord's Prayer so that they could not only repeat it after him, but could say it by themselves. The middle one was the first to know it, and to repeat the whole of it alone. The Bishop made him say it again and again, and at last the others could say it too.

It was getting dark and the moon was appearing over the water, before the Bishop rose to return to the vessel. When he took leave of the old men they all bowed down to the ground before him. He raised them, and kissed each of them, telling them to pray as he had taught them. Then he got into the boat and returned to the ship.

And as he sat in the boat and was rowed to the ship he could hear the three voices of the hermits loudly repeating the Lord's Prayer. As the boat drew near the vessel their voices could no longer be heard, but they could still be seen in the moonlight, standing as he had left them on the shore, the shortest in the middle, the tallest on the right, the middle one on the left. As soon as the Bishop had reached the vessel and got on board, the anchor was weighed and the sails unfurled. The wind filled them and the ship sailed away, and the Bishop took a seat in the stern and watched the island they had left. For a time he could still see the hermits, but presently they disappeared from sight, though the island was still visible. At last it too vanished, and only the sea was to be seen, rippling in the moonlight.

The pilgrims lay down to sleep, and all was quiet on deck. The Bishop did not wish to sleep, but sat alone at the stern, gazing at the sea where the island was no longer visible, and thinking of the good old men. He thought how pleased they had been to learn the Lord's Prayer; and he thanked God for having sent him to teach and help such godly men.

So the Bishop sat, thinking, and gazing at the sea where the island had disappeared. And the moonlight flickered before his eyes, sparkling, now here, now there, upon the waves. Suddenly he saw something white and shining, on the bright path which the moon cast across the sea. Was it a seagull, or the little gleaming sail of some small boat? The Bishop fixed his eyes on it, wondering.

"It must be a boat sailing after us," thought he, "but it is overtaking us very rapidly. It was far, far away a minute ago, but now it is much nearer. It cannot be a boat, for I can see no sail; but whatever it may be, it is following us and catching us up."

And he could not make out what it was. Not a boat, nor a bird, nor a fish! It was too large for a man, and besides a man could not be out there in the midst of the sea. The Bishop rose, and said to the helmsman:

"Look there, what is that, my friend? What is it?" the Bishop repeated, though he could now see plainly what it was—the three hermits running upon the water, all gleaming white, their grey beards shining, and approaching the ship as quickly as though it were not moving.

The steersman looked, and let go the helm in terror.

"Oh, Lord! The hermits are running after us on the water as though it were dry land!"

The passengers, hearing him, jumped up and crowded to the stern. They saw the hermits coming along hand in hand, and the two outer ones beckoning the ship to stop. All three were gliding along upon the water without moving their feet. Before the ship could be stopped, the hermits had reached it, and raising their heads, all three as with one voice, began to say:

"We have forgotten your teaching, servant of God. As long as we kept repeating it we remembered, but when we stopped saying it for a time, a word dropped out, and now it has all gone to pieces. We can remember nothing of it. Teach us again."

The Bishop crossed himself, and leaning over the ship's side, said:

"Your own prayer will reach the Lord, men of God. It is not for me to teach you. Pray for us sinners."

And the Bishop bowed low before the old men; and they turned and went back across the sea. And a light shone until daybreak on the spot where they were lost to sight.

Tit for Tat

by Sholom Aleichem

❖❖❖

Once I was a rabbiner. A rabbiner, not a rabbi. That is, I was called rabbi—but a rabbi of the crown.

To old-country Jews I don't have to explain what a rabbi of the crown is. They know the breed. What are his great responsibilities? He fills out birth certificates, officiates at circumcisions, performs marriages, grants divorces. He gets his share from the living and the dead. In the synagogue he has a place of honor, and when the congregation rises, he is the first to stand. On legal holidays he appears in a stovepipe hat and holds forth in his best Russian: *"Gospoda Prihozhane!"* To take it for granted that among our people a rabbiner is well loved— let's not say any more. Say rather that we put up with him, as we do a government inspector or a deputy sheriff. And yet he is chosen from among the people, that is, every three years a proclamation is sent us: *"Na Osnavania Predpisania . . ."* Or, as we would say: "Your Lord, the Governor, orders you to come together in the synagogue, poor little Jews, and pick out a rabbiner for yourselves . . ."

Then the campaign begins. Candidates, hot discussions, brandy, and maybe even a bribe or two. After which come charges and countercharges, the elections are annulled, and we are ordered to hold new elections. Again the proclamations: *"Na Osnavania Predpisania . . ."* Again candidates, discussions, party organizations, brandy, a bribe or two . . . That was the life!

Well, there I was—a rabbiner in a small town in the province of Poltava. But I was anxious to be a modern one. I wanted to serve the public. So I dropped the formalities of my position and began to mingle with the people—as we say: to stick my head into the community pot. I got busy with the *Talmud Torah,* the charity fund, interpreted a law, settled disputes or just gave plain advice.

The love of settling disputes, helping people out, or advising them, I inherited from my father and my uncles. They— may they rest in peace—also enjoyed being bothered all the time with other people's business. There are two kinds of people in the world: those that you can't bother at all, and others whom you can bother all the time. You can climb right on their heads—naturally not in one jump, but gradually. First you climb into their laps, then on to their shoulders, then their heads—and after that you can jump up and down on their heads and stamp on their hearts with your heavy boots— as long as you want to.

I was that kind, and without boasting I can tell you that I had plenty of ardent followers and plain hangers-on who weren't ashamed to come every day and fill my head with their clamoring and sit around till late at night. They never refused a glass of tea, or cigarettes. Newspapers and books they took without asking. In short, I was a regular fellow.

Well, there came a day . . . The door opened, and in walked the very foremost men of the town, the sparkling best, the

141

very cream of the city. Four householders—men of affairs—you could almost say: real men of substance. And who were these men? Three of them were the *Troika*—that was what we called them in our town because they were together all the time—partners in whatever business any one of them was in. They always fought, they were always suspicious of each other, and watched everything the others did, and still they never separated—working always on this principle: if the business is a good one and there is profit to be made, why shouldn't I have a lick at the bone too? And on the other hand, if it should end in disaster—you'll be buried along with me, and lie with me deep in the earth. And what does God do? He brings together the three partners with a fourth one. They operate together a little less than a year and end up in a brawl. That is why they're here.

What had happened? "Since God created thieves, swindlers and crooks, you never saw a thief, swindler or crook like this one." That is the way the three old partners described the fourth one to me. And he, the fourth, said the same about them. Exactly the same, word for word. And who was this fourth one? He was a quiet little man, a little innocent-looking fellow, with thick, dark eyebrows under which a pair of shrewd, ironic, little eyes watched everything you did. Everyone called him Nachman Lekach.

His real name was Nachman Noss'n, but everybody called him Nachman Lekach, because as you know, *Noss'n* is the Hebrew for "he gave," and *Lekach* means "he took," and in all the time we knew him, no one had ever seen him give anything to anyone—while at taking no one was better.

Where were we? Oh, yes . . . So they came to the rabbiner with the complaints, to see if he could find a way of straighten-

142

ing out their tangled accounts. "Whatever you decide, Rabbi, and whatever you decree, and whatever you say, will be final."

That is how the three old partners said it, and the fourth, Reb Nachman, nodded with that innocent look on his face to indicate that he too left it all up to me: "For the reason," his eyes said, "that I know that I have done no wrong." And he sat down in a corner, folded his arms across his chest like an old woman, fixed his shrewd, ironic, little eyes on me, and waited to see what his partners would have to say. And when they had all laid out their complaints and charges, presented all their evidence, said all they had to say, he got up, patted down his thick eyebrows, and not looking at the others at all, only at me, with those deep, deep, shrewd little eyes of his, he proceeded to demolish their claims and charges—so completely, that it looked as if they were the thieves, swindlers and crooks—the three partners of his—and he, Nachman Lekach, was a man of virtue and piety, the little chicken that is slaughtered before *Yom Kippur* to atone for our sins—a sacrificial lamb. "And every word that you heard them say is a complete lie, it never was and never could be. It's simply out of the question." And he proved with evidence, arguments and supporting data that everything he said was true and holy, as if Moses himself had said it.

All the time he was talking, the others, the *Troika,* could hardly sit in their chairs. Every moment one or another of them jumped up, clutched his head—or his heart: "Of all things! How can a man talk like that! Such lies and falsehoods!" It was almost impossible to calm them down, to keep them from tearing at the fourth one's beard. As for me—the rabbiner—it was hard, very hard to crawl out from this horrible tangle, because by now it was clear that I had a fine band to deal with, all four of them swindlers, thieves and crooks, and informers to boot, and all four of them deserving a severe punishment. But what? At last this idea occurred to me, and I said to them:

"Are you ready, my friends? I am prepared to hand down my decision. My mind is made up. But I won't disclose what I have to say until each of you has deposited twenty-five *rubles*— to prove that you will act upon the decision I am about to hand down."

"With the greatest of pleasure," the three spoke out at once, and Nachman Lekach nodded his head, and all four reached into their pockets, and each one counted out his twenty-five on the table. I gathered up the money, locked it up in a drawer, and then I gave them my decision in these words:

"Having heard the complaints and the arguments of both parties, and having examined your accounts and studied your evidence, I find according to my understanding and deep conviction, that all four of you are in the wrong, and not only in the wrong, but that it is a shame and a scandal for Jewish people to conduct themselves in such a manner—to falsify accounts, perjure yourselves and even act as informers. Therefore I have decided that since we have a *Talmud Torah* in our town with many children who have neither clothes nor shoes, and whose parents have nothing with which to pay their tuition, and since there has been no help at all from you gentlemen (to get a few pennies from you one has to reach down into your very gizzards) therefore it is my decision that this hundred *rubles* of yours shall go to the *Talmud Torah,* and as for you, gentlemen, you can go home, in good health, and thanks for your contribution. The poor children will now have some

shoes and socks and shirts and pants, and I'm sure they'll pray
to God for you and your children. Amen."

Having heard the sentence, the three old partners—the
Troika—looked from one to the other—flushed, unable to speak.
A decision like this they had not anticipated. The only one
who could say a word was Reb Nachman Lekach. He got up,
patted down his thick eyebrows, held out a hand, and looking
at me with his ironic little eyes, said this:

"I thank you, Rabbi Rabbiner, in behalf of all four of us,
for the wise decision which you have just made known. Such
a judgment could have been made by no one since King Solo-
mon himself. There is only one thing that you forgot to say,
Rabbi Rabbiner, and that is: what is your fee for this wise and
just decision?"

"I beg your pardon," I tell him. "You've come to the wrong
address. I am not one of those rabbiners who tax the living
and the dead." That is the way I answered him, like a real
gentleman. And this was his reply:

"If that's the case, then you are not only a sage and a Rabbi
among men, you're an honest man besides. So, if you would
care to listen, I'd like to tell you a story. Say that we will pay
you for your pains at least with a story."

"Good enough. Even with two stories."

"In that case, sit down, Rabbi Rabbiner, and let us have
your cigarette case. I'll tell you an interesting story, a true
one, too, something that happened to me. What happened
to others I don't like to talk about."

And we lit our cigarettes, sat down around the table, and
Reb Nachman spread out his thick eyebrows, and looking at
me with his shrewd, smiling, little eyes, he slowly began to
tell his true story of what had once happened to him himself.

All this happened to me a long time ago. I was still a young man and I was living not far from here, in a village near the railroad. I traded in this and that, I had a small tavern, made a living. A Rothschild I didn't become, but bread we had, and in time there were about ten Jewish families living close by—because, as you know, if one of us makes a living, others come around. They think you're shoveling up gold . . . But that isn't the point. What I was getting at was that right in the midst of the busy season one year, when things were moving and traffic was heavy, my wife had to go and have a baby—our boy—our first son. What do you say to that? "Congratulations! Congratulations everybody!" But that isn't all. You have to have a *bris,* the circumcision. I dropped everything, went into town, bought all the good things I could find, and came back with the *Mohel* with all his instruments, and for good measure I also brought the *shammes* of the synagogue. I thought that with these two holy men and myself and the neighbors we'd have the ten men that we needed, with one to spare. But what does God do? He has one of my neighbors get sick—he is sick in bed and can't come to the *bris,* you can't carry him. And another has to pack up and go off to the city. He can't wait another day! And here I am without the ten men. Go do something. Here it is—Friday! Of all days, my wife has to pick Friday to have the *bris*—the day before the Sabbath. The *Mohel* is frantic—he has to go back right away. The *shammes* is actually in tears. "What did you ever drag us off here for?" they both want to know. And what can I do?

All I can think of is to run off to the railroad station. Who knows—so many people come through every day—maybe God will send some one. And that's just what happened. I

come running up to the station—the agent has just called out
that a train is about to leave. I look around—a little roly-poly
man carrying a huge traveling bag comes flying by, all sweating and out of breath, straight toward the lunch counter. He
looks over the dishes—what is there a good Jew can take in a
country railroad station? A piece of herring—an egg. Poor
fellow—you could see his mouth was watering. I grab him
by the sleeve. "Uncle, are you looking for something to eat?"
I ask him, and the look he gives me says: "How did you know
that?" I keep on talking: "May you live to be a hundred—
God himself must have sent you." He still doesn't understand,
so I proceed: "Do you want to earn the blessings of eternity—
and at the same time eat a beef roast that will melt in your
mouth, with a fresh, white loaf right out of the oven?" He
still looks at me as if I'm crazy. "Who are you? What do you
want?"

So I tell him the whole story—what a misfortune had overtaken us: here we are, all ready for the *bris,* the *Mohel* is waiting, the food is ready—and such food!—and we need a tenth
man! "What's that got to do with me?" he asks, and I tell
him: "What's that got to do with you? Why—everything
depends on you—you're the tenth man! I beg you—come
with me. You will earn all the rewards of heaven—and have
a delicious dinner in the bargain!" "Are you crazy," he asks
me, "or are you just out of your head? My train is leaving in
a few minutes, and it's Friday afternoon—almost sundown.
Do you know what that means? In a few more hours the
Sabbath will catch up with me, and I'll be stranded." "So
what!" I tell him. "So you'll take the next train. And in the
meantime you'll earn eternal life—and taste a soup, with fresh
dumplings, that only my wife can make . . ."

Well, why make the story long? I had my way. The roast and the hot soup with fresh dumplings did their work. You could see my customer licking his lips. So I grab the traveling bag and I lead him home, and we go through with the *bris*. It was a real pleasure! You could smell the roast all over the house, it had so much garlic in it. A roast like that, with fresh warm twist, is a delicacy from heaven. And when you consider that we had some fresh dill pickles, and a bottle of beer, and some cognac before the meal and cherry cider after the meal—you can imagine the state our guest was in! His cheeks shone and his forehead glistened. But what then? Before we knew it the afternoon was gone. My guest jumps up, he looks around, sees what time it is, and almost has a stroke! He reaches for his traveling bag: "Where is it?" I say to him, "What's your hurry? In the first place, do you think we'll let you run off like that—before the Sabbath? And in the second place—who are you to leave on a journey an hour or two before the Sabbath? And if you're going to get caught out in the country somewhere, you might just as well stay here with us."

He groans and he sighs. How could I do a thing like that to him—keep him so late? What did I have against him? Why hadn't I reminded him earlier? He doesn't stop bothering me. So I say to him: "In the first place, did I have to tell you that it was Friday afternoon? Didn't you know it yourself? And in the second place, how do you know—maybe it's the way God wanted it? Maybe He wanted you to stay here for the Sabbath so you could taste some of my wife's fish? I can guarantee you, that as long as you've eaten fish, you haven't eaten fish like my wife's fish—not even in a dream!" Well, that ended the argument. We said our evening prayers, had a glass of wine, and my wife brings the fish to the table. My guest's nostrils swell out, a new light shines in his eyes and he goes after that fish as if he hadn't eaten a thing all day. He can't get over it. He praises it to the skies. He fills a glass with brandy and drinks a toast to the fish. And then comes the soup, a specially rich Sabbath soup with noodles. And he likes that, too, and the *tzimmes* also, and the meat that goes with the *tzimmes,* a nice, fat piece of brisket. I'm telling you, he just sat there licking his fingers! When we're finishing the last course he turns to me: "Do you know what I'll tell you? Now that it's all over, I'm really glad that I stayed over for *Shabbes.* It's been a long time since I've enjoyed a Sabbath as I've enjoyed this one." "If that's how you feel, I'm happy," I tell him. "But wait. This is only a sample. Wait till tomorrow. Then you'll see what my wife can do."

And so it was. The next day, after services, we sit down at the table. Well, you should have seen the spread. First the appetizers: crisp wafers and chopped herring, and onions and chicken fat, with radishes and chopped liver and eggs and *gribbenes.* And after that the cold fish and the meat from yesterday's *tzimmes,* and then the jellied neat's foot, or *fisnoga* as you call it, with thin slices of garlic, and after that the potato *cholent* with the *kugel* that had been in the oven all night—and you know what that smells like when you take it out of the oven and take the cover off the pot. And what it tastes like. Our visitor could not find words to praise it. So I tell him: "This is still nothing. Wait until you have tasted our borsht tonight, then you'll know what good food is." At that he laughs out loud—a friendly laugh, it is true—and says to me: "Yes, but how far do you think I'll be from here by the time your borsht is ready?" So I laugh even louder than he does, and say: "You can forget that right now! Do you think you'll be going off tonight?"

And so it was. As soon as the lights were lit and we had a glass of wine to start off the new week, my friend begins to pack his things again. So I call out to him: "Are you crazy? Do you think we'll let you go off, the Lord knows where, at night? And besides, where's your train?" "What?" he yells at me. "No train? Why, you're murdering me! You know I have to leave!" But I say, "May this be the greatest misfortune in your life. Your train will come, if all is well, around dawn tomorrow. In the meantime I hope your appetite and digestion are good, because I can smell the borsht already! All I ask," I say, "is just tell me the truth. Tell me if you've ever touched a borsht like this before. But I want the absolute truth!" What's the use of talking—he had to admit it: never before in all his life had he tasted a borsht like this. Never. He even started to ask how you made the borsht, what you put into it, and how long you cooked it. Everything. And I say: "Don't worry about that! Here, taste this wine and tell me what you think of *it*. After all, you're an expert. But the truth! Remember—nothing but the truth! Because if there is anything I hate, it's flattery . . ."

So we took a glass, and then another glass, and we went to bed. And what do you think happened? My traveler overslept, and missed the early morning train. When he wakes up he boils over! He jumps on me like a murderer. Wasn't it up to me, out of fairness and decency, to wake him up in time? Because of me he's going to have to take a loss, a heavy loss—he doesn't even know himself how heavy. It was all my fault. I ruined him. I! . . . So I let him talk. I listen, quietly, and when he's all through, I say: "Tell me yourself, aren't you a queer sort of

150

person? In the first place, what's your hurry? What are you rushing for? How long is a person's life altogether? Does he have to spoil that little with rushing and hurrying? And in the second place, have you forgotten that today is the third day since the *bris*? Doesn't that mean a thing to you? Where we come from, on the third day we're in the habit of putting on a feast better than the one at the *bris* itself. The third day— it's something to celebrate! You're not going to spoil the celebration, are you?"

What can he do? He can't control himself any more, and he starts laughing—a hysterical laugh. "What good does it do to talk?" he says. "You're a real leech!" "Just as you say," I tell him, "but after all, you're a visitor, aren't you?"

At the dinner table, after we've had a drink or two, I call out to him: "Look," I say, "it may not be proper—after all, we're Jews—to talk about milk and such things while we're eating meat, but I'd like to know your honest opinion: what do you think of *kreplach* with cheese?" He looks at me with distrust. "How did we get around to that?" he asks. "Just like this," I explain to him. "I'd like to have you try the cheese *kreplach* that my wife makes—because tonight, you see, we're going to have a dairy supper . . ." This is too much for him, and he comes right back at me with, "Not this time! You're trying to keep me here another day, I can see that. But you can't do it. It isn't right! It isn't right!" And from the way he fusses and fumes it's easy to see that I won't have to coax him too long, or fight with him either, because what is he but a man with an appetite, who has only one philosophy, which he practices at the table? So I say this to him: "I give you my word of honor, and if that isn't enough, I'll give you my hand as well—here, shake—that tomorrow I'll wake you up

151

in time for the earliest train. I promise it, even if the world turns upside down. If I don't, may I—you know what!" At this he softens and says to me: "Remember, we're shaking hands on that!" And I: "A promise is a promise." And my wife makes a dairy supper—how can I describe it to you? With such *kreplach* that my traveler has to admit that it was all true: he has a wife too, and she makes *kreplach* too, but how can you compare hers with these? It's like night to day!

And I kept my word, because a promise is a promise. I woke him when it was still dark, and started the samovar. He finished packing and began to say goodbye to me and the rest of the household in a very handsome, friendly style. You could see he was a gentleman. But I interrupt him: "We'll say goodbye a little later. First, we have to settle up." "What do you mean—settle up?" "Settle up," I say, "means to add up the figures. That's what I'm going to do now. I'll add them up, let you know what it comes to, and you will be so kind as to pay me."

His face flames red. "Pay you?" he shouts. "Pay you for what?" "For what?" I repeat. "You want to know for what? For everything. The food, the drink, the lodging." This time he becomes white—not red—and he says to me: "I don't understand you at all. You came and invited me to the *bris*. You stopped me at the train. You took my bag away from me. You promised me eternal life." "That's right," I interrupt him. "That's right. But what's one thing got to do with the other? When you came to the *bris* you earned your reward in heaven. But food and drink and lodging—do I have to give you these things for nothing? After all, you're a businessman, aren't you? You should understand that fish costs money, and that the wine you drank was the very best, and the beer,

152

too, and the cherry cider. And you remember how you praised the *tzimmes* and the puddings and the borsht. You remember how you licked your fingers. And the cheese *kreplach* smelled pretty good to you, too. Now, I'm glad you enjoyed these things; I don't begrudge you that in the least. But certainly you wouldn't expect that just because you earned a reward in heaven, and enjoyed yourself in the bargain, that *I* should pay for it?" My traveling friend was really sweating; he looked as if he'd have a stroke. He began to throw himself around, yell, scream, call for help. "This is Sodom!" he cried. "Worse than Sodom! It's the worst outrage the world has ever heard of! How much do you want?" Calmly I took a piece of paper and a pencil and began to add it up. I itemized everything, I gave him an inventory of everything he ate, of every hour he spent in my place. All in all it added up to something like thirty-odd *rubles* and some *kopeks*—I don't remember it exactly.

When he saw the total, my good man went green and yellow, his hands shook, and his eyes almost popped out, and again he let out a yell, louder than before. "What did I fall into—a nest of thieves? Isn't there a single human being here? Is there a God anywhere?" So I say to him, "Look, sir, do you know what? Do you know what you're yelling about? Do you have to eat your heart out? Here is my suggestion: let's ride into town together—it's not far from here— and we'll find some people—there's a rabbiner there—let's ask the rabbi. And we'll abide by what he says." When he heard me talk like that, he quieted down a little. And—don't worry—we hired a horse and wagon, climbed in, and rode off to town, the two of us, and went straight to the rabbi.

When we got to the rabbi's house, we found him just finishing his morning prayers. He folded up his prayer shawl and put his phylacteries away. "Good morning," we said to him, and he: "What's the news today?" The news? My friend tears loose and lets him have the whole story—everything from A to Z. He doesn't leave a word out. He tells how he stopped at the station, and so on and so on, and when he's through he whips out the bill I had given him and hands it to the rabbi. And when the rabbi had heard everything, he says: "Having heard one side I should now like to hear the other." And turning to me, he asks, "What do you have to say to all that?" I answer: "Everything he says is true. There's not a word I can add. Only one thing I'd like to have him tell you—on his word of honor: did he eat the fish, and did he drink the beer and cognac and the cider, and did he smack his lips over the borsht that my wife made?" At this the man becomes almost frantic, he jumps and he thrashes about like an apoplectic. The rabbi begs him not to boil like that, not to be so angry, because anger is a grave sin. And he asks him again about the fish and the borsht and the *kreplach,* and if it was true that he had drunk not only the wine, but beer and cognac and cider as well. Then the rabbi puts on his spectacles, looks the bill over from top to bottom, checks every line, and finds it correct! Thirty-odd *rubles* and some *kopeks,* and he makes his judgment brief: he tells the man to pay the whole thing, and for the wagon back and forth, and a judgment fee for the rabbi himself . . .

The man stumbles out of the rabbi's house looking as if he'd been in a steam bath too long, takes out his purse, pulls out two twenty-fives and snaps at me: "Give me the change." "What change?" I ask, and he says: "For the thirty you charged me—for that bill you gave me." "Bill? What bill?

What thirty are you talking about? What do you think I am, a highwayman? Do you expect me to take money from you? I see a man at the railroad station, a total stranger; I take his bag away from him, and drag him off almost by force to our own *bris,* and spend a wonderful *Shabbes* with him. So am I going to charge him for the favor he did me, and for the pleasure I had?" Now he looks at me as if I really am crazy, and says: "Then why did you carry on like this? Why did you drag me to the rabbi?" "Why this? Why that?" I say to him. "You're a queer sort of person, you are! I wanted to show you what kind of man our rabbi was, that's all . . ."

When he finished the story, my litigant, Reb Nachman Lekach, got up with a flourish, and the other three partners followed him. They buttoned their coats and prepared to leave. But I held them off. I passed the cigarettes around again, and said to the story-teller:

"So you told me a story about a rabbi. Now maybe you'll be so kind as to let me tell you a story—also about a rabbi, but a much shorter story than the one you told."

And without waiting for a yes or no, I started right in, and made it brief:

This happened, I began, not so long ago, and in a large city, on *Yom Kippur* eve. A stranger falls into the town—a businessman, a traveler, who goes here and there, everywhere, sells merchandise, collects money . . . On this day he comes into the city, walks up and down in front of the synagogue, holding his sides with both hands, asks everybody he sees where he can find the rabbi. "What do you want the rabbi for?" people ask. "What business is that of yours?" he wants to know. So they don't tell him. And he asks one man, he asks another: "Can you tell where the rabbi lives?" "What do you want the rabbi for?" "What do you care?" This one and that one, till finally he gets the answer, finds the rabbi's house, goes in, still holding his sides with both hands. He calls the rabbi aside, shuts the door, and says, "Rabbi, this is my story. I am a traveling man, and I have money with me, quite a pile. It's not my money. It belongs to my clients—first to God and then to my clients. It's *Yom Kippur* eve. I can't carry money with me on *Yom Kippur,* and I'm afraid to leave it at my lodgings. A sum like that! So do me a favor—take it, put it away in your strong box till tomorrow night, after *Yom Kippur.*"

And without waiting, the man unbuttons his vest and draws out one pack after another, crisp and clean, the real red, crackling, hundred *ruble* notes!

Seeing how much there was, the rabbi said to him: "I beg your pardon. You don't know me, you don't know who I am." "What do you mean, I don't know who you are? You're a rabbi, aren't you?" "Yes, I'm a rabbi. But I don't know *you* —who you are or what you are." They bargain back and forth. The traveler: "You're a rabbi." The rabbi: "I don't know who you are." And time does not stand still. It's almost *Yom Kippur!* Finally the rabbi agrees to take the money. The only thing is, who should be the witnesses? You can't trust just anyone in a matter like that.

So the rabbi sends for the leading townspeople, the very cream, rich and respectable citizens, and says to them: "This is what I called you for. This man has money with him, a tidy sum, not his own, but first God's and then his clients'. He wants me to keep it for him till after *Yom Kippur.* Therefore

I want you to be witnesses, to see how much he leaves with me, so that later—you understand?" And the rabbi took the trouble to count it all over three times before the eyes of the townspeople, wrapped the notes in a kerchief, sealed the kerchief with wax, and stamped his initials on the seal. He passed this from one man to the other, saying, "Now look. Here is my signature, and remember, you're the witnesses." The kerchief with the money in it he handed over to his wife, had her lock it in a chest, and hide the keys where no one could find them. And he himself, the rabbi, went to *shul,* and prayed and fasted as it was ordained, lived through *Yom Kippur,* came home, had a bite to eat, looked up, and there was the traveler. "Good evening, Rabbi." "Good evening. Sit down. What can I do for you?" "Nothing. I came for my package." "What package?" "The money." "What money?" "The money I left with you to keep for me." "You gave *me* money to keep for you? When was that?"

The traveler laughs out loud. He thinks the rabbi is joking with him. The rabbi asks: "What are you laughing at?" And the man says: "It's the first time I met a rabbi who liked to play tricks." At this the rabbi is insulted. No one, he pointed out, had ever called him a trickster before. "Tell me, my good man, what do you want here?"

When he heard these words, the stranger felt his heart stop. "Why, Rabbi, in the name of all that's holy, do you want to kill me? Didn't I give you all my money? That is, not mine, but first God's and then my clients'? I'll remind you, you wrapped it in a kerchief, sealed it with wax, locked it in your wife's chest, hid the key where no one could find it. And here is better proof: there were witnesses, the leading citizens of the city!" And he goes ahead and calls them all off by name. In the midst of it a cold sweat breaks out on his forehead, he feels faint, and asks for a glass of water.

The rabbi sends the *shammes* off to the men the traveler had named—the leading citizens, the flower of the community. They come running from all directions. "What's the matter? What's happened?" "A misfortune. A plot! A millstone around our necks! He insists that he brought a pile of money to me yesterday, to keep over *Yom Kippur,* and that you were witnesses to the act."

The householders look at each other, as if to say: "Here is where we get a nice bone to lick!" And they fall on the traveler: how could he do a thing like that? He ought to be ashamed of himself! Thinking up an ugly plot like that against their rabbi!

When he saw what was happening, his arms and legs went limp, he just about fainted. But the rabbi got up, went to the chest, took out the kerchief and handed it to him.

"What's the matter with you! Here! Here is your money! Take it and count it, see if it's right, here in front of your witnesses. The seal, as you see, is untouched. The wax is whole, just as it ought to be."

The traveler felt as if a new soul had been installed in his body. His hands trembled and tears stood in his eyes.

"Why did you have to do it, Rabbi? Why did you have to play this trick on me? A trick like this."

"I just wanted to show you—the kind—of—leading citizens —we have in our town."

The Minister's Black Veil

A PARABLE[1]

by NATHANIEL HAWTHORNE

᠂᠅᠊᠅

THE SEXTON STOOD IN THE PORCH OF MILFORD MEETING-house, pulling busily at the bell rope. The old people of the village came stooping along the street. Children with bright faces tripped merrily beside their parents, or mimicked a graver gait, in the conscious dignity of their Sunday clothes. Spruce bachelors looked sidelong at the pretty maidens, and fancied that the Sabbath sunshine made them prettier than on week days. When the throng had mostly streamed into the porch, the sexton began to toll the bell, keeping his eye on the Reverend Mr. Hooper's door. The first glimpse of the clergy-man's figure was the signal for the bell to cease its summons.

---

[1] Another clergyman in New England, Mr. Joseph Moody, of York, Maine, who died about eighty years since, made himself remarkable by the same eccentricity that is here related of the Reverend Mr. Hooper. In his case, however, the symbol had a different import. In early life he had accidentally killed a beloved friend; and from that day till the hour of his own death, he hid his face from men.

"But what has good Parson Hooper got upon his face?" cried the sexton in astonishment.

All within hearing immediately turned about, and beheld the semblance of Mr. Hooper, pacing slowly his meditative way towards the meeting-house. With one accord they started, expressing more wonder than if some strange minister were coming to dust the cushions of Mr. Hooper's pulpit.

"Are you sure it is our parson?" inquired Goodman Gray of the sexton.

"Of a certainty it is good Mr. Hooper," replied the sexton. "He was to have exchanged pulpits with Parson Shute, of Westbury; but Parson Shute sent to excuse himself yesterday, being to preach a funeral sermon."

The cause of so much amazement may appear sufficiently slight. Mr. Hooper, a gentlemanly person of about thirty, though still a bachelor, was dressed with due clerical neatness, as if a careful wife had starched his band, and brushed the weekly dust from his Sunday's garb. There was but one thing remarkable in his appearance. Swathed about his forehead, and hanging down over his face, so low as to be shaken by his breath, Mr. Hooper had on a black veil. On a nearer view, it seemed to consist of two folds of crape, which entirely concealed his features, except the mouth and chin, but probably did not intercept his sight, further than to give a darkened aspect to all living and inanimate things. With this gloomy shade before him, good Mr. Hooper walked onward, at a slow and quiet pace, stooping somewhat, and looking on the ground, as is customary with abstracted men, yet nodding kindly to those of his parishioners who still waited on the meeting-house steps. But so wonder-struck were they, that his greeting hardly met with a return.

160

"I can't really feel as if good Mr. Hooper's face was behind that piece of crape," said the sexton.

"I don't like it," muttered an old woman, as she hobbled into the meeting-house. "He has changed himself into something awful, only by hiding his face."

"Our parson has gone mad!" cried Goodman Gray, following him across the threshold.

A rumor of some unaccountable phenomenon had preceded Mr. Hooper into the meeting-house, and set all the congregation astir. Few could refrain from twisting their heads towards the door; many stood upright, and turned directly about; while several little boys clambered upon the seats, and came down again with a terrible racket. There was a general bustle, a rustling of the women's gowns and shuffling of the men's feet, greatly at variance with that hushed repose which should attend the entrance of the minister. But Mr. Hooper appeared not to notice the perturbation of his people. He entered with an almost noiseless step, bent his head mildly to the pews on each side, and bowed as he passed his oldest parishioner, a white-haired great-grandsire, who occupied an armchair in the centre of the aisle. It was strange to observe how slowly this venerable man became conscious of something singular in the appearance of his pastor. He seemed not fully to partake of the prevailing wonder, till Mr. Hooper had ascended the stairs, and showed himself in the pulpit, face to face with his congregation, except for the black veil. That mysterious emblem was never once withdrawn. It shook with his measured breath as he gave out the psalm; it threw its obscurity between him and the holy page, as he read the Scriptures; and while he prayed, the veil lay heavily on his uplifted countenance. Did he seek to hide it from the dread Being whom he was addressing?

Such was the effect of this simple piece of crape, that more than one woman of delicate nerves was forced to leave the meeting-house. Yet perhaps the pale-faced congregation was almost as fearful a sight to the minister as his black veil to them.

Mr. Hooper had the reputation of a good preacher, but not an energetic one: he strove to win his people heavenward, by mild, persuasive influences, rather than to drive them thither by the thunders of the Word. The sermon which he now delivered was marked by the same characteristics of style and manner as the general series of his pulpit oratory. But there was something, either in the sentiment of the discourse itself, or in the imagination of the auditors, which made it greatly the most powerful effort that they had ever heard from their pastor's lips. It was tinged, rather more darkly than usual, with the gentle gloom of Mr. Hooper's temperament. The subject had reference to secret sin, and those sad mysteries which we hide from our nearest and dearest, and would fain conceal from our own consciousness, even forgetting that the Omniscient can detect them. A subtle power was breathed into his words. Each member of the congregation, the most innocent girl, and the man of hardened breast, felt as if the preacher had crept upon them, behind his awful veil, and discovered their hoarded iniquity of deed or thought. Many spread their clasped hands on their bosoms. There was nothing terrible in what Mr. Hooper said; at least, no violence; and yet, with every tremor of his melancholy voice, the hearers quaked. An unsought pathos came hand in hand with awe. So sensible were the audience of some unwonted attribute in their minister, that they longed for a breath of wind to blow aside the veil, almost believing that a stranger's visage would be discovered, though the form, gesture, and voice were those of Mr. Hooper.

At the close of the services, the people hurried out with indecorous confusion, eager to communicate their pent-up amazement, and conscious of lighter spirits the moment they lost sight of the black veil. Some gathered in little circles, huddled closely together, with their mouths all whispering in the centre; some went homeward alone, wrapt in silent meditation; some talked loudly, and profaned the Sabbath day with ostentatious laughter. A few shook their sagacious heads, intimating that they could penetrate the mystery; while one or two affirmed that there was no mystery at all, but only that Mr. Hooper's eyes were so weakened by the midnight lamp as to require a shade. After a brief interval, forth came good Mr. Hooper also, in the rear of his flock. Turning his veiled face from one group to another, he paid due reverence to the hoary heads, saluted the middle aged with kind dignity, as their friend and spiritual guide, greeted the young with mingled authority and love, and laid his hands on the little children's heads to bless them. Such was always his custom on the Sabbath day. Strange and bewildered looks repaid him for his courtesy. None, as on former occasions, aspired to the honor of walking by their pastor's side. Old Squire Saunders, doubtless by an accidental lapse of memory, neglected to invite Mr. Hooper to his table, where the good clergyman had been wont to bless the food, almost every Sunday since his settlement. He returned, therefore, to the parsonage, and, at the moment of closing the door, was observed to look back upon the people, all of whom had their eyes fixed upon the minister. A sad smile gleamed faintly from beneath the black veil, and flickered about his mouth, glimmering as he disappeared.

"How strange," said a lady, "that a simple black veil, such as any woman might wear on her bonnet, should become such a terrible thing on Mr. Hooper's face!"

"Something must surely be amiss with Mr. Hooper's intellects," observed her husband, the physician of the village. "But the strangest part of the affair is the effect of this vagary, even on a sober-minded man like myself. The black veil, though it covers only our pastor's face, throws its influence over his whole person, and makes him ghostlike from head to foot. Do you not feel it so?"

"Truly do I," replied the lady; "and I would not be alone with him for the world. I wonder he is not afraid to be alone with himself!"

"Men sometimes are so," said her husband.

The afternoon service was attended with similar circumstances. At its conclusion, the bell tolled for the funeral of a young lady. The relatives and friends were assembled in the house, and the more distant acquaintances stood about the door, speaking of the good qualities of the deceased, when their talk was interrupted by the appearance of Mr. Hooper, still covered with his black veil. It was now an appropriate emblem. The clergyman stepped into the room where the corpse was laid, and bent over the coffin, to take a last farewell of his deceased parishioner. As he stooped, the veil hung straight down from his forehead, so that, if her eyelids had not been closed forever, the dead maiden might have seen his face. Could Mr. Hooper be fearful of her glance, that he so hastily caught back the black veil? A person who watched the interview between the dead and living, scrupled not to affirm, that, at the instant when the clergyman's features were disclosed, the corpse had slightly shuddered, rustling the shroud and muslin cap, though the countenance retained the composure of death. A superstitious old woman was the only witness of this prodigy. From the coffin Mr. Hooper passed into the chamber of the mourners, and thence to the head of the staircase, to make the funeral prayer. It was a tender and heart-dissolving prayer, full of sorrow, yet so imbued with celestial hopes, that the music of a heavenly harp, swept by the fingers of the dead, seemed faintly to be heard among the saddest accents of the minister. The people trembled, though they but darkly understood him when he prayed that they, and himself, and all of mortal race, might be ready, as he trusted this young maiden had been, for the dreadful hour that should snatch the veil from their faces. The bearers went heavily forth, and the mourners followed, saddening all the street, with the dead before them, and Mr. Hooper in his black veil behind.

"Why do you look back?" said one in the procession to his partner.

"I had a fancy," replied she, "that the minister and the maiden's spirit were walking hand in hand."

"And so had I, at the same moment," said the other.

That night, the handsomest couple in Milford village were to be joined in wedlock. Though reckoned a melancholy man, Mr. Hooper had a placid cheerfulness for such occasions, which often excited a sympathetic smile, where livelier merriment would have been thrown away. There was no quality of his disposition which made him more beloved than this. The company at the wedding awaited his arrival with impatience, trusting that the strange awe, which had gathered over him throughout the day, would now be dispelled. But such was not the result. When Mr. Hooper came, the first thing that their eyes rested on was the same horrible black veil, which had added deeper gloom to the funeral, and could portend nothing but evil to the wedding. Such was its immediate effect on the guests, that a cloud seemed to have rolled duskily from beneath the black crape, and dimmed the light of the candles. The bridal pair stood up before the minister. But the bride's cold fingers quivered in the tremulous hand of the bridegroom, and her deathlike paleness caused a whisper, that the maiden who had been buried a few hours before, was come from her grave to be married. If ever another wedding were so dismal, it was that famous one, where they tolled the wedding knell. After performing the ceremony, Mr. Hooper raised a glass of wine to his lips, wishing happiness to the new-married couple, in a strain of mild pleasantry that ought to have brightened the features of the guests, like a cheerful gleam from the hearth. At that instant, catching a glimpse of his figure in the looking glass, the black veil involved his own spirit in the horror with which it overwhelmed all others. His frame shuddered—his lips grew white—he spilt the untasted wine upon the carpet—and rushed forth into the darkness. For the Earth, too, had on her Black Veil.

The next day, the whole village of Milford talked of little else than Parson Hooper's black veil. That, and the mystery concealed behind it, supplied a topic for discussion between acquaintances meeting in the street, and good women gossiping at their open windows. It was the first item of news that the tavern keeper told to his guests. The children babbled of it on their way to school. One imitative little imp covered his face with an old black handkerchief, thereby so affrighting his playmates that the panic seized himself, and he well nigh lost his wits by his own waggery.

It was remarkable that, of all the busybodies and impertinent people in the parish, not one ventured to put the plain question to Mr. Hooper, wherefore he did this thing. Hitherto, whenever there appeared the slightest call for such interference, he had never lacked advisers, nor shown himself averse to be guided by their judgment. If he erred at all, it was by so painful a degree of self-disgust, that even the mildest censure would lead him to consider an indifferent action as a crime. Yet, though so well acquainted with this amiable weakness, no individual among his parishioners chose to make the black veil a subject of friendly remonstrance. There was a feeling of dread, neither plainly confessed nor carefully concealed, which caused each to shift the responsibility upon another, till at length, it was found expedient to send a deputation of the church, in order to deal with Mr. Hooper about the mystery, before it should grow into a scandal. Never did an embassy so ill discharge its duties. The minister received them with friendly courtesy, but became silent, after they were seated, leaving to his visitors the whole burden of introducing their important business. The topic, it might be supposed, was obvious enough. There was the black veil, swathed round Mr. Hooper's forehead, and concealing every feature above his placid mouth, on which, at times, they could perceive the glimmering of a melancholy smile. But that piece of crape, to their imagination, seemed to hang down before his heart, the symbol of a fearful secret between him and them. Were the veil but cast aside, they might speak freely of it, but not till then. Thus they sat a considerable time, speechless, confused, and shrinking uneasily from Mr. Hooper's eye, which they felt to be fixed upon them with an invisible glance. Finally, the deputies returned abashed to their constituents, pronouncing the matter too weighty to be handled, except by a council of the churches, if, indeed, it might not require a general synod.

But there was one person in the village, unappalled by the awe with which the black veil had impressed all beside herself. When the deputies returned without an explanation, or even venturing to demand one, she, with the calm energy of her character, determined to chase away the strange cloud that appeared to be settling round Mr. Hooper, every moment more darkly than before. As his plighted wife, it should be her privilege to know what the black veil concealed. At the minister's first visit, therefore, she entered upon the subject, with a direct simplicity, which made the task easier both for him and her. After he had seated himself, she fixed her eyes steadfastly upon the veil, but could discern nothing of the dreadful gloom that had so overawed the multitude: it was but a double fold of crape, hanging down from his forehead to his mouth, and slightly stirring with his breath.

"No," said she, aloud and smiling, "there is nothing terrible in this piece of crape, except that it hides a face which I am always glad to look upon. Come, good sir, let the sun shine from behind the cloud. First lay aside your black veil: then tell me why you put it on."

Mr. Hooper's smile glimmered faintly.

"There is an hour to come," said he, "when all of us shall cast aside our veils. Take it not amiss, beloved friend, if I wear this piece of crape till then."

"Your words are a mystery too," returned the young lady. "Take away the veil from them, at least."

"Elizabeth, I will," said he, "so far as my vow may suffer me. Know, then, this veil is a type and a symbol, and I am bound to wear it ever, both in light and darkness, in solitude and before the gaze of multitudes, and as with strangers, so with my familiar friends. No mortal eye will see it withdrawn. This dismal shade must separate me from the world: even you, Elizabeth, can never come behind it!"

"What grievous affliction hath befallen you," she earnestly inquired, "that you should thus darken your eyes forever?"

"If it be a sign of mourning," replied Mr. Hooper, "I, perhaps, like most other mortals, have sorrows dark enough to be typified by a black veil."

"But what if the world will not believe that it is the type of an innocent sorrow?" urged Elizabeth. "Beloved and respected as you are, there may be whispers that you hide your face under the consciousness of secret sin. For the sake of your holy office, do away this scandal!"

The color rose into her cheeks as she intimated the nature of the rumors that were already abroad in the village. But Mr. Hooper's mildness did not forsake him. He even smiled again —that same sad smile, which always appeared like a faint glimmering of light, proceeding from the obscurity beneath the veil.

"If I hide my face for sorrow, there is cause enough," he merely replied; "and if I cover it for secret sin, what mortal might not do the same?"

And with this gentle but unconquerable obstinacy did he resist all her entreaties. At length Elizabeth sat silent. For a few moments she appeared lost in thought, considering, probably, what new methods might be tried, to withdraw her lover from so dark a fantasy, which, if it had no other meaning, was perhaps a symptom of mental disease. Though of a firmer character than his own, the tears rolled down her cheeks. But, in an instant, as it were, a new feeling took the place of sorrow: her eyes were fixed insensibly on the black veil, when, like a sudden twilight in the air, its terrors fell around her. She arose, and stood trembling before him.

"And do you feel it then at last?" said he, mournfully.

She made no reply, but covered her eyes with her hand, and turned to leave the room. He rushed forward and caught her arm.

"Have patience with me, Elizabeth!" cried he passionately. "Do not desert me, though this veil must be between us here on earth. Be mine, and hereafter there shall be no veil over my face, no darkness between our souls! It is but a mortal veil— it is not for eternity! Oh! you know not how lonely I am, and how frightened, to be alone behind my black veil. Do not leave me in this miserable obscurity forever!"

"Lift the veil but once, and look me in the face," said she.

"Never! It cannot be!" replied Mr. Hooper.

"Then, farewell!" said Elizabeth.

She withdrew her arm from his grasp, and slowly departed, pausing at the door to give one long, shuddering gaze, that seemed almost to penetrate the mystery of the black veil. But, even amid his grief, Mr. Hooper smiled to think that only a material emblem had separated him from happiness, though the horrors, which it shadowed forth, must be drawn darkly between the fondest of lovers.

From that time no attempts were made to remove Mr. Hooper's black veil, or, by a direct appeal, to discover the secret which it was supposed to hide. By persons who claimed a superiority to popular prejudice, it was reckoned merely an eccentric whim, such as often mingles with the sober actions of men otherwise rational, and tinges them all with its own semblance of insanity. But with the multitude, good Mr. Hooper was irreparably a bugbear. He could not walk the street with any peace of mind, so conscious was he that the gentle and timid would turn aside to avoid him, and that others would make it a point of hardihood to throw themselves in his way. The impertinence of the latter class compelled him to give up his customary walk, at sunset, to the burial ground; for when he leaned pensively over the gate, there would always be faces behind the gravestones, peeping at his black veil. A fable went the rounds, that the stare of the dead people drove him thence. It grieved him, to the very depth of his kind heart, to observe how the children fled from his approach, breaking up their merriest sports, while his melancholy figure was yet afar off. Their instinctive dread caused him to feel, more strongly than aught else, that a preternatural horror was interwoven with the threads of the black crape. In truth, his own antipathy to the veil was known to be so great, that he never willingly passed before a mirror, nor stooped to drink at a still fountain, lest, in its peaceful bosom, he should be affrighted by himself. This was what gave plausibility to the whispers, that Mr. Hooper's conscience tortured him for some great crime too horrible to be entirely concealed, or otherwise than so obscurely intimated. Thus, from beneath the black veil, there rolled a cloud into the sunshine, an ambiguity of sin or sorrow, which enveloped the poor minister, so that love or sympathy could never reach him. It was said that ghost and fiend consorted with him there. With self-shudderings and outward terrors, he walked continually in its shadow, groping darkly within his own soul, or gazing through a medium that saddened the whole world. Even the lawless wind, it was believed, respected his dreadful secret, and never blew aside the veil. But still good Mr. Hooper sadly smiled at the pale visages of the worldly throng as he passed by.

Among all its bad influences, the black veil had the one desirable effect, of making its wearer a very efficient clergyman. By the aid of his mysterious emblem—for there was no other apparent cause—he became a man of awful power over souls that were in agony for sin. His converts always regarded him with a dread peculiar to themselves, affirming, though but figuratively, that, before he brought them to celestial light, they had been with him behind the black veil. Its gloom, indeed, enabled him to sympathize with all dark affections. Dying sinners cried aloud for Mr. Hooper, and would not yield their breath till he appeared; though ever, as he stooped to whisper consolation, they shuddered at the veiled face so near their own. Such were the terrors of the black veil, even when Death had bared his visage! Strangers came long distances to attend service at his church, with the mere idle purpose of gazing at his figure, because it was forbidden them to behold his face. But many were made to quake ere they departed! Once, during Governor Belcher's administration, Mr. Hooper was appointed to preach the election sermon. Covered with his black veil, he stood before the chief magistrate, the council, and the representatives, and wrought so deep an impression, that the legislative measures of that year were characterized by all the gloom and piety of our earliest ancestral sway.

In this manner Mr. Hooper spent a long life, irreproachable in outward act, yet shrouded in dismal suspicions; kind and loving, though unloved, and dimly feared; a man apart from men, shunned in their health and joy, but ever summoned to their aid in mortal anguish. As years wore on, shedding their snows above his sable veil, he acquired a name throughout the New England churches, and they called him Father Hooper. Nearly all of his parishioners, who were of mature age when he was settled, had been borne away by many a funeral: he had one congregation in the church, and a more crowded one in the church-yard; and having wrought so late into the evening, and done his work so well, it was now good Father Hooper's turn to rest.

Several persons were visible by the shaded candlelight, in the death chamber of the old clergyman. Natural connections he had none. But there was the decorously grave, though unmoved physician, seeking only to mitigate the last pangs of the patient whom he could not save. There were the deacons, and other eminently pious members of his church. There, also, was the Reverend Mr. Clark, of Westbury, a young and zealous divine, who had ridden in haste to pray by the bedside of the expiring minister. There was the nurse, no hired handmaiden of death, but one whose calm affection had endured thus long in secrecy, in solitude, amid the chill of age, and would not perish, even at the dying hour. Who, but Elizabeth! And there lay the hoary head of good Father Hooper upon the death pillow, with the black veil still swathed about his brow, and reaching down over his face, so that each more difficult gasp of his faint breath caused it to stir. All through life that piece of crape had hung between him and the world: it had separated him from cheerful brotherhood and woman's love, and kept him in that saddest of all prisons, his own heart; and still it lay upon his face, as if to deepen the gloom of his

173

darksome chamber, and shade him from the sunshine of eternity.

For some time previous, his mind had been confused, wavering doubtfully between the past and the present, and hovering forward, as it were, at intervals, into the indistinctness of the world to come. There had been feverish turns, which tossed him from side to side, and wore away what little strength he had. But in his most convulsive struggles, and in the wildest vagaries of his intellect, when no other thought retained its sober influence, he still showed an awful solicitude lest the black veil should slip aside. Even if his bewildered soul could have forgotten, there was a faithful woman at his pillow, who, with averted eyes, would have covered that aged face, which she had last beheld in the comeliness of manhood. At length the death-stricken old man lay quietly in the torpor of mental and bodily exhaustion, with an imperceptible pulse, and breath that grew fainter and fainter, except when a long, deep, and irregular inspiration seemed to prelude the flight of his spirit.

The minister of Westbury approached the bedside.

"Venerable Father Hooper," said he, "the moment of your release is at hand. Are you ready for the lifting of the veil, that shuts in time from eternity?"

Father Hooper at first replied merely by a feeble motion of his head; then, apprehensive, perhaps, that his meaning might be doubtful, he exerted himself to speak.

"Yea," said he, in faint accents, "my soul hath a patient weariness until that veil be lifted."

"And is it fitting," resumed the Reverend Mr. Clark, "that a man so given to prayer, of such a blameless example, holy in deed and thought, so far as mortal judgment may pronounce; is it fitting that a father in the church should leave a shadow on his memory, that may seem to blacken a life so pure? I pray you, my venerable brother, let not this thing be! Suffer us to be gladdened by your triumphant aspect, as you go to your reward. Before the veil of eternity be lifted, let me cast aside this black veil from your face!"

And thus speaking, the Reverend Mr. Clark bent forward to reveal the mystery of so many years. But, exerting a sudden energy, that made all the beholders stand aghast, Father Hooper snatched both his hands from beneath the bed clothes, and pressed them strongly on the black veil, resolute to struggle if the minister of Westbury would contend with a dying man.

"Never!" cried the veiled clergyman. "On earth, never!"

"Dark old man!" exclaimed the affrighted minister, "with what horrible crime upon your soul are you now passing to the judgment?"

Father Hooper's breath heaved; it rattled in his throat; but, with a mighty effort, grasping forward with his hands, he caught hold of life, and held it back till he should speak. He even raised himself in bed; and there he sat, shivering with the arms of death around him, while the black veil hung down, awful, at that last moment, in the gathering terrors of a lifetime. And yet the faint, sad smile, so often there, now seemed to glimmer from its obscurity, and linger on Father Hooper's lips.

"Why do you tremble at me alone?" cried he, turning his veiled face round the circle of pale spectators. "Tremble also at each other! Have men avoided me, and women shown no pity, and children screamed and fled, only for my black veil? What, but the mystery which it obscurely typifies, has made this piece of crape so awful? When the friend shows his inmost heart to his friend; the lover to his best beloved; when man does not vainly shrink from the eye of his Creator, loathsomely treasuring up the secret of his sin; then deem me a monster, for the symbol beneath which I have lived, and die! I look around me, and, lo! on every visage a Black Veil!"

While his auditors shrank from one another, in mutual affright, Father Hooper fell back upon his pillow, a veiled corpse, with a faint smile lingering on the lips. Still veiled, they laid him in his coffin, and a veiled corpse they bore him to the grave. The grass of many years has sprung up and withered on that grave, the burial stone is moss-grown, and good Mr. Hooper's face is dust; but awful is still the thought, that it mouldered beneath the Black Veil!

His Mother's Sermon

by IAN MACLAREN

┈┈┈┈┈┈┈┈┈┈┈┈┈┈┈┈┈┈┈┈┈┈┈┈┈┈┈┈┈┈┈┈

H E WAS AN INGENUOUS LAD, WITH THE CALLOW SIM-
plicity of a theological college still untouched, and had arrived on the preceding Monday at the Free Kirk manse with
four cartloads of furniture and a maiden aunt. For three days
he roamed from room to room in the excitement of house-
holding, and made suggestions which were received with
hilarious contempt; then he shut himself up in his study to
prepare the great sermon, and his aunt went about on tiptoe.
During meals on Friday he explained casually that his own
wish was to preach a simple sermon, and that he would have
done so had he been a private individual, but as he had held
the MacWhammel scholarship a deliverance was expected by
the country. He would be careful and say nothing rash, but
it was due to himself to state the present position of theological
thought, and he might have to quote once or twice from
Ewald.

His aunt was a saint, with that firm grasp of truth, and
tender mysticism, whose combination is the charm of Scottish
piety, and her face was troubled. While the minister was

speaking in his boyish complacency, her thoughts were in a room where they had both stood, five years before, by the death-bed of his mother.

He was broken that day, and his sobs shook the bed, for he was his mother's only son and fatherless, and his mother, brave and faithful to the last, was bidding him farewell.

"Dinna greet like that, John, nor break yir hert, for it's the will o' God, and that's aye best."

"Here's my watch and chain," placing them beside her son, who could not touch them, nor would lift his head, "and when ye feel the chain about yir neck it will mind ye o' yir mother's arms."

"Ye'ill no forget me, John, I ken that weel, and I'll never forget you. I've loved ye here and I'll love ye yonder. Th'ill no be an 'oor when I'll no pray for ye, and I'll ken better what to ask than I did here, sae dinna be comfortless."

Then she felt for his head and stroked it once more, but he could not look nor speak.

"Ye'ill follow Christ, and gin He offers ye His cross ye'ill no refuse it, for He aye carries the heavy end Himsel'. He's guided yir mother a' thae years, and been as gude as a husband since yir father's death, and He 'ill hold me fast tae the end. He 'ill keep ye too, and, John, I'll be watchin' for ye. Ye'ill no fail me," and her poor cold hand that had tended him all his days tightened on his head.

But he could not speak, and her voice was failing fast.

"I canna see ye noo, John, but I know yir there, an' I've just one other wish. If God calls ye to the ministry, ye 'ill no refuse, an' the first day ye preach in yir ain kirk, speak a gude word for Jesus Christ, an', John, I'll hear ye that day, though ye'ill no see me, and I'll be satisfied."

A minute after she whispered, "Pray for me," and he cried, "My mother, my mother."

It was a full prayer, and left nothing unasked of Mary's Son.

"John," said his aunt, "your mother is with the Lord," and he saw death for the first time, but it was beautiful with the peace that passeth all understanding.

Five years had passed, crowded with thought and work, and his aunt wondered whether he remembered that last request, or indeed had heard it in his sorrow.

"What are you thinking about, aunt? Are you afraid of my theology?"

"No, John, it's no that, laddie, for I ken ye 'ill say what ye believe to be true withoot fear o' man," and she hesitated.

"Come, out with it, auntie: you're my only mother now, you know," and the minister put his arm round her, "as well as the kindest, bonniest, goodest auntie ever man had."

Below his student self-conceit he was a good lad, and sound of heart.

"Shame on you, John, to make a fool o' an auld dune body, but ye'ill no come round me with yir flattery. I ken you ower weel," and as she caught the likeness in his face, her eyes filled suddenly.

"What's the matter, auntie? Will ye no tell me?"

"Dinna be angry wi' me, John, but a'm concerned aboot Sabbath, for a've been praying ever syne ye were called to Drumtochty that it micht be a great day, and that I micht see ye comin' tae yir people, laddie, wi' the beauty o' the Lord upon ye, according tae the auld prophecy: 'How beautiful upon the mountains are the feet of him that bringeth good tidings, that publisheth peace,' " and again she stopped.

179

"Go on, auntie, go on," he whispered; "say all that's in yir mind."

"It's no for me tae advise ye, who am only a simple auld woman, who ken's naethin' but her Bible and the Catechism, and it's no that a'm feared for the new views, or aboot yir faith, for I aye mind that there's mony things the Speerit hes still tae teach us, and I ken weel the man that follows Christ will never lose his way in ony thicket. But it's the fouk, John, a'm anxious aboot, the flock o' sheep the Lord hes given ye tae feed for Him."

She could not see his face, but she felt him gently press her hand, and took courage.

"Ye maun mind, laddie, that they're no clever and learned like what ye are, but juist plain country fouk, ilka ane wi' his ain temptation, an' a' sair trachled wi' mony cares o' this world. They 'ill need a clear word tae comfort their herts and show them the way everlasting. Ye 'ill say what's richt, nae doot o' that, and a'body 'ill be pleased wi' ye, but, oh, laddie, be sure ye say a gude word for Jesus Christ."

The minister's face whitened, and his arm relaxed. He rose hastily and went to the door, but in going out he gave his aunt an understanding look, such as passes between people who have stood together in a sorrow. The son had not forgotten his mother's request.

The manse garden lies toward the west, and as the minister paced its little square of turf, sheltered by fir hedges, the sun was going down behind the Grampians. Black massy clouds had begun to gather in the evening, and threatened to obscure the sunset, which was the finest sight a Drumtochty man was ever likely to see, and a means of grace to every sensible heart in the glen. But the sun had beat back the clouds on either side, and shot them through with glory, and now between piled billows of light he went along a shining pathway into the Gates of the West. The minister stood still before that spectacle, his face bathed in the golden glory, and then before his eyes the gold deepened into an awful red, and the red passed into shades of violet and green, beyond painter's hand or the imagination of man. It seemed to him as if a victorious saint had entered through the gates into the city, washed in the blood of the Lamb, and the after-glow of his mother's life fell solemnly on his soul. The last trace of sunset had faded from the hills when the minister came in, and his face was of one who had seen a vision. He asked his aunt to have worship with the servant, for he must be alone in his study.

It was a cheerful room in the daytime, with its southern window, through which the minister saw the roses touching the very glass and dwarf apple trees lining the garden walks; there was also a western window that he might watch each day close. It was a pleasant room now, when the curtains were drawn, and the light of the lamp fell on the books he loved, and which bade him welcome. One by one he had arranged the hard-bought treasures of student days in the little book case, and had planned for himself that sweetest of pleasures, an evening of desultory reading. But his books went out of mind as he looked at the sermon shining beneath the glare of the lamp, and demanding judgment. He had finished its last page with honest pride that afternoon, and had declaimed it, facing the southern window, with a success that amazed himself. His hope was that he might be kept humble, and not called to Edinburgh for at least two years; and now he lifted the sheets with fear. The brilliant opening, with its historical parallel, this review of modern thought reinforced by telling quotations, that trenchant criticism of old-fashioned views, would not deliver. For the audience had vanished, and left one careworn, but ever beautiful face, whose gentle eyes were waiting with a yearning look. Twice he crushed the sermon in his hands, and turned to the fire his aunt's care had kindled, and twice he repented and smoothed it out. What else could he say now to the people? And then in the stillness of the room he heard a voice, "Speak a gude word for Jesus Christ."

Next minute he was kneeling on the hearth, and pressing the *magnum opus,* that was to shake Drumtochty, into the heart of the red fire, and he saw, half-smiling and half-weeping, the impressive words, "Semitic environment," shrivel up and disappear. As the last black flake fluttered out of sight, the face looked at him again, but this time the sweet brown eyes were full of peace.

It was no masterpiece, but only the crude production of a lad who knew little of letters and nothing of the world. Very likely it would have done neither harm nor good, but it was his best, and he gave it for love's sake, and I suppose that there is nothing in a human life so precious to God, neither clever words nor famous deeds, as the sacrifices of love.

The moon flooded his bedroom with silver light, and he felt the presence of his mother. His bed stood ghostly with its white curtains, and he remembered how every night his mother knelt by its side in prayer for him. He is a boy once more, and repeats the Lord's Prayer, then he cries again, "My mother! my mother!" and an indescribable contentment fills his heart.

His prayer next morning was very short, but afterwards he stood at the window for a space, and when he turned, his aunt said:

182

"Ye will get yir sermon, and it will be worth hearing."

"How did ye know?"

But she only smiled, "I heard you pray."

When he shut himself into the study that Saturday morning, his aunt went into her room above, and he knew she had gone to intercede for him.

An hour afterwards he was pacing the garden in such anxious thought that he crushed with his foot a rose lying on the path, and then she saw his face suddenly lighten, and he hurried to the house, but first he plucked a bunch of forget-me-nots. In the evening she found them on his sermon.

Two hours later—for still she prayed and watched in faithfulness to mother and son—she observed him come out and wander round the garden in great joy. He lifted up the soiled rose and put it in his coat; he released a butterfly caught in some mesh; he buried his face in fragrant honeysuckle. Then she understood that his heart was full of love, and was sure that it would be well on the morrow.

When the bell began to ring, the minister rose from his knees and went to his aunt's room to be robed, for this was a covenant between them.

His gown was spread out in its black silken glory, but he sat down in despair.

"Auntie, whatever shall we do, for I've forgotten the bands?"

"But I've not forgot them, John, and here are six pair wrought with my own hands, and now sit still and I'll tie them round my laddie's neck."

When she had given the last touch, and he was ready to go, a sudden seriousness fell upon them.

"Kiss me, auntie."

"For your mother, and her God be with you," and then he

183

went through the garden and underneath the honeysuckle and into the kirk, where every Free Churchman in Drumtochty that could get out of bed, and half the Established Kirk, were waiting in expectation.

I sat with his aunt in the minister's pew, and shall always be glad that I was at that service. When winter lies heavy upon the glen I go upon my travels, and in my time have seen many religious functions. I have been in Mr. Spurgeon's Tabernacle, where the people wept one minute and laughed the next; have heard Canon Liddon in St. Paul's, and the sound of that high, clear voice is still with me, "Awake, awake, put on thy strength, O Zion"; have seen High Mass in St. Peter's, and stood in the dusk of the Duomo at Florence when Padre Agostino thundered against the evils of the day. But I never realised the unseen world as I did that day in the Free Kirk of Drumtochty.

It is impossible to analyse a spiritual effect, because it is largely an atmosphere, but certain circumstances assisted. One was instantly prepossessed in favour of a young minister who gave out the second paraphrase at his first service, for it declared his filial reverence and won for him the blessing of a cloud of witnesses. No Scottish man can ever sing,

> "God of our fathers, be the God
> Of their succeeding race,"

with a dry heart. It satisfied me at once that the minister was of a fine temper when, after a brave attempt to join, he hid his face and was silent. We thought none the worse of him that he was nervous, and two or three old people who had suspected self-sufficiency took him to their hearts when the minister concluded the Lord's prayer hurriedly, having omitted two petitions. But we knew it was not nervousness which made him pause for ten seconds after praying for widows and orphans, and in the silence which fell upon us the Divine Spirit had free access. His youth commended him, since he was also modest, for every mother had come with an inarticulate prayer that the "puir laddie wud dae weel on his first day, and him only twenty-four." Texts I can never remember, nor, for that matter, the words of sermons; but the subject was Jesus Christ, and before he had spoken five minutes I was convinced, who am outside dogmas and churches, that Christ was present. The preacher faded from before one's eyes, and there rose the figure of the Nazarene, best lover of every human soul, with a face of tender patience such as Sarto gave the Master in the Church of the Annunziata, and stretching out His hands to old folk and little children as He did, before His death, in Galilee. His voice might be heard any moment, as I have imagined it in my lonely hours by the winter fire or on the solitary hills—soft, low, and sweet, penetrating like music to the secret of the heart, "Come unto Me . . . and I will give you rest."

During a pause in the sermon I glanced up the church, and saw the same spell held the people. Donald Menzies had long ago been caught into the third heaven, and was now hearing words which it is not lawful to utter. Campbell in his watch-tower at the back had closed his eyes, and was praying. The women were weeping quietly, and the rugged faces of our men were subdued and softened, as when the evening sun plays on the granite stone.

But what will stand out for ever before my mind was the sight of Marget Howe. Her face was as white as death, and her wonderful grey eyes were shining through a mist of tears, so that I caught the light in the manse pew. She was thinking of George, and had taken the minister to her heart.

The elders, one by one, gripped the minister's hand in the vestry, and, though plain, homely men, they were the godliest in the glen; but no man spoke save Burnbrae.

"I a' but lost ae fairm for the Free Kirk, and I wud hae lost ten tae be in the Kirk this day."

Donald walked with me homewards, but would only say: "There was a man sent from God whose name was John." At the cottage he added, "The friend of the bridegroom rejoiced greatly because of the bridegroom's voice."

Beneath the honeysuckle at his garden gate a woman was waiting.

"My name is Marget Howe, and I'm the wife of William Howe of Whinnie Knowe. My only son wes preparin' for the ministry, but God wanted him nearly a year syne. When ye preached the Evangel o' Jesus the day I heard his voice, and I loved you. Ye hev nae mither on earth, I hear, and I hae nae son, and I wantit tae say that if ye ever wish tae speak to ony woman as ye wud tae yir mither, come to Whinnie Knowe, an' I'll coont it ane of the Lord's consolations."

His aunt could only meet him in the study, and when he looked on her his lip quivered, for his heart was wrung with one wistful regret.

"Oh, auntie, if she had only been spared to see this day, and her prayers answered."

But his aunt flung her arms round his neck.

"Dinna be cast doon, laddie, nor be unbelievin'. Yir mither has heard every word, and is satisfied, for ye did it in remembrance o' her, and yon was yir mither's sermon."

The Reverend John Smith Prepares His Sermon

by S. R. CROCKETT

❖❖

IT WAS FRIDAY, AND THE MINISTER OF ARKLAND WAS WRIT-
ing his sermon. Things had not gone well in Arkland that
week. The meeting of the church court charged with the
temporalities had not passed off well on Tuesday. One man
especially had hurt the minister in a sensitive place. This was
Peter M'Robert, the shoemaker. The minister had represented that a bath in a manse was not a luxury but a necessity,
when Peter M'Robert said that as for him he had never "had
sic a thing in his life, an' as for the minister that auld Maister
Drouthy had dune withoot yin in the manse for thirty-three
year to the satisfaction o' the pairish."

Then there had been certain differences of opinion within
the manse itself, and altogether the sermon had been begun
with the intention of dressing down the offending parishioners. Nearly all sermons are personal to the preacher. They
have been awakened within him by some circumstance which
has come to his knowledge during the week. Preachers use
this fact for good or evil according to their kind.

A plain man was John Smith of Arkland—as plain and hodden grey as his name. He had succeeded to the church with the largest majority that had been known in the presbytery, for in that neighbourhood to have given a man a unanimous call would have been considered a disgrace and a reflection on the critical discrimination of the congregation. He had tried to do his duty without fear or favour, only asking that his hands should not be tied. He visited the sick with a plain quiet helpfulness which brought sympathy with it as surely as the minister entered the house. His sermons were not brilliant, but they were staves and crutches to many.

Now as he sat at his manse window that bitter November morning he watched the rain volleying on the round causeway stones and the wide spaces of the village street dimly white with the dancing spray. The minister felt grimly in unison with the elements as he sat framing his opening sentences. He had chosen his text from a wonderful chapter. "Wisdom is justified of her children." And in this wise he began to write: "To be ignorant is to be dangerous. The ignorant man, though he be but one, can make of no account the wisdom of many men. After the wise of many generations have been striving to teach a people wisdom, a knave or a fool may come and cry aloud, 'There is no god but ourselves, there is no law but our own desires, there is no hereafter but the grave which we share with our sister the worm and our brother the dead dog!' Yet so great is the folly of man that such an one may draw away much people after him into the wilderness of sin and self-indulgence. It is in accordance with the nature of man that ignorance and narrowness should often succeed where wisdom is wholly rejected."

188

"That will do," said the minister, looking over his work. He had Peter M'Robert in his mind, and he rose and walked his study, "mandating" his opening sentences with appropriate gestures, much to the astonishment of Marget Lowrie in the kitchen, who said, "Save us! What's wrang wi' the minister? This is no' Setturday!"

As he came in his sentry walks to the window which looked up the rainswept street, he saw a dark-coloured oblong patch with a strange protuberance on the right side, hirpling like a decrepit beetle athwart the road, till, being caught at the manse corner by a bitter swirl, this irregular shape—

"If shape it could be called, that shape had none,"

stumbled and fell within thirty yards of the study window, discharging on the muddy road an avalanche of shavings, small branches, knobs, angles, and squares of wood. In a moment the minister was out at the door and was helping old Nance Kissock to her feet, and then under the eyes of all the wives in the village assisting her to collect again her bagful of chips and kindlings which the good-natured joiner allowed her to take once a week from his floor.

"I hope you are none the worse, Nance?" said the minister.

"I thank ye, Maister Smith; I'm sair forfoughten wi' the wun', but gin the Almichty be willing I'll be at the kirk on the Sabbath to hear ye. It's guid to think on a' the week what ye tell us. Whiles it gars me forget the verra rheumatics!"

When the minister got back into the friendly shelter of his study he took up the sheet which he had laid down in order to rush out to Nance Kissock's assistance. He read it over, but when he took his pen again, he did not seem to like it so well. If Nance were speaking the truth, and she fed during the week on the spiritual food which she received in his kirk on the Sabbath, he could not conceal from himself that next week she had a good chance of going hungry. Yet he could not allow Peter M'Robert to get off without a word, so he put the thought away from him and went on with his task. "How often does a man of limited view mistake his own limitations for the possibilities of others. He never judges himself—he could not if he would—and naturally when he judges others it is only to condemn them." A gust more than ordinarily powerful took the minister again to the window, and he saw John Scott, the herd from the Dornel, wringing the wet from his plaid. He knew that he had come down to the village from the hills three miles out of his road to get his wife's medicine. Presently he would trudge away manfully back again to the cot-house on the edge of the heather. Now the minister knew that come storm or calm John Scott would be at the kirk on the next day but one, and that he would carry away in the cool quiet brain that lay behind the broad brow the heads and particulars of the sermon he heard. As he went steadily knitting his stocking, conquering the heather with strides long and high, visiting his black-faced flock, he would go revolving the message that his minister had given him in the house of God.

"Wisdom is justified of her children," repeated the minister, doggedly; but his text now awakened no fervour. There was no enthusiasm in it. He thought that he would go out and let the November winds drive the rain into his face for a tonic. So he slipped on his Inverness and let himself out. His feet carried him towards the garret of one of his best friends, where an aged woman, blind and infirm, was spending the latter end of her days. She could not now come to church, therefore the minister went often to her—for it was sunshine to him also to bring light into that very dark place where the aged servant of God waited her end.

Mary Carment knew his step far down the stair, and she said to herself: "It is himsel'!" and deep within her she gave thanks. "It is a great thing to hae the bread o' life broken to us so simply that we a' understan' it, Maister Smith," she said.

"But, Mary, how long is it since you heard a sermon of mine?"

"It's true it's a lang time since I heard ye preach, minister, but I hear o' yer sermons every Sabbath. Yin and anither tells me pairt o't till I get as muckle as I can think on."

As the minister said good-bye to Mary Carment, she said: "Ye'll hae ower muckle to think on to mind me on the Lord's day when ye're speakin' for yer Maister; but I hae nane but you to mind, sir, so I'll be prayin' for you a' the time that ye're uphaudin' His name."

"Thank you, Mary, I'll not forget!" said her minister.

And he went out much strengthened.

As he went mansewards he passed the little cobbler's den where Peter M'Robert was *tap-tapping* all the day, and the sound of Peter's terrible cough called to him with a voice that claimed him. He stepped in, and after the word of salutation, he asked his office-bearer:

"Are you not thinking of getting that cough attended to, Peter?" he said.

"Wha—me? Na, no' me; hoots, it's but a bit host, nocht to speak aboot, thank ye for speerin', Maister Smith."

191

Just then the minister saw the doctor walking rapidly up the far side of the street, calm-faced and dignified, as if this howling November north-easter were a beautiful June morning. Him he summoned.

"Here's Peter'll no' speak to you about his cough. He must have some of your drugs, doctor."

The doctor called the unwilling cobbler from his last, and after a brief examination he said:

"No, I don't think there will be any need for drugs, Mr. Smith; if you, Peter, will use a gargle to get rid of a trifling local inflammation. Less lapstone dust and less snuff, Peter, and warm water three times a day," said the doctor, succinctly, and proceeded on his rounds.

As the minister went out, Peter looked up with a queer twinkle in his eye.

"Maister Smith," he said, "gin water be sae needful for the inside o' a cobbler's thrapple, maybe I was wrang in thinkin' that it wasna as necessary for the ootside o' a minister!"

"Then we'll say no more about it, Peter," said the minister, smiling, as he closed the door. "Mind your gargle!"

When the minister got to his study, he never stopped even to wipe his feet, and when the mistress followed to remonstrate, she found him putting his sermon in the fire.

The minister's text on the following Sabbath morning was an old one, but it was no old sermon that the Arkland folk got that day. The text was, "Come unto me all ye that labour and are heavy laden, and I will give you rest."

Nance Kissock was there, and did not go home hungry; John Scott had come down from the muirs, and had something better than physic to take back to his ailing wife; Peter M'Robert sat in his corner looking cleaner than he had done within the memory of man—also he never coughed once; no less than eight different folk came in to tell blind Mary Carment about the sermon.

But none but the minister knew who it was that had been praying for him.

The Third Commandment

THOU SHALT NOT TAKE THE NAME
OF THE LORD THY GOD IN VAIN

by FRANZ WERFEL

❖❖❖

HE TOLD ME THE STORY HIMSELF. HE WAS A SHORT, STURDY redhead with a coarse complexion and the heavy hands of a peasant. His eyes, dark green, were usually downcast; but sometimes they would flash fire, giving a boyish, defiant air to this man of forty, who had evidently had some hard knocks from life.

Looking at him, you would never have supposed he was a Catholic priest. He wore neither ecclesiastical collar nor black habit, but a gray suit of the kind affected by German tourists, with shorts and Tirolean socks that exposed the knees and ankles. When I first saw him, in Paris, the suit was already quite threadbare. In America, two years later, it had by no means improved.

We had met briefly in Paris. Although I took an immediate

liking to his looks and manner, we did not become really acquainted. For I had been warned against Chaplain Ottokar Felix.

Mistrust is one of the most poisonous plants that flourish in the dark shadows of political exile. Every *émigré* mistrusts every other, and if he could he would even suspect himself, for his spirit is in turmoil; it has no home.

Who is this Austrian chaplain? people asked. Why did he leave the country? Nobody knows anything about him. He had taken no part in the fight against the Nazis, either by word or by deed. The Austrian clergy made peace with them after the *Anschluss*. Suppose this wonderful priest in his Tirolean socks is an emissary of the Party, sent to spy on us. How did he get across the frontier? By the way, somebody saw him recently in the Rue de Lille. The German Embassy is in the Rue de Lille. . . .

I thought all this chatter sheer nonsense, yet still I avoided him. But when he suddenly appeared in my room at Hunter's Hotel in St. Louis, I felt an unexpected pleasure. This occurred in the late fall of 1941. The evening before, I had given a lecture on "The Crisis of Modern Man," trying to show that the deepest cause of our misery was our loss of faith in God.

Chaplain Felix, who had been in the audience, said a few kind words about my efforts, and told me I was on the right path, but that it would lead me still deeper into the mystery of our modern despairs.

He looked pale, tired, underfed. But when I asked, with the idea of helping him, how he was getting along, he dismissed the question with an abrupt gesture. He had all he needed, he said. During our two or three encounters in Paris, too, he had declined to talk about himself or his affairs.

We were discussing perfectly general subjects, therefore, when suddenly I remembered the suspicion of him that the refugees had expressed in France. As I looked at the man now, it seemed to me more irrelevant than ever. Yet I could not help myself: against my will and against the dictates of my feelings I asked what had driven him from home.

He turned his honest, weather-beaten face and looked squarely at me. His freckles and his coarse complexion almost seemed like pockmarks; his bristly red hair topped a low but attractively wrinkled forehead. His eyes, which had no lashes, sat deep in their sockets. That made them disturbing when they gleamed.

"I'm grateful to you," said the chaplain, "for asking me about something so far back and not about something like the concentration camps that I escaped from in France, or how I slipped through the heart of the German lines, or about the bypaths in the Pyrenees—about the various adventures that every one of us, after all, has had."

"Why are you grateful?"

He was silent some time before answering.

"Well, because I've been thinking all day about Aladar Fuerst. . . . Your lecture had something to do with it."

Seeing my bewilderment, he smiled indulgently: "There was a fine man for you, a good man, Dr. Aladar Fuerst. And he was the first to fall before the enemy, the enemy of the world, in this great war that's going on. Nobody knows about this first casualty, and he will never get a medal for dying a hero's death. But he did more than just get killed in the war."

"What war are you talking about? When Austria was swallowed up, in 1938, there wasn't any war—"

"Oh, you'll see in a minute," the chaplain nodded, "the war began then. Ever since yesterday, I've been wanting to entrust this forgotten story to you, that is, to put it in your hands. You understand?"

"What story?" I asked.

The chaplain's hand shaded his weak eyes against the bright afternoon sunshine that poured in through the window overlooking the big park in St. Louis.

"It's the story of a Jew who did not want to take the name of the Lord in vain," Felix said rather softly, and added a few seconds later: "It's the true story of the profaned and reconsecrated cross."

2

Father Ottokar Felix had the parish of Parndorf, a market village in the northern Burgenland between a range of wooded hills and the long, reedy lake of Neusiedl. The Burgenland— the name "Castle Country" comes from the many medieval castles crowning its southwestern heights—is the newest, poorest, and in many ways the most remarkable province of Austria. Before the First World War it belonged to Hungary, which was forced by the peace treaty to surrender it to neighboring Austria. It is a typical border region, where Hungary, Slovakia, Yugoslavia, and Austria all meet. Accordingly, its inhabitants are a rather motley group. Hungarian landowners, Austrian peasants, Slovak harvest hands, Jewish traders, Croat artisans, gypsies, and finally the nondescript stock of the Kumans, who were swept westward by the Turkish invasions in the seventeenth century.

Parndorf itself, with its ring-shaped market place, its goose pond, and the low thatched roofs crowned with storks' nests, is one of the more dismal villages of the region. Its almost Asiatic melancholy contrasts sharply with the large graciousness of the Austrian countryside. These hamlets give no hint that Vienna and the lofty Alps lie close at hand. The boundary between East and West seems to cut through them like a razor.

Parndorf's sole importance is that it lies on the main line between Vienna and Budapest. The shiny cars of the great express trains connecting Orient and Occident go roaring past its tiny station—a world-wide distinction that has not fallen to the lot of the chief towns in the province.

Why Ottokar Felix was transferred from the Viennese workmen's suburb of Jedlesee, where he was chaplain at the main church, to the God-forsaken village of Parndorf, I do not know. As the transfer took place in 1934, after the distressing battles between the Vienna workmen and the federal troops—everyone remembers that historic stage on the road to collapse—I think it not unlikely that the chaplain was compromised in the eyes of his superiors by his support of the Socialists, and underwent a sort of punitive banishment. He gave no hint of this, and I felt shy about pumping him.

The Jews had a small congregation in Parndorf, perhaps ten families, totaling thirty or forty people. There were similar congregations in every county and hamlet of the long, narrow Burgenland, in Eisenstadt and Mattersdorf, the big cities, in Kittsee and Petronell, the so-called Three Corners where Hungary, Czechoslovakia, and Austria meet, and in Rechnitz, far down in the south, on the border of the kingdom of Yugoslavia. Most of these congregations consisted of a few old families, related or intermarried all over the country. Everywhere you found the same names—Kopf, Zopf, Roth, Wolf, Fuerst. Next to the millionaire Wolf family in Eisenstadt, the Fuersts were the most distinguished, though in quite a different way. They had never acquired large property, but as early as the seventeenth century had produced a line of rabbis and scholars who played an important part in the peculiar intellectual history of the ghetto.

The Burgenland Jews were proud of two things: their learned men and their roots in the country. For in contrast with other Jewish communities, they had long since forgotten the curse of wandering and homelessness. They had never immigrated from Russia and Poland or from Moravia and Hungary; they boasted that they had always been in the country, except for a few who had moved from neighboring Styria into this freer boundary region, along with the persecuted Protestants, at the time of the Reformation.

The prominent Fuerst family came from the very Parndorf to which an unkind fate had banished Chaplain Ottokar Felix. Here too lived Dr. Aladar Fuerst, a man in his thirties, married but a few years, the father of three children. The youngest, a boy, was exactly three weeks old on the Black Friday when Austrian liberty was murdered. Aladar Fuerst must have been a visionary and fond of solitude; though a doctor of philosophy and law, a graduate of the celebrated Hebrew Seminar at Breslau, a man of the world who had lived in various European capitals, he could think of nothing better than to come back to the thatched roofs of his native village, bury himself in his choice library, and fill the office of country rabbi for Parndorf and a few neighboring congregations. He held services in a tiny, ancient synagogue, and gave religious instruction to the Jewish children at various neighboring schools.

In such a little place the chaplain and the young rabbi met almost daily as a matter of course. And in view of the delicate similarity and dissimilarity between their two offices, it was equally a matter of course that for a long time they confined themselves to a courteous salutation in passing.

A wedding, to which Dr. Aladar Fuerst was also invited, brought about their first conversation of any length. Afterward Fuerst paid a call on the priest, which was immediately returned. The rabbi invited the cleric to dinner. Regular, though sedate and formal, social intercourse followed.

Presumably, something more than a difference in religion raised a barrier between Felix and Fuerst. Even free spirits find it hard to overcome a strangeness centuries deep and an ancient mutual mistrust. Nevertheless, as he admitted to me, the Christian priest quickly became fond of the Jewish rabbi. He was profoundly astonished, not so much by his intellectual friend's brilliance and wide reading (which did not greatly concern him as a practical man), as by something else.

Whenever he had had dealings with a son of the house of Jacob, he had always read in the man's eyes a lurking hostility, even a painfully concealed horror inspired by the anointed priest of a once-implacable church, and this had set narrow limits to any conversation. Fuerst was conspicuously different. He was amazingly at home in every department of Catholic theology, and seemed to take great pleasure in displaying his knowledge. He quoted Paul, Thomas, Saint Bonaventure, and Newman more expertly than a harassed village chaplain could have done.

200

The priest believed he was right in thinking that something more than vanity had caused Aladar Fuerst to go so far in overcoming his father's wariness of Christ, as ancient as it was natural after their endless sufferings. Yet at the same time he had not departed even a step from his own faith.

Felix quoted one remark by the rabbi that moved him deeply. It was spoken during a conversation about the Mission to the Jews, a delicate subject that not he but Fuerst had introduced with quite alarming outspokenness.

"I can't see, Your Reverence," the rabbi had said, "why the Church is so interested in baptizing the Jews. Can it be content with winning perhaps two or three real converts among a hundred weak renegades or climbers? Besides, what would happen if all the Jews in the world were to accept baptism? Israel would disappear. And with it the last actual, physical witness to divine Revelation would vanish from the earth. The Holy Scriptures, not only the Old but the New Testament, would become an empty, insubstantial legend like any myth of the ancient Egyptians or Greeks. Doesn't the Church see the terrible danger—and particularly at a moment of complete breakup like this?

"We belong together, Your Reverence, but we are not one entity. The Epistle to the Romans, as you must know better than I, says that fellowship of Christ is founded upon Israel. I am convinced that Israel will survive as long as the Church survives, but also that the Church is bound to fall if Israel falls."

"What makes you think that?" asked the chaplain.

"The sufferings we have gone through down to this very day," replied the rabbi. "Or do you think God would have

201

allowed us to endure so much and so long, for so many thousands of years, all for nothing?"

3

On Austria's Black Friday, the eleventh day of March, when the inconceivable happened, Chaplain Ottokar Felix was sitting in his living room. It was seven o'clock at night. An hour before, he had heard Chancellor Schuschnigg's farewell words spoken in a leaden voice over the radio, "We must yield to superior force," and then, "God keep Austria," and then a great silence, and the strains of Haydn, solemn and heartrending. Felix had turned off the radio and sat motionless beside it. His rusty, paralyzed mind futilely turned over the question of how he must behave in the catastrophe that had come so suddenly upon the unhappy country.

Then the door opened, and Dr. Aladar Fuerst came into the room. He had not waited for the housekeeper to announce him. He wore a Prince Albert coat; the Sabbath, of course, had already begun. His thin face, with its dark eyes behind long lashes and its sparse black side whiskers, was a few shades paler than usual.

"Forgive me, Your Reverence," he began rather breathlessly, "for bursting in on you like this. We had already begun the holy day, and I've only just——"

"I should say it was events that broke the Sabbath," the priest remarked, as if to help him out. He pushed forward the armchair for his unexpected guest, who, however, declined to sit down.

"I need your advice, Your Reverence. You see, here's what I expect; I was so trusting, and now . . . Had you heard that young Schoch is in the neighborhood, has been for a week?

It was all arranged long ago. Schoch is the Storm Leader of the S.A. here. He's drummed up the whole crew, the farmer boys, the laborers from the cartridge factory, the unemployed; they're all getting drunk in the tavern, threatening to kill all the Jews this very night."

"I'll go straight to old Schoch," said the chaplain; "the rascal is still afraid of his father——"

This was not true, and Felix himself knew perfectly well that it was not the son who was in mortal terror of the father, but the father of the son. He only said this because he could think of no better way to calm Fuerst.

Old Schoch was the richest winegrower in the neighborhood and a good Catholic. But he had had decidedly bad luck with his youngest son, young Peterl. At least so far. The biography of Peter Schoch had its charms. A strikingly good-looking lad at seventeen, he had got one of his father's servant girls with child—which is far from a sin according to the local view—but then he had threatened the girl and the child with violence and had broken open her trunk and stolen all her savings.

Old Schoch, who doted most idiotically on his youngest son, this time flew into a rage (as he had not done over the lad's earlier pranks), primarily because the unsavory tale had leaked out. With the help of his older sons he first thrashed Peter soundly, and then sent him to the forestry school in the city of Leoben. (In addition to their vineyards, the Schochs also had timberlands.)

But as the handsome ne'er-do-well had spent six full years in the first grade of primary school, and could hardly read and write even yet, he promptly failed the entrance examinations at Leoben, which any first-class logger could pass with

203

ease. Far from sending word of his defeat home, Peter stayed in the bustling town, which he liked much better than dismal Parndorf, and threw away a lot of money that he managed to extract from his parent for his alleged studies.

In quieter times Peter Schoch's career would certainly have come to a bad end. But in these memorable days the "Movement," handsomely supported in all neighboring countries by the Third Reich, came to his rescue. It was the Movement's custom, with farseeing wisdom, to secure such ne'er-do-wells to itself. It knew by experience that an aversion for the alphabet and regular employment almost invariably brought with it a talent for reckless rowdyism. And for the first blow to break the resistance of the Austrian people, nothing was more urgently needed than a body of determined rowdies.

A not inconsiderable share of the favor with which certain Party chieftains regarded Peter arose from his golden-blond hair, his slim figure, his stubby little face. In contrast to the bald pates, pot bellies, and limping legs of the leaders, he was a glorious embodiment of racial doctrines and of the perfect Nordic man. Photographers did honor to him almost daily, and many copies of his pictures adorned the files of the German race bureaus.

And thus it was that the son of the rich Parndorf winegrower became an "irregular." The Munich Party funds gave him so large a subsidy that he played the part of Croesus among his peers. A few foolhardy misdeeds on behalf of the Party made his name known, and when he finally went to prison for some months as a saboteur and bomb thrower, he had at last advanced to the ranks of the martyrs who were "delivered from shame and misery" after the Berchtesgaden meeting and the collapse of the Austrian government. This, in brief, is the story of Peter Schoch, whose mere name was enough to make Dr. Aladar Fuerst—and others, too—turn pale with horror.

The rabbi at last sat down. The chaplain handed him a small glass of brandy. "We mustn't begin by expecting the very worst," he said.

"Why mustn't we?" asked Fuerst, lifting his head with a jerk. "Perhaps we should . . . Listen, Your Reverence," he went on tensely after a while, "a train leaves for the Hungarian frontier in an hour. Oughtn't we—I mean the whole family—though of course my poor wife has only been up for three days . . . What shall I do, Your Reverence? Give me your advice—I do need it."

Father Ottokar Felix then did something for which he has never forgiven himself. Instead of shrugging his shoulders, instead of saying, I don't know what's best, he gave his advice, definite counsel, and it was bad. But at such moments who can tell whether he is advising well or ill?

"Are you really going to throw everything overboard in such a hurry, my dear Dr. Fuerst?" said the chaplain, unfortunately comparing his own situation with the doctor's. "We don't even know about the new government yet. Who can tell—in Austria everything may turn out differently from what we think. Why don't you wait and see for a few days?"

At these words Aladar Fuerst heaved a sigh of relief. "I do thank you for your advice. I'm sure you're right; Austrians are not Germans, and I'm a good patriot. It would be terribly hard for me to leave our house. Within the memory of man, my family has always lived here; our tombstones in the cemetery go back to the Middle Ages, and when I left the outside world I deliberately chose to return to Parndorf. Perhaps . . ."

205

The chaplain accompanied him out into the clear, starlit night.

"I'll look in to see how you're doing tomorrow," he said as they parted.

But Aladar Fuerst said, uneasily shaking hands with Felix: "There's only one thing I'm afraid of, Father Felix. I'm afraid people like us have grown too soft, and won't have the old strength and fortitude of our fathers under persecution. Good night."

4

At nine o'clock the following morning—just when Chaplain Ottokar Felix was considering how far his Sunday sermon might go in attacking the victors—a sound of tumult and shouting penetrated his closed study window. Instantly he rushed outdoors, hatless and coatless. The Market Ring was filled with a crowd even bigger than the one that usually assembled for market days or church festivals. Expecting something interesting, they had poured in from the hamlets of the desolate Parndorf Heath, and even from the remote shore villages of the great reedy lake—peasants, farm laborers and girls, workmen from the cartridge and sugar factories of the neighborhood, and in addition a crowd of the unemployed who were no longer getting government relief and who usually supplied the most turbulence at any riot.

The center of this mob was a detachment of Brown Shirts lined up in ranks, all of them already wearing swastika armbands on their left arms. They were drawn up opposite Parndorf's most imposing building. It was probably not fitting that the Fuerst family should own this edifice, one of the few in the village with two stories and a mansard roof. However, one could hardly hold Aladar Fuerst responsible for the fact that his grandfather, in the happy days, fifty years ago, had been incautious or presumptuous enough to build this metropolitan house amid a world of wretched thatched huts.

On the ground floor, at the sides of the archway to the court-yard, were two large shops, the Town Bakery of David Kopf and the Grocery and General Store of Samuel Roth's son. The proprietors of these shops, their wives, sons, daughters, rela-tives, and assistants, were standing in a tight little knot outside the gateway; in their midst was Rabbi Aladar, the only one who held his head really high. In contrast with the night before, he did not seem crushed. Peter Schoch, the commander of the present military engagement, had taken up his post as the antagonist of this symbol of forlorn hope. Obviously delighted, he held an automatic rifle in the bend of his arm, the barrel pointing at Aladar Fuerst. Beside Schoch stood a scrubby little man with a pinched, witch's face that looked as if it could be distended or collapsed at will like an accordion. The man wore a pair of steel spectacles on his nose and a red cap on his head, for he was Ignaz Inbichler, the Parndorf stationmaster.

When Chaplain Felix arrived, Peter Schoch was just finishing a pungent harangue. Its intonation, at once deeply injured and bitingly scornful, reproduced to the life the radio speeches of the great Party deities.

"German men and women! It is insufferable for our fellow Germans to receive their daily bread from the hands of a Jewish bakery. How that would delight the international Jews, to go on poisoning our innocent children with his matzos! Those days are past, because this is a historic moment. In the name of the German people's community I declare Kopf's bakery Aryanized. Fellow German Ladislaus Tschitschevitzky takes authority in his place. *Sieg Heil!*"

Peter Schoch spoke in a labored newspaper idiom mingled with naked, vulgar dialect. The Brown Shirts bellowed the *Sieg Heils* after him, keeping time. The crowd remained oddly silent, apparently filled with unconcerned curiosity.

Now the man with the red cap took the floor. This obscure frontier village differed not a whit from Berlin: the two basic aspects of the National Socialist Party were both present. Schoch represented utter heroism; Inbichler stood for the twinkling-eyed diplomacy that pats the victim artlessly on the back as heroism rips his stomach open.

And so Inbichler, the stationmaster, addressed the little handful before the gate: "Gentlemen! Everything will proceed in order. There will be no uncontrolled action. Everything will take place according to regulation. Germanism is organization. Not a hair of your heads will be touched. You have only to sign a form certifying that you are turning over your trash to us quite voluntarily and will leave German soil at once. If any inmate of this house should be found here after five o'clock this afternoon, he would have no one but himself to blame for the disagreeable, I may say *very* disagreeable, consequences. Even I could then do nothing for him. . . . There are only two ways to solve the Jewish question. In the infinite kindness of his heart, our Leader had chosen the second way."

The chaplain realized that by interfering he not only could accomplish nothing, but would endanger himself to no purpose. He therefore raced home and excitedly telephoned the police, the county authorities, and finally the provincial government at Eisenstadt.

Everywhere he got the same evasive answer. With the best will in the world, they said, nothing could be done against the dubious elements momentarily in control of the streets. They were Party members, and the Party was getting its orders direct from Berlin. The voices on the telephone shook with the most grievous discomfort. Undoubtedly all the lines were tapped, and the officials dared not speak openly.

Losing no time, Father Felix hurried to see a well-known local landowner, and in his car was roaring toward Eisenstadt within half an hour. There, at the capital, he went from pillar to post, finally winding up with the Apostolic Administrator of the Burgenland. He was the ecclesiastical head of the province, a Monsignor So-and-so.

The placid prelate received him with darkly unctuous suspicion. Since the supreme ecclesiastical authority, His Eminence the Cardinal Archbishop of Vienna, he said, had chosen to meet the new temporal power (which, according to dogma, must after all derive from God) in a spirit of confidence, he himself could only recommend an obedient emulation of this attitude to the provincial clergy. He was well aware, he said, of what was going on today in the villages of the country, but he strongly urged that there be no interference on behalf of the expelled Jews. No doubt these occurrences merited condemnation, but they were in no way within the province of the parish priests.

Folding his hands, the prelate concluded: "We will pray for the Jews, but in other respects we must keep constantly before our eyes the fact that all authority derives from God."

"Even if the Lord puts Satan in authority, Monsignor?" asked the chaplain a trifle rebelliously.

"Even then," said Monsignor, with a heart for any compromise.

On his way home the chaplain leaned more and more toward accepting the decision of the cardinal and the prelate as a wise one. There were things more important to protect than a few robbed and expelled Jews. The Church itself stood in danger. Would it not be best to lie low and stay home for the next few days, perform the Sunday offices without a sermon, and guard against all friction?

Probably he would have yielded to this impulse if Aladar Fuerst's words had not kept running through his head: "I am convinced that Israel will survive as long as the Church survives, but also that the Church is bound to fall if Israel falls."

5

When Chaplain Felix arrived at the Market Ring in Parndorf, the church clock was just striking three. The two trucks belonging to Moritz Zopf's trucking concern were standing in front of the Fuerst house. Furnishings, beds, cupboards, tables, chairs were being carried out of the bakery, the shop, and the courtyard driveway and stowed in one of the trucks. Stationmaster Inbichler was scrutinizing each piece with shortsighted intentness and the conscientious zeal of a good customs inspector, for the exiles were not allowed an ash tray or a box of matches without his approval. And, in fact, he put aside for himself any article that took his fancy, shrouding the appropriation with a muttered incantation that sounded something like "German national property." The Brown Shirts had stacked their rifles and were lounging about, smoking. Schoch and his staff were at the inn, where Peter had been presiding for several hours over a lavish banquet to which the mayor and other Parndorf notables had rushed with fawning haste.

There was no wind, and a peculiar milky vapor hung over the village. The group of outcasts had grown considerably, numbering more than thirty souls. Chaplain Felix was surprised

to see them all busily scuttling about, running a hundred sense-
less errands, and moved apparently more by insectlike unrest
than by any purposeful plan. The children in the group watched
the bustle excitedly, but they were eager, not frightened. All
of them, however, looked as if they had been up all night;
they were like shadows stirred by a gusty wind of destiny
imperceptible to Christians even as it blew across the market
place.

Felix went into Rabbi Aladar's house. The young mother, a
delicate, bright-eyed woman from the Rhineland, scarcely risen
from childbed, was working breathlessly. Her white forehead
under the parted brown hair was deeply furrowed with exer-
tion. She was standing amid a mountain of bed and table linen
and underwear, trying vainly to cram all of it into an already
overcrowded traveling hamper. Now and then she looked up.
Her eyes shone moistly with weakness and bewilderment. From
the next room came the peaceful chatter of children and an
occasional insistent squall of an infant.

The chaplain found Aladar Fuerst in front of his bookcases,
which filled all four walls of the big living room from floor to
ceiling. A few hundred volumes that he had picked out from
the many thousands rose in tottering piles at his feet. He held a
book in his hand and was reading, reading raptly, with a ghost
of a smile on his face. He seemed to have completely forgotten
reality. The spectacle of this Jew reading with absorption amid
the collapse of his world deeply impressed the chaplain, as he
emphasized to me.

"Your Reverence Dr. Fuerst," he said, "unfortunately I gave
you bad advice. The fact that that advice is tormenting my
conscience is no help to you or to me, either. Luckily you have
a Hungarian passport. Perhaps the Lord means better by you

and yours than by us. It would not be the first time He has brought to safety the people in which He manifested Himself, when He seemed to be punishing it."

Dr. Aladar Fuerst gave the priest a long, remote look, which moved and disturbed him so much that he turned to and helped carry down the favorite books chosen to go.

An hour later everyone was ready. Inbichler had kept the best property of the exiles, the more valuable furniture, all the silver, all the women's jewelry, and whatever money and securities he could lay hands on; for all those who were being banished, Fuerst included, were stripped to their shirts and subjected to a thorough search. The rabbi took this ignominious proceeding, aggravated by derisive remarks from the Brown Shirts, with such absent-minded equanimity that Felix was almost annoyed at him. I'd be hitting about me, he thought. The only thing that Inbichler passed uninspected, with a gesture of disdain, was the books.

But since, as Inbichler had said, everything had to "proceed in order," and "Germanism was organization," he made out a careful receipt for each article he was keeping. This raised naked robbery to the level of law and governmental action, making it all the sweeter to the robber.

Peter Schoch, having taken his seat beside the driver of the first truck, began blowing the horn furiously. It was four o'clock. Night would fall within two hours at latest.

The Brown Shirts kicked and cuffed their victims into the first truck, where they tumbled against one another, and then had to sit on the floor. Now at last the small children began to be uncomfortable, and a few of them started crying. The closely packed spectators remained deathly silent, and from their curious faces there was no telling whether they approved or condemned what was going on. Schoch's men were getting their motorcycles ready.

At this Chaplain Ottokar Felix stepped up sharply to Ignaz Inbichler. "Chief," he said, "I do not know whether you are acting under official orders, and if so, whose. But I will point out to you that if you are acting on your own authority, you will be held responsible, tomorrow, the next day, someday, in one way or another. It is a well-known fact that these people have lived here for centuries, and no one has ever had cause to complain of them. Things may be different in Vienna and the big cities, but not here. You have given them a bad fright, Chief; I think that's punishment and revenge enough. Let it go at that, and we can all wait for the legal settlement of the Jewish question."

The pinched man with the accordion face sucked luxuriously at his cigarette and blew a cloud of smoke in the priest's face. "Don't be impatient, Your Reverence," he cooed sweetly, "everyone will have his turn. Our black-coated friends might very well come next. That idea had already occurred to me. However, if you're so fond of the Jew swine, you can go right with them."

"So I will," said the chaplain, leaping into the truck. He had no idea what had brought him to this perilous resolution. And indeed it was not a resolution at all. It was an action apparently not caused by his own will.

The Jews stared at him incredulously. Mrs. Fuerst was the only one sitting on a chair, which had been put into the truck for her. She was holding the baby in her arms, while her husband tried to quiet the second child, a tiny girl. The chaplain took the rabbi's eldest, a four-year-old boy, in his lap and began to joke with him.

The motor whirred. The powerful truck started off with a bounce, for the road was full of deep holes. The second car followed. The Brown Shirts' motorcycles came chattering after.

6

They went bumping along the rough country road that follows the big lake, though it is not visible from there. This road leads to a desolate boundary station on the Hungarian frontier. Why the main route to the important frontier town of Hegyeshalom had not been chosen remained Peter Schoch's own spiteful secret. In the first truck, jammed with roughly shaken people, no one said a word. When Chaplain Ottokar Felix tried to encourage the outcasts, they all listened to him with the strained, watery eyes of deaf-mutes. The tremendous quarries of Rust must have been passed by the time twilight fell, and with it, from the reedy lake, drifted one of the thick, choking fogs which the people of the region so superstitiously dread.

Schoch halted the column. The Brown Shirts got off their motorcycles. A curt command: "Everybody out! Unload! The trucks go back."

Through the steam from some witch's caldron in which the daylight had trickled away, the storm troopers rushed at the second truck. Bureaus, sideboards, cupboards, cherished household furnishings, boxes of china and kitchenware went flying through the air into the muddy road, where they smashed to the accompaniment of scornful laughter. The women let out a woebegone cry.

The chaplain, absolutely beside himself, grabbed Schoch by the wrist. "What does this mean? Are you crazy?"

214

With his fist, Schoch landed a blow on the priest's chest that sent him staggering. "I'll have you before communion, you damned incense-swinger," he laughed.

Next the rabbi's books followed the ruined household goods. Aladar Fuerst came running up, his arms outspread. But when Felix stooped to pick up at least a few of the volumes, Rabbi Aladar made a gesture of resignation that seemed to the chaplain positively grotesque in its Jewishness. "What's lost is better lost," he intoned to himself, with his slender head on his right shoulder.

"Left of the road," Peter Schoch commanded in echoing tones. "Forward march!"

Those who hesitated, old and young, were driven into the open fields by the Brown Shirts. None might lag. No consideration was given the old people or the children, either. If a few of the Jew brats pegged out on the forced march, so much the better. These were outcasts completely beyond the law, people protected by no state on earth, for the governments of England, France, and America had, after all, not only made no vigorous protest, but had hastened to announce that they would sagely refrain from interfering in another country's domestic affairs. Not only the governing circles of the Party, but even the simplest Party sympathizer, knew that the English Prime Minister, Mr. Chamberlain, along with his adherents, was covertly a friend and regarded the fight against Jewish Bolshevism (represented in Parndorf by Aladar Fuerst) with tacit approval. When but here and now would there be another such opportunity, right in Europe and in this effete age, for the primitively heroic and, furthermore, legitimate sport of a real, ready-made man hunt? It was enough to stir your blood, with a rousing hip-hurrah! The eager hunters rocked with laughter at the Jewish shadows panting before them in the fog.

The fog began to grow black. Suddenly the chaplain felt himself wading ankle-deep, then almost knee-deep, in ice-cold water. They had reached the wet swamps that fringe the lake near Moerbisch. Ottokar Felix picked up the four-year-old, whom he had been leading by the hand. Now he carried the child on his left arm, and with his free hand helped the young mother who was mechanically dragging herself and the infant along.

I remember that Felix stopped at this point in his story. The gray eyes in that coarse-skinned face stared at me.

I made use of the pause to ask: "What were you thinking in the swamps of Moerbisch, Chaplain?"

"I don't know what I was thinking," he replied, "probably nothing at all. But now I think mankind must keep incessantly punishing itself. It is bound to, quite logically, for the sin of lovelessness that has brought about all our misery, that makes it keep on growing piece by piece."

7

It was almost a miracle that after this "short cut" they got out of the swamp comparatively quickly and regained the road. It was a still greater miracle that no one had been injured or lost. At nightfall it grew bitterly cold, and the fog lifted. Yonder glowed the lights of Moerbisch. Everyone started to run. Beyond the last houses of Moerbisch lay the longed-for frontier. Home, but yesterday the familiar scene of an accustomed life, was already a strange inferno, looked back to with horror.

The night was very dark. An icy wind blew in gusts. The flag of the conqueror was already flying from the Austrian customhouse. But when the old frontier guard, who had not yet been relieved, caught sight of Peter Schoch with his Brown Shirts and their victims, they vanished from the scene as swiftly as if the bog had swallowed them up. The road to the Hungarian boundary station lay open, not a hundred yards away.

Aladar Fuerst gathered up the exiles' passports. Most of them, his own included, were Hungarian papers, since a good many Burgenlanders had for various reasons retained their original Hungarian citizenship, notwithstanding the treaties of Trianon and Saint-Germain. No doubt the Magyar frontier would be open without question at least to all those whose papers were in order. That was no more than simple law and justice.

Rabbi Aladar, with the bundle of passports in his hand, went over to the Hungarian customhouse. The chaplain silently accompanied him. Peter Schoch followed them at a shambling gait, whistling cheerfully.

The functionary in the office never even glanced at the passports. "Have you gentlemen had permission from the Royal Hungarian Consulate General in Vienna, please?" he asked with the greatest courtesy.

Aladar Fuerst's lips turned white. "What permission, for goodness' sake?"

"By an ordinance of ten o'clock this morning, the frontier may not be crossed except by permission of the Consulate General."

"But this is quite impossible," stammered Fuerst. "We knew nothing about it, and would not have been allowed to get such permission, anyway. After all, we were given six hours' notice, under threat of death."

"I'm very sorry," said the immigration officer, shrugging his shoulders, "but I can't do anything about it. You gentlemen will have to show the permission of the Consulate General."

Peter Schoch stepped up and slapped the "forms" on the table by which the exiles affirmed, over their own signatures, that they proposed to leave the country voluntarily and without compulsion.

"Go fetch your commander," said the chaplain in a tone that made the young official stand up and comply without remonstrance. Ten minutes later he was back with a slender, grizzled officer who had obviously, by the look of him, served in the old, glorious army. He took the passports in his hand like a pack of cards and ruffled them nervously.

The chaplain tackled him sharply: "Major, I am a witness that these people were looted down to the skin a few hours ago, and hounded through the swamp to the frontier as if they were worse than animals. Dr. Fuerst is a Hungarian subject, and so are many of the others, as you can see by the passports. There is no ordinance among civilized people that can refuse entry to these citizens in search of protection."

"Now, now, Father," said the officer, looking at Felix with dark, bitter eyes, "there are all kinds of things among civilized people . . ." He added coldly, "I have to follow regulations."

"There aren't many of us," pleaded Aladar Fuerst. "Most of us have relatives somewhere in Hungary. We shan't be a burden on the state."

The major pushed away the pack of passports with a gesture of revulsion. He did not deign to glance at any of those present, neither Fuerst nor Felix nor Schoch. After frowning thoughtfully, he said rather roughly, "You go on back across the border and wait."

It was only when the chaplain looked at him, aghast, that he muttered: "I'll telephone to Sopron, to the Obergespan."

8

There was an open space in front of the Austrian custom-house. To the left the road went off toward the reedy shores of the lake; to the right it vanished among vineyards. Using their motorcycle headlights, the Brown Shirts had turned this space into a sort of lighted stage. They rounded up the old men in this circle of light, and were amusing themselves after the fashion of the German concentration camps by making them do rapid knee bends and other gymnastics: "Up! Down! One! Two!" After a time eighty-year-old David Kopf, the baker's father, collapsed with a heart attack. The chaplain was very nearly ready to join the ranks of those being tormented and share their humiliation. But he knew all too well that he would merely have called forth the asinine laughter and scorn of the victors drunk with their triumph.

One thought kept running through his mind: "These lucky ones are driven to sin, while these unlucky ones do penance. Which, then, are lucky and which unlucky?"

A crowd of spectators had gathered around, people from Moerbisch and soldiers from the Hungarian frontier post. They did not conceal their horror and fury. Felix heard a non-commissioned officer spit and say savagely to his neighbor, "If I had to go through anything like that, I'd kill myself, and my whole family too, on the spot."

An hour later an auto arrived, bringing the Obergespan (the Hungarian provincial governor). Sopron, the capital of the neighboring county, was but a few miles from the frontier. The local potentate was a fat, amiable gentleman, with the elastic grace too often favored by corpulent dignitaries. His face was turkey red, his mustache snow white, and he was visibly perspiring in spite of the glacial cold. Stepping with easy nonchalance into the focused glare of the headlights and jovially beckoning everyone close, he planted his fists on his hips, setting off his bulging figure to better advantage, and rocked to and fro on his toes like a calvaryman.

"Now, now, good people, what's all this?" he began in fatherly tones, addressing himself to the exiles. "I can't over-step legal enactments. I'm only an administrative organ. I'm responsible to the Ministry of the Interior at Budapest. Hungary is a constitutional state, and a Christian one, certainly. But *ultra posse nemo teneatur*. I can't create a precedent. Why, after all? If I let you across the border today, others will come tomorrow on the strength of it, tomorrow and the day after and maybe for months. That would be a fine how-do-you-do—surely you can see that yourselves. Hungary is a country with its arms and legs cut off, and it has almost a million Israelite citizens, and it has innumerable unemployed, and really now . . . I'm sure you understand what I mean, don't you? Well, then! Now do go back home, all of you, and don't make trouble for me. Personally I'm very sorry I can't do anything for you."

The Obergespan had spoken like a kindly old gentleman trying to induce naughty children to give up some prank and go home at once. He had addressed his speech to the wrong audience, giving only an occasional uncomfortable glance at the armed Brown Shirts.

Then Peter Schoch broke the deep stillness. "Sooner than let 'em go home we'll knock off the whole lot."

220

And everyone realized that the storm leader's words were no empty threat. At first Aladar Fuerst tried to explain calmly to the Obergespan that it was the middle of the night, and quite out of the question to let infants, small children, a woman barely risen from childbed, and a number of sick old people spend the night at large (if you could call it) in the open air, in the midst of nothingness. Here, in neither one country nor the other, was after all true nothingness. His voice was not beseeching, but weary, the voice of a man who knows that no plea and no appeal to reason will do any good.

But the chaplain's voice now was imploring. He begged the official in the name of Christ to shelter the outcasts beyond the frontier at least for one night, because they would not be taken in at Moerbisch or any other Austrian town, and the murderous threats of the armed gang were meant in deadly earnest.

The Obergespan rocked busily on his toes, and wiped away the sweat. "But, Reverend Father," he complained in almost wounded tones, "why must you make my situation more difficult than it already is, you of all people? Do you think I'm not human? Once and for all, the government has closed the frontier. I regret it extremely."

By way of consolation the Obergespan thereupon had his chauffeur distribute to the women and children some provisions he had brought from Sopron. It may have been chance or it may have been part of his character that they consisted mostly of the stick candy sold on street corners.

The grizzled major stood the whole time not saying a word, surveying the tips of his boots. Finally the Obergespan drew him and the chaplain aside. They walked back and forth in the road between the two customhouses.

221

"I've just thought of something," the Obergespan began. "It may be a way out that will satisfy His Reverence. But I mustn't know anything about it, understand, Major?"

Thereupon he unfolded his plan. The major was to let "the company" apparently cross the frontier, but to smuggle them back to Austria during the night, preferably on one of the flat barges that traveled on the lake. This would satisfy both the law and the dictates of humanity.

The major halted and drew himself up. "Your Excellency has only to wink, and I will evade the law in the present case. But I am a family man myself, and I will not be a party to the outright massacre of women and children; and they will be massacred if we take them in and then put them out again."

"Just as you please, my dear fellow; it was only an idea," smiled the Obergespan, deeply offended, and got into his car without noticing the chaplain's upraised hands.

9

The night had brightened somewhat. A very white quarter moon had risen, seeming to sharpen the cold. In the nearby vineyards a hut used by the vintagers for shelter from wind and weather during the season stood out against the blackness. Aladar Fuerst took his exhausted wife and children to it. The chaplain carried the four-year-old who had fallen asleep in his arms, into the hut. Meanwhile the major had sent straw ticks and blankets from the Hungarian frontier garrison and distributed bread and coffee. He also ordered his men to put up two tents for the exiles, one for the men and one for the women. The Brown Shirts looked on these preparations with extreme disfavor, but dared not prevent them, since they were being made by an armed foreign power whose friendship was for the moment still needed.

The chaplain withstood the temptation to go to Moerbisch and ask a night's lodging of the parish priest. Aladar Fuerst had tried to persuade him, saying that nothing more could happen till morning. But Felix was physically tough, and an uncomfortable night meant little to him.

He had asked and received from the major a large bottle of milk for Fuerst's children. But as he was approaching the hut with this gift, a quick blast on a horn sounded from the open space, and a sharp command rang out in Schoch's piercing voice: "Assembly! All men fall in!"

The shadows that had just lain down to sleep in and around the tents staggered to their feet and assembled, hollow-eyed, in the glaring beams of the headlights. Aladar Fuerst came last, with Felix behind him. While some of the older men were groaning as if awakened from deep sleep, Rabbi Aladar now had a gentle, dreamy look.

Peter Schoch marched solemnly toward him, very slowly, his small eyes squinting voluptuously, his mouth twisting with great promise. The Brown Shirts laughed at the top of their voices. This was sure to be the great treat, one well worth staying up several nights for. Storm Leader Peterl was famous for his brilliant and comical notions. He stood blond and straight before Fuerst now, towering high above the small figure of the rabbi. In his right hand he held a wooden swastika, a simple cross that he had abstracted from a pauper's grave in the Moerbisch churchyard and had hastily transformed into the symbol of victory by nailing on short arms. No doubt it had been made specially for the sport he had in mind. There were no swastikas in the country yet, and in this predicament Schoch had had the happy notion of taking the Christian adornment from the sunken grave mound of some forgotten soul.

He raised this strangely macabre swastika high above his head like a Crusader. "Jew swine and garlic-eater," he cried, his voice showing plainly how much he was enjoying himself, "you're the rabbi, hey? Are you the rabbi?"

No answer.

"You're the rabbi with curls and caftan, jumping around in front of the Ark of the Covenant on the Shabbos, invoking your great Jehovah—is that right, Ikeymatzo Crappamoe?"

The motorcyclists roared, delighted beyond measure at this parodied Hebrew. Fuerst stood silent, almost inattentive.

"You're the rabbi who kisses your Ark on the Shabbos, hey?"

No answer.

At this Schoch gave Aladar Fuerst such a blow in the stomach with his left fist that Fuerst fell to his knees. Then he turned to the Brown Shirts. "Nobody can say we don't treat you right. Jew swine, I am allowing you the honor of kissing the symbol of the exalted Germanic race with your dirty mug. Appeal to your great Jehovah. And our horse-collared friend there can sing *Kyrie eleison* for accompaniment."

Aladar Fuerst, still on his knees, quietly took the swastika held out to him by Schoch, who now fell back a step. At first he held it irresolutely in his hands, this rude, crumbling cross from the grave of the unknown dead, smelling of damp spring earth. During those tense seconds Ottokar prayed that Fuerst would do nothing rash, but would kiss the swastika.

Instead something utterly unexpected happened.

The chaplain interrupted his story; these were his actual words: "A Jewish rabbi did what I, a priest of Christ, ought to have done. He restored the profaned cross."

224

Aladar Fuerst's eyes were half closed; he seemed to be acting as if sunk in some distant dream, and his motions were not quick, but reflective. One after another he broke off the loosely attached strips that made the cross a swastika. But as the wood had suffered from wind and weather, one end of the rotten cross arm snapped off; it became evident that the retransformed cross had been damaged and was no longer quite what it had been.

There was dead silence. No one attempted to stop him as he raptly destroyed the triumphant symbol. Peter Schoch and his men did not seem to understand what the action signified. For more than a minute they stood helpless, not knowing what to do. A smile hovered on Rabbi Aladar's face, which was turned toward the chaplain standing beside him. And he handed Felix the cross as if it were something belonging to the priest, not to himself. Chaplain Felix took it in his right hand. In his left he still carried the milk bottle.

Just then someone in the ranks of the Brown Shirts cried: "Jew swine, can't you hear that the Hungarian wants you over there? Run, Jew swine, run!"

Sure enough. Aladar Fuerst staggered to his feet, looked around, breathed heavily, saw the group of Hungarian soldiers under the distant lights of the other customhouse, to which they had withdrawn. He hesitated for a moment and then began to bound wildly toward Hungary, toward life.

Too late! There was a shot. Then another. And then the rattle of automatic rifles. Fuerst did not get twenty steps. The Brown Shirts jumped at him where he fell and trampled him with their hobnailed boots as if to stamp him into the ground.

On the far side, Magyar words of command snapped like whips. With leveled bayonets, Hungarian frontier guards, quivering with rage and spoiling for a fight, advanced on the murderers. The major took the lead, pistol in hand.

Seeing this, Shoch and his men left their victim where he was, whirled about, swung themselves on their motorcycles, and faded away with a bad smell of exhaust gas. For it lay not only in the genius of their Party policy but in the nature of their murdering courage always to know within a hair-breadth how far they could go without endangering the great cause.

The wounded man was carried into the Hungarian custom-house and stretched out on one of the benches. He was unconscious. A doctor summoned by the major soon arrived. He found a spinal injury and two shots through the lungs. There were also several broken ribs and severe contusions.

The chaplain tried to look after Mrs. Fuerst, who had lost her voice and the power of speech. She crouched wide-eyed beside her husband, despairingly moving her lips without a sound. The thin, piercing cries of the infant cut through the room. Its mother was incapable of giving it the breast.

Toward morning Aladar Fuerst, Rabbi of Parndorf, passed away. Before the end he opened his great, dark eyes. They sought the eyes of the Chaplain of Parndorf; their expression was quiet, very remote, and not dissatisfied.

By his death Aladar Fuerst saved his congregation. The major defied government orders and risked his own livelihood by allowing women, children, and old men to cross the border. They were taken to Sopron. Nine men in the prime of life remained behind. The major advised them to head northward. He had heard a report, he said, that the Czechoslovak frontier had been opened to fugitives. Let them trust in God, and look for some sort of vehicle beyond the reedy lake.

"And you, Father?" I asked.

"And I?" repeated Ottokar Felix absently. Then he reached for his hat. "This story wasn't about me. But since you're interested, obviously I couldn't go back to Parndorf. So I went along with the nine other men, and got across the Slovak frontier at an unguarded point. We swam a river. Since then I have been roaming from land to land with the children of Israel."

We went out of Hunter's Hotel into the street. The sun was setting gloriously behind the huge park. It was Friday evening, and a pleasant hour of the day. People were going home. The traffic was heavy; four lines of cars made no headway in the street. The women were very lovely with their bare, gleaming hair. Their laughing voices embroidered the blanket of sound. America was all peace and contentment.

"Look," said Felix, blinking at the passing scene. "Just look at all these kindly people, well fed, well dressed, good-tempered. These innocents don't realize that they have long since been involved in the war—the first war in their history that has really been a question of whether to be or not to be. They don't realize that Peter Schoch is upon them, perhaps among them. Many of these men are going to fall in battle. They will go out to defend the decent life and liberty of their nation. But there's much more at stake than freedom and a decent life; there's the desecrated cross without which the night will engulf us. And only God knows whether it will be granted to the whole world to do what Aladar Fuerst, the little Jew, did with his feeble hands."

The Making of a Minister

by J. M. BARRIE

❖❖❖

ON THE EAST COAST OF SCOTLAND, HIDDEN, AS IF IN A quarry, at the foot of cliffs that may one day fall forward, is a village called Harvie. So has it shrunk since the day when I skulked from it that I hear of a traveller's asking lately at one of its doors how far he was from a village; yet Harvie throve once, and was celebrated even in distant Thrums for its fish. Most of our weavers would have thought it as unnatural not to buy harvies in the square on the Muckle Friday, as to let Saturday night pass without laying in a sufficient stock of halfpennies to go round the family twice.

Gavin was born in Harvie, but left it at such an early age that he could only recall thatched houses with nets drying on the roofs, and a sandy shore in which coarse grass grew. In the picture he could not pick out the house of his birth, though he might have been able to go to it had he ever returned to the village. Soon he learned that his mother did not care to speak of Harvie, and perhaps he thought that she had forgotten it too, all save one scene to which his memory still guided him. When his mind wandered to Harvie, Gavin saw the door of his home open and a fisherman enter, who scratched his head and then said, "Your man's drowned, missis." Gavin seemed to see many women crying, and his mother staring at them with a face suddenly painted white, and next to hear a voice that was his own saying, "Never mind, mother; I'll be a man to you now, and I'll get into breeks for the burial." But Adam required no funeral, for his body lay deep in the sea.

Gavin thought that this was the tragedy of his mother's life, and the most memorable event of his own childhood. But it was neither. When Margaret, even after she came to Thrums, thought of Harvie, it was not at Adam's death she shuddered, but at the recollection of me.

It would ill become me to take a late revenge on Adam Dishart now by saying what is not true of him. Though he died a fisherman he was a sailor for a great part of his life, and doubtless his recklessness was washed into him on the high seas, where in his time men made a crony of death, and drank merrily over dodging it for another night. To me his roars of laughter without cause were as repellent as a boy's drum; yet many faces that were long in my company brightened at his coming, and women, with whom, despite my learning, I was in no wise a favourite, ran to their doors to listen to him as readily as to the bell-man. Children scurried from him if his mood was savage, but to him at all other times, while me they merely disregarded. There was always a smell of the sea about him. He had a rolling gait, unless he was drunk, when he walked very straight, and before both sexes he boasted that any woman would take him for his beard alone. Of this beard he took prodigious care, though otherwise thinking little of his appearance, and I now see that he understood women better than I did, who had nevertheless reflected much about them.

229

It cannot be said that he was vain, for though he thought he attracted women strangely, that, I maintain, is a weakness common to all men, and so no more to be marvelled at than a stake in a fence. Foreign oaths were the nails with which he held his talk together, yet I doubt not they were a curiosity gathered at sea, like his chains of shells, more for his own pleasure than for others' pain. His friends gave them no weight, and when he wanted to talk emphatically he kept them back, though they were then as troublesome to him as eggs to the bird-nesting boy who has to speak with his spoil in his mouth.

Adam was drowned on Gavin's fourth birthday; a year after I had to leave Harvie. He was blown off his smack in a storm, and could not reach the rope his partner flung him. "It's no go, lad," he shouted; "so long, Jim," and sank.

A month afterwards Margaret sold her share in the smack, which was all Adam left her, and the furniture of the house was rouped. She took Gavin to Glasgow, where her only brother needed a housekeeper, and there mother and son remained until Gavin got his call to Thrums. During these seventeen years I lost knowledge of them as completely as Margaret had lost knowledge of me. On hearing of Adam's death I went back to Harvie to try to trace her, but she had feared this, and so told no one where she was going.

According to Margaret, Gavin's genius showed itself while he was still a child. He was born with a brow whose nobility impressed her from the first. It was a minister's brow, and though Margaret was herself no scholar—being as slow to read as she was quick at turning bannocks on the griddle—she decided, when his age was still counted by months, that the ministry had need of him. In those days the first question

230

asked of a child was not "Tell me your name," but "What are you to be?" and one child in every family replied "A minister." He was set apart for the Church as doggedly as the shilling a week for the rent, and the rule held good though the family consisted of only one boy. From his earliest days Gavin thought he had been fashioned for the ministry as certainly as a spade for digging, and Margaret rejoiced and marvelled thereat, though she had made her own puzzle. An enthusiastic mother may bend her son's mind as she chooses, if she begins at once; nay, she may do stranger things. I know a mother in Thrums who loves "features," and had a child born with no chin to speak of. The neighbors expected this to bring her to the dust, but it only showed what a mother can do. In a few months that child had a chin with the best of them.

Margaret's brother died, but she remained in his single room, and, ever with a picture of her son in a pulpit to repay her, contrived to keep Gavin at school. Everything a woman's fingers can do Margaret's did better than most, and among the wealthy people by whom she was employed her gentle manner was spoken of. For though Margaret had no schooling, she was a lady at heart, moving and almost speaking as one even in Harvie, where they did not perhaps like her the better for it.

At six Gavin hit another boy hard for belonging to the Established Church, from which the stern Auld Lichts were the original seceders. At seven he could not lose himself in the Shorter Catechism. His mother expounded the Scriptures to him till he was eight, when he began to expound them to her. By this time he was studying the practical work of the pulpit

231

as enthusiastically as ever medical student cut off a leg. From a front pew in the gallery Gavin watched the minister's every movement, noting that the first thing to do on ascending the pulpit is to cover your face with your hands, as if the exalted position affected you like a strong light, and the second to move the big Bible slightly, to show that the kirk officer, not having had a university education, cannot be expected to know the very spot on which it ought to lie. Gavin saw that the minister joined in the singing more like one countenancing a seemly thing than because he needed it himself, and that he only sang a mouthful now and again after the congregation was in full pursuit of the precentor. It was noteworthy that the first prayer lasted longer than all the others, and that to read the intimations about the Bible class and the collection elsewhere than immediately before the last Psalm would have been as sacrilegious as to insert the dedication to King James at the end of Revelation. Sitting under a minister justly honoured in his day, the boy was often some words in advance of him, not vainglorious of his memory, but fervent, eager, and regarding the preacher as hardly less sacred than the Book. Gavin was encouraged by his frightened and yet admiring mother to saw the air from their pew as the minister sawed it in the pulpit, and two benedictions were pronounced twice a Sabbath in that church, in the same words, the same manner, and simultaneously.

There was a black year when the things of this world, especially its pastimes, took such a grip of Gavin that he said to Margaret he would rather be good at the high jump than the author of "The Pilgrim's Progress." That year passed, and Gavin came to his right mind. One afternoon Margaret was at

232

home making a glengarry for him out of a piece of carpet, and giving it a tartan edging, when the boy bounded in from school, crying "Come quick, mother, and you'll see him." Margaret reached the door in time to see a street musician flying from Gavin and his friends. "Did you take stock of him, mother?" the boy asked when he re-appeared with the mark of a muddy stick on his back. "He's a Papist! a sore sight, mother, a sore sight. We stoned him for persecuting the noble Martyrs."

When Gavin was twelve he went to the University, and also got a place in a shop as errand boy. He used to run through the streets between his work and his classes. Potatoes and salt fish, which could be got at twopence the pound if bought by the half-hundredweight, were his food. There was not always a good meal for two, yet when Gavin reached home at night there was generally something ready for him, and Margaret had supped "hours ago." Gavin's hunger urged him to fall to, but his love for his mother made him watchful.

"What did you have yourself, mother?" he would demand suspiciously.

"Oh, I had a fine supper, I assure you."

"What had you?"

"I had potatoes, for one thing."

"And dripping?" *

"You may be sure."

"Mother, you're cheating me. The dripping hasn't been touched since yesterday."

"I dinna—don't—care for dripping—no much."

---

* *Dripping,* of roasted meat. It was sold by cooks to the poor.

Then would Gavin stride the room fiercely, a queer little figure.

"Do you think I'll stand this, mother? Will I let myself be pampered with dripping and every delicacy when you starve?"

"Gavin, I really dinna care for dripping."

"Then, I'll give up my classes, and we can have butter."

"I assure you I'm no hungry. It's different wi' a growing laddie."

"I'm not a growing laddie," Gavin would say, bitterly; "but, mother, I warn you that not another bite passes my throat till I see you eating too."

So Margaret had to take her seat at the table, and when she said "I can eat no more," Gavin retorted sternly, "Nor will I, for fine I see through you."

These two were as one far more than most married people, and, just as Gavin in his childhood reflected his mother, she now reflected him. The people for whom she sewed thought it was contact with them that had rubbed the broad Scotch from her tongue, but she was only keeping pace with Gavin. When she was excited the Harvie words came back to her, as they come back to me. I have taught the English language all my life, and I try to write it, but everything I say in this book I first think to myself in the Doric. This, too, I notice, that in talking to myself I am broader than when gossiping with the farmers of the glen, who send their children to me to learn English, and then jeer at them if they say old lights instead of auld lichts.

To Margaret it was happiness to sit through the long evenings sewing, and look over her work at Gavin as he read or wrote or recited to himself the learning of the schools. But

234

she coughed every time the weather changed, and then Gavin would start.

"You must go to your bed, mother," he would say, tearing himself from his books; or he would sit beside her and talk of the dream that was common to both; a dream of a manse where Margaret was mistress and Gavin was called the minister. Every night Gavin was at his mother's bedside to wind her shawl round her feet, and while he did it Margaret smiled.

"Mother, this is the chaff pillow you've taken out of my bed, and give me your feather one."

"Gavin, you needna change them. I winna have the feather pillow."

"Do you dare to think I'll let you sleep on chaff? Put up your head. Now, is that soft?"

"It's fine. I dinna deny but what I sleep better on feathers. Do you mind, Gavin, you bought this pillow for me the moment you got your bursary money?"

The reserve that is a wall between many of the Scottish poor had been broken down by these two. When he saw his mother sleeping happily, Gavin went back to his work. To save the expense of a lamp he would put his book almost beneath the dying fire, and taking the place of the fender, read till he was shivering with cold.

"Gavin, it is near morning, and you not in your bed yet! What are you thinking about so hard?"

"Oh, mother, I was wondering if the time would ever come when I would be a minister, and you would have an egg for your breakfast every morning."

So the years passed, and soon Gavin would be a minister. He had now sermons to prepare, and everyone of them was first preached to Margaret. How solemn was his voice, how his eyes flashed, how stern were his admonitions.

"Gavin, such a sermon I never heard. The spirit of God is on you. I'm ashamed you should have me for a mother."

"God grant, mother," Gavin said, little thinking what was soon to happen, or he would have made this prayer on his knees, "that you may never be ashamed to have me for a son."

"Ah, mother," he would say wistfully, "it is not a great sermon, but do you think I'm preaching Christ? That is what I try, but I'm carried away and forget to watch myself."

"The Lord has you by the hand, Gavin: and mind I dinna say that because you're my laddie."

"Yes, you do mother, and well I know it, and yet it does me good to hear you."

That it did him good, I, who would fain have shared those days with them, am very sure. The praise that comes of love does not make us vain, but humble rather. Knowing what we are, the pride that shines in our mother's eyes as she looks at us, is about the most pathetic thing a man has to face, but he would be a devil altogether if it did not burn some of the sin out of him.

Not long before Gavin preached for our kirk and got his call, a great event took place in the little room at Glasgow. The student appeared for the first time before his mother in his ministerial clothes. He wore the black silk hat, that was destined to become a terror to evil-doers in Thrums, and I daresay he was rather puffed up about himself that day. You would probably have smiled at him.

"It's a pity I'm so little, mother," he said with a sigh.

"You're no what I would call a particularly long man," Margaret said, "but you're just the height I like."

236

Then Gavin went out in his grandeur, and Margaret cried for an hour. She was thinking of me as well as of Gavin, and as it happens I know that I was thinking at the same time of her. Gavin kept a diary in those days, which I have seen, and by comparing it with mine, I discovered that while he was showing himself to his mother in his black clothes, I was on my way back from Tilliedrum, where I had gone to buy a sand-glass for the school. The one I bought was so like another Margaret had used at Harvie that it set me to thinking of her again all the way home. This is a matter hardly worth mentioning, and yet it interests me.

Busy days followed the call to Thrums, and Gavin had difficulty in forcing himself to his sermons when there was always something more to tell his mother about the weaving town they were going to, or about the manse or the furniture that had been transferred to him by the retiring minister. The little room which had become so familiar that it seemed one of a family party of three had to be stripped, and many of its contents were sold. Among what were brought to Thrums was a little exercise-book, in which Margaret had tried unknown to Gavin, to teach herself writing and grammar, that she might be less unfit for a manse. He found it accidentally one day. It was full of "I am, thou art, he is," and the like, written many times in a shaking hand. Gavin put his arms round his mother when he saw what she had been doing. The exercise-book is in my desk now, and will be my little maid's when I die.

"Gavin, Gavin," Margaret said many times in those last days at Glasgow, "to think it has all come true!"

"Let the last word you say in the house be a prayer of

thankfulness," she whispered to him when they were taking a final glance at the old home.

In the bare room they called the house, the little minister and his mother went on their knees, but, as it chanced, their last word there was not addressed to God.

"Gavin," Margaret whispered as he took her arm, "do you think this bonnet sets me?"